L.A. FADE AWAY

JORDAN OKUN

A TOUCHSTONE BOOK
Published by Simon & Schuster
New York   London   Toronto   Sydney   New Delhi

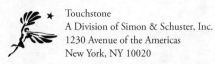

Touchstone
A Division of Simon & Schuster, Inc.
1230 Avenue of the Americas
New York, NY 10020

First Touchstone trade paperback edition September 2012

TOUCHSTONE and colophon are registered trademarks of Simon & Schuster, Inc.

For information about special discounts for bulk purchases, please contact Simon & Schuster Special Sales at 1-866-506-1949 or business@simonandschuster.com.

The Simon & Schuster Speakers Bureau can bring authors to your live event. For more information or to book an event contact the Simon & Schuster Speakers Bureau at 1-866-248-3049 or visit our website at www.simonspeakers.com.

Designed by Renata Di Biase

Manufactured in the United States of America

10   9   8   7   6   5   4   3   2   1

Library of Congress Cataloging-in-Publication Data
Okun, Jordan.
    L.A. fadeaway : a novel / Jordan Okun.—1st Touchstone trade paperback ed.
        p. cm.
    "A Touchstone book."
    1. Young men—California, Southern—Fiction. 2. Theatrical agents—Fiction.
    3. Family secrets—Fiction. 4. Hollywood (Los Angeles, Calif.)—Fiction. I. Title.
    PS3615.K86L33 2012
        813'.6—dc23   2012006463

ISBN 978-1-4516-5198-0
ISBN 978-1-4516-5199-7 (ebook)

For Li, Pops, Ma, Kors, and E

GITTES
I want to know what you're worth—
over ten million?

CROSS
Oh, my, yes.

GITTES
Then why are you doing it?
How much better can you eat?
What can you buy that you can't
already afford?

CROSS
The future, Mr. Gittes—the future.

Robert Towne
Chinatown (1974)

L.A.
FADE
AWAY

Welcome to the Mailroom

Don't be afraid to not be yourself. I hear this while walking back into the mailroom after a few early morning runs upstairs that consisted of carrying a metal statue of Groucho Marx to the third-floor reception, replenishing Red Vines and dark chocolate Hershey's Kisses to the seven kitchens throughout the building, and setting up the main conference room with a spread from Barney Greengrass for the weekly motion picture breakfast meeting, which, in my opinion, featured too much kippered salmon and white fish salad. Stan, the head of the mailroom, is patting a new trainee on the arm with a pudgy hand and saying, "Don't be afraid to not be yourself." The words, which I'm struggling to identify as a joke or real advice, hang in the air like a Coldwater Canyon fog as I adjust and tighten the knot of my solid navy Thom Browne tie, smooth my eyebrows out with the tips of my fingers, and inhale deeply, readying myself for another day.

Two months into the job, and I already know how the beast breathes.

That's why more than half the agents and executives in town start in agency mailrooms. It's the first six months of our lives—it's where it all begins.

It's where you discover who to respect, who to ignore,

who to watch out for, who's the hottest client, who to fuck, who wants it for the power, who wants it for the money, who drinks, who's on drugs, who cheats, who's gay, who cares, who's dangerous, who's manic, who's afraid, who to avoid, who's weak, who steals, who's next, who's watching who, who actually reads, and who, if anybody, knows anything at all.

"What makes a better lube—blood, cum, or spit?" Ty asks, flashing a Joker grin after Stan exits the mailroom.

All heads turn toward Tyler. Eager fucks in tailor-made and designer suits, all holding today's issue of *Variety* and cups of some caffeine-infused drink.

"Blood, I'm sure of it. Positive." Kev strikes first.

"HIV positive!" Ty adds in a flash, slapping fives with Kev, as most of us are now laughing in unison. It's more sick than funny, but we're all cackling regardless, especially Perry from the Palisades, who is really dying, while the other Perry, Perry Eisenberg, really isn't enjoying the show. He's just sitting there, acting aloof and ignoring everything, waiting for the impending 10:00 a.m. mail run while twirling a thin gray tie with a manicured finger, probably thinking he's too good for all this, which I assure you is not the case. The new trainee, a black dude who I haven't yet introduced myself to, stares at all of us, lost in first-day awkwardness.

"Well, let's make sure of it," Kevin continues, as all eyes, except Eisenberg's, turn to Andrew, who just came out of the deep dark closet, which really wasn't necessary because he's so obviously a homosexual that the thought of him going down on a girl is about as far off as the thought of him ever being promoted to agent—it's not happening. But they love gays around here, so he's definitely got a chance to be pounded in the ass for a few years; and they love nothing more than to pound anything in the ass. Actually, he fits in quite well, since there are more gay people here than I've ever been exposed to in my entire life. More than the audience at a Kathy Griffin show, more than any Saturday night on Santa Monica Boulevard between Fairfax and Doheny, and many more than that beach in Mykonos where my boy Cohen beat up some German dude who tried to fist him when we blacked out at the Tropicana Beach Bar while vacationing during my year abroad.

I fit in quite nicely around here, too. Lucky enough to be Jewish and from Beverly Hills, lucky enough to have rich parents who will support me until I'm forty if need be (but that will not be necessary), lucky enough to have a father in the business with a Rolodex of contacts longer than Milton Berle's dick (Industry Fact: Milton Berle had a huge fucking dick). Most important, I'm lucky enough not to have to give a shit about most people around me, which is absolutely essential, 'cause sooner or later I will have to fuck them all up in order to ascend the canyons, scale the Hollywood sign, and piss on anyone trying to follow me.

I'll be promoted before my peers through hard work or by making them look bad—whichever's quickest. I'll steal information and clients, fuck girlfriends and wives (wives get me harder than girlfriends, they need it more), and I'll talk so much shit behind all their backs, drop so much information to Nikki Finke, Perez Hilton, and editors at *Us Weekly,* create so much chaos in their lives, that no one will be left standing.

Kevin asks Andrew again about natural human lubes and there's no answer; he just laughs it off, blows each of us a kiss, and goes back to daintily turning the pages of *Variety* as if everyone was kidding about wanting to know what the best lube is, which is mostly true, but I'm sure Kevin and Tyler weren't kidding. They seem remarkably curious about lubes and continue to press for an answer.

"This is so blah," Alisa declares while skimming an issue of *Entertainment Weekly*, not enjoying the banter, which she usually does. Either her mother really is a lesbian (a rumor that's been swirling and even though Alisa and I are fucking, I haven't cared enough to ask) or she's just on her period and not in the mood. That would certainly explain why her skin is so blotchy today.

"Blood, huh? I think so," Kevin adds, ignoring Alisa while sipping a triple cappuccino from Bristol Farms, causing Perry from the Palisades to snicker.

"It hurts so good," Tyler says, making humping motions in Andrew's direction as Alisa shakes her head, a slight grin breaking through.

I tighten the knot on the Thom Browne again, centering it against my neck, digesting the clownish routine of these buffoons who I've grown close with since losing track of the majority of my high school and college friends. Stan reenters the scene, a gust of smoke trailing him into the mailroom, and erupts, "Knock it the fuck off! You're all fags until you get a desk and then you'll be fucking idiots, but you'll always be my bitches. It's 10:00 a.m., so man your carts, ladies."

That's the beauty of being in the mailroom at a Hollywood talent agency, whether you're twenty-two and fresh out of USC like me or a twenty-six-year-old Stanford Law School graduate, you're destined to make $450 for an approximately seventy-hour week while answering to Stan, a forty-five-year-old, bald, failed actor with three kids who lives in Glendale and shops at

Old Navy, who makes an embarrassing amount of money and wields no power whatsoever outside this tiny room in Beverly Hills where he's telling you who, what, where, when, why, and how. And you better fucking listen or you'll be gone like Keyser Söze.

The Life

The agency business goes back well over a century to the vaudeville days of the entertainment industry. Book a performer in a gig that pays ten bucks and take a dollar for your time. It's that simple. Book Tom Cruise in *Mission: Impossible,* which paid him well over $60 million with his back-end participation, and take at least $6 million for your time. It's that simple. It's also that lucrative . . . so find some fucking clients.

If Hollywood had a Mount Rushmore, the faces of Swifty Lazar, Lew Wasserman, and Michael Ovitz would be chiseled into a rock formation that isn't currently housing the estates of numerous, less-deserving agents in the hills. Those animals paved the way, they changed everything and everyone knows it. They're why style is a must, why sharks get fed, and, most important, why power and respect have been seized from studios and producers. Ever see the movie *A Day Without a Mexican*? Don't worry, no one did. But try to imagine a day without an agent and see how far you get. Swifty, Lew, and Mike wrestled the keys to the castle away, and, trust me, we aren't giving those back anytime soon.

The day begins with the 10:00 a.m. mail run and it's the first of five throughout the day, and by far the busiest. Every agent receives his or her *Daily Variety, Hollywood Reporter* (once a week of course), and any other mail, business or personal, that came in that morning. Runs are divided by floors, floors are divided by departments, and departments are divided for the most part by assholes. So, if you want to be a TV agent, make sure you're delivering mail and being seen on the second floor, which holds the entire Television Department. If you want to be a motion picture agent, make sure you're on the third floor. And if you want to work in voice-over, below-the-line, or comedy bookings, your life is going to suck and it really doesn't matter what floor that happens on.

I take the third floor because I'm going to be an MP lit agent, which, for you civilians, means I'm going to represent writers and directors who make movies. Lots of kids come here only wanting to represent actors, thinking that shit is glamorous, thinking they're going to catch some contact fame by getting photographed on a red carpet and end up on WireImage or Getty Images, or if they're crazy lucky like John Campisi, Jim Toth, or Jason Trawick they'll end up getting blessed in *Us Weekly*. But my dad, who was a talent agent once upon a time, warned me on numerous occasions to stick to working with writers and directors. One of my more vivid memories was during my eleventh birthday party at Universal Studios, when my father studied a woman dressed as Dorothy from *The Wizard of Oz* posing for pictures with kids. He leaned over as my friends and I were eating Doc Brown's chicken and said, "Actors are good for two things, boys, fucking in the mouth and divorcing." The truth is, I have some interest in representing actors and being the next Huvane or Whitesell, being bigger than my dad ever was as a talent agent, but I can't walk that line right now. Dad has his beliefs and would stop payment on my blacked-out X5 if I strayed from this path, and I simply can't have that.

Today it's my absolute pleasure to show around the new trainee. His name is Derek and he seems nice, but one of the first things he tells me is how much he wants to work in MP lit, so I'm lying about the company, my experience, and pretty much everything else but my name to casually discourage him. A lot of people say, be nice to everyone you meet in this business because you never know, that person may be your boss tomorrow or you may need a favor from them one day. Well, my father has been one of the biggest executives in town for over twenty years, which puts me in the unique position of knowing that most of my peers can get tea-bagged by my neatly trimmed Kosher nuts.

I'm showing Derek around, highlighting a few methods of properly controlling the metal-wheeled carts so they don't make a tremendous amount of noise, which pisses off the agents, what routes to take on each floor, where to deliver and pick up the mail at each office—knowledge that truly defines a Hollywood player. I formally introduce him to all the mailroom trainees, who—including myself—ignored him earlier this morning, the assistants worth knowing on every floor, and the rare few young agents who actually acknowledge a trainee's or assistant's existence. Derek got his first basic mail run shadow job, which I'm sure was absolutely mesmerizing for him.

Next up is the 11:00 a.m. "pickup," the first of three throughout the day. I take Derek with me, and after an exciting bit of a hollow back-and-forth about college (he just graduated from Princeton and jokes that checking the African American box on his application didn't help), nearby breakfast spots (I jokingly mention that the Blvd is affordable and he believes me), and favorite writers (he mentions Brandt and Haas); I quickly come to the realization that he poses no threat to me whatsoever. Fortunately, he doesn't seem too hip, he's not better looking than I am (his hairline looks to be receding), the pin-striped Brooks Brothers suit is acceptable, but certainly not special, and toward the end of our journey he mentions that he commutes from Chatsworth every day, and while shaking my head in disbelief I quietly say, "I'm sorry."

In between mail runs, pickups, and requests to photocopy six-hundred-page books one page at a time or demands to file a year's worth of check receipts in Accounting or reminders to clean puke off a couch in the lobby and recognizing it as a La Scala chopped salad while a movie star watches or assignments to sit in the parking garage checking in messenger deliveries while the wannabe actor who usually works there is taking a personal day to pose for new head shots because somehow, in his deranged mind, the only reason why no one has hired him in the last decade is because he doesn't possess the right picture of himself, there's an inordinate amount of downtime in the mailroom to bond with your coworkers.

Discussions usually heard floating around the mailroom: the true joy that celebrity divorces bring us; Red Bull vs. 5-Hour Energy (too close to call); clients who have recently left for another agency and who's most at fault; Jillian Barberie's vagina (beef curtains or not? This can last awhile); directors who lost it and aren't getting it back (De Palma, Bogdanovich, and Friedkin); directors who slip from time to time, which pisses us off (Woody, Burton, and Spielberg); Giorgio Baldi vs. E. Baldi (only the wealthier in the group discuss this, which is pretty much everyone except Stan); number of Broadway shows attended (Vegas versions don't count); hate mail vs. fan mail and which are scarier (we all agree on the fan mail); biggest asshole in the building (this lasts longer than the Jillian Barberie vagina discussion); Starbucks vs. Coffee Bean caffeine levels; filthiest slut in the building (separate nominees for assistants, agents, and administrative staff); speed vs. cocaine (cocaine wins by a mile); best restaurant burger in the city (Father's Office, Comme Ça, Wolfgang's, or Rustic Canyon); and who we'd rather see in an issue of *Playboy,* which is also basically the same discussion as who has the best natural tits in Hollywood (Scarlett Johansson, Jessica Simpson, Sofia Vergara, Maria Menounos, or Anne Hathaway).

Later in the day a Hispanic messenger wearing a Tarzana Hebrew school shirt delivers Larry Lazar's prescription medicine to the mailroom. I'm watching Alisa help Derek check the medicine in to the computer's receiving log. She laughs at Derek as he playfully raises his tie (probably purchased from Macy's) in the air and sticks his tongue out and to the side in mock suicide after a failed attempt at checking in the delivery. I wonder if Alisa has ever fucked a black guy and, if she hasn't, if she ever would. If she hasn't, I also wonder if the thought excites her and, if it does, if she'd ever be attracted to Derek.

When anything is delivered to the mailroom, we log it in to the computer at the front counter and put it in the agent's mailbox so it can be picked up or delivered on the next mail run. In the case of prescription medicine, I always like to investigate. Through the blue-and-white Mickey Fine Pharmacy packaging, Derek, Alisa, and I can read the bottles: Propecia, Thorazine, and Risperdal. Because of my grandmother's mental breakdown during my freshman year at USC, I know that Larry (no relation to Swifty), besides not wanting to go bald, doesn't want to hear the uninvited voices in his head anymore.

And I guess the voices are growing louder by the second because within a minute of its delivery, Larry glides through the mailroom, grabs the bag without slowing down, and heads outside, into the courtyard, flipping a cigarette in his mouth while ripping the bag open.

LARRY LAZAR

44 years old

Motion Picture Talent Agent

- Earns $400,000 a year

- Drives an Audi8 (Why spend $90k on *that*?)

- Cheats on his wife and twin sons at least once a month, sometimes with guys, but only once in a while and mostly for signing purposes

- Specializes in representing "urban" clients and young actresses that are often typecast as sluts and/or rape victims

- Has a reputation for being a massive asshole to mostly everyone in town, but especially to his male assistant, Sam, who he fondly calls Samantha. He pretty much calls everyone else either Guy or Bro

- Only eats at The Ivy (never at the Shore), Mr Chow, Urasawa, Chaya (never Venice), Ago, Chateau Marmont, Katsuya (except the Izakaya), Scarpetta, and Spago. Banned from Tower Bar, Capo, and Koi for what the staff have termed, "wildly aggressive behavior while dining"

Done for the Day

t's finally 8:00 p.m. and mailroom trainees are allowed to leave after at least twelve hours of slave labor while maintaining chemically whitened smiles. Through the glass exterior of the lobby walls I can see an event or screening across the street from the agency, and, as the elevator doors slowly shut in front of my face, I watch an older woman on a red carpet who looks like Benecio Del Toro in *Sin City* posing with a Saint Bernard for a multitude of battery-powered flashes, showering them in a bright, white haze.

It's dark this time of year and unseasonably warm tonight and I almost hit a Persian kid walking a chocolate Lab in the crosswalk on Canon, near Bouchon. Watching him pass in front of my bumper, I'm tempted to run him over as he stares me down, but I'd die if I hurt that dog, so I patiently wait while the smell of buttered steak wafting out of Mastro's makes my mouth water. Minutes later, I pull into my apartment's parking garage, amused by the thought of how much hairier that kid was than his dog.

I live in the Versailles Apartments at 8811 Burton Way on the corner of Burton Way and Robertson in a two-bedroom executive suite on the fifth floor, with two balconies: one in the living room overlooking Burton Way, facing Beverly Hills, and the second in the bedroom overlooking Robertson, facing West Hollywood. The rent for the year is more than twice as much as I make (I could care less, my parents pay it), but the amenities are great, a lot of actresses are tenants, including one or two actual celebrities, and a girl I met from Palos Verdes at Barney's Beanery a few months ago fucked me just for living here, so it's worth it. I get inside, immediately move toward the air-conditioning controls, and turn it down to somewhere in the mid-sixties, sit down on the dark brown leather couch, flick on the plasma, grab the glass pipe from a nook on the side of the couch where an original *Godfather* poster signed by Marlon Brando, Al Pacino, Francis Ford Coppola, and Mario Puzo hangs, and get so high so quick that I can't really recall smoking. Consciousness is restored an hour later and so is my appetite, so I drive to Xi'an to pick up an order of chopped chicken salad and steamed vegetable dumplings, drive home blasting the new Drake album, eat while watching a recorded *60 Minutes* piece on torture techniques, ignore a text from Alisa begging me to let her come over and wondering if I miss her, jump on the computer to check Perez Hilton, Just Jared, ESPN, Deadline, Facebook, and Twitter—where I tweet out a message regarding air-conditioning, and how it may be a better invention than the Internet. Soon I get bored, jerk off to a porn site where very old guys fuck underage-looking girls, start reading a script written by the daughter of a family friend about an Amish girl who moves to Vegas and falls into prostitution—it's *Kingpin* meets *Showgirls,* and I throw it away after twenty pages. Then I'm watching *The Biggest Loser* and laugh the entire time, jerk off again to a different site that may have been illegal (maybe the Internet is better than air-conditioning), smoke another bowl, do a bunch of push-ups, shower, lay down half wet and naked in bed, start watching Michael Mann's *Thief,* which I have never seen, and fall asleep while James Caan talks to Tuesday Weld in a diner.

Good Night and Good Luck

t's Tuesday afternoon and everyone is freaking out because Brian Katz left the agency for one of our competitors and he's taking most of his client list with him. I grab a package in the mailroom that needs delivering, head upstairs, and catch security escorting Katz's assistant out of the building in tears. The tears, of course, are due to the fact that this chick, who I had only talked to once or twice during mail runs, isn't being brought along with Katz to the agency that just hired him and she knows it's going to take at least a couple of months collecting unemployment—which isn't much less than her agency pay—for her to land somewhere again; especially with that skin, those tits, and this fact: she doesn't want it bad enough. She knew Brian was leaving, she had to know, and she was dumb enough to assume he was taking her with him. She was also too scared to tell the agency he was leaving. Too dumb and too scared, not exactly a recipe for success in this town.

As security escorts her out I try my best to give her a sincere nod and hope for her sake she uses the time off wisely. Maybe to hop on a treadmill, pay for a makeover, read the Jerry Weintraub biography—anything to help her score her next gig in a timely fashion.

As for Katz, he was long gone by this point, but the reason

an agent and their assistant (in this case) are immediately escorted out of the building once they quit is so they can't take any company information with them. This is standard agency protocol because years ago, a few agents left ICM to start Endeavor, and in the days before they quit, rumor has it they "stole" a bunch of files and critical information regarding the clients they were leaving with to start the new company. Those guys now run one of the biggest and most successful agencies in town; so the moral of the story is simple. Plan your escape well, steal whatever you can whenever you can, betray the company and people who brought you along and taught you everything you know, and, finally, always remember to smile when posing for pictures with your ex-bosses at Golden Globe and Oscar parties.

BRIAN KATZ

39 years old

Motion Picture Talent Agent

- Earns $550,000 a year

- Paid a $200,000 bonus for signing an A-list client last year who he is now taking with him

- Only eats at Italian restaurants and only at Ago, Madeo, Cecconi's, Giorgio Baldi (he hates E. Baldi for some reason), Angelini Osteria, Peppone, Capo, Dan Tana's, Enoteca Drago (never Centro), Mozza (only Osteria), and La Scala (only for lunch and only orders the chop salad with turkey instead of salami)

- Drinks an average of 9 cups of coffee a day

- Often brags that he has fucked cast members of *Gossip Girl, Friends, Dawson's Creek, American Pie,*

The O.C., Charmed, America's Next Top Model, I Know What You Did Last Summer, and at least 5 assistants, 3 agents, and 1 intern whom he let live in his house for a week before feeding her a few Ambiens and leaving her in an alley near The Grove with herpes pulsing through her bloodstream. I hear he's infested.

Prelude to an Interview

During a run upstairs to deliver a four-foot cactus to second-floor reception—the agency chose a southwestern motif for the month—this kid Jake, who's an assistant for Nick Rizzo, one of the few partners at the agency, places a hand on my back and says, "Follow me, you're going to like this."

"What do you want? I have six other runs I need to get done in the next five minutes."

"No, bro, what do *you* want?" he asks with a smile and I know it can only be one thing.

"You're leaving?" I ask.

"I talked to the mailroom; you're off the hook for a little while. Nick wants to meet a possible replacement. So, I'll ask again . . . what do *you* want?"

He smiles, as do I.

Minutes later, I'm waiting in Jake's office, which is connected to Nick's by a short hallway with a fully stocked bar, and I'm staring at a signed, original *Taxi Driver* poster, the one where Robert De Niro is walking down a filthy New York street in the early morning with his head down and hands in his pockets. The inscription reads:

NICKY,
YOU'RE THE ONE.
LOVE YOU,
MARTY

I can hear him speaking in the connecting office. It's more harsh than loud, more wild than stern, and it doesn't faze me at all; he sounds like my father. Five minutes flash by, and I'm still waiting. Jake, who is leaving the business to become a psychologist, receives calls from the offices of Harvey Weinstein, Roger Goodell, and James Carville, and tells each office that Nick will have to return their call. But when Scott Rudin calls a minute later, Jake intercoms it to Nick, knowing that they're lucky this call isn't coming in at 8:00 p.m. or later (when Scott returns the majority of his calls to the West Coast), and he was right, because Nick jumps on the call. Jake exhales while closing his eyes and turns toward me, eyes still glued shut, before slowly opening them.

"Are you down for this?" he asks me.

"You know it," I tell him.

"Do you have any idea what I feel like right now?"

"I think I do," I respond, staring at the *Taxi Driver* poster, getting lost in Travis's vacant being.

"You couldn't possibly," he says.

"Do you know who my dad is?"

"Okay, so you have a little idea," he admits.

"I have a very good idea," I reply while pressing a hand against, and then down, my Ralph Lauren checkered tie.

"Fine, just don't remind Nick who your dad is, I think he hates him."

The door to Nick's office violently swings open and an empty water bottle flies through it, landing in front of Jake's desk, spinning on the crisp white carpet before coming to a rest. Nick's screaming, "Let's go, let's go, let's do this now, let's go."

Jake bolts from his desk, picks the empty bottle up off the carpet, and starts filling it with water from the Poland Spring dispenser nearby. Nick is from New York and hates how Arrowhead tastes, so he spends thousands a year shipping five-gallon jugs of his favorite water from the East Coast.

"You're up, bring this in, it means he wants it filled," he tells me as he hands me the bottle, a menacing smirk now forming on his face. I take the bottle and see Nick for the first time standing in the doorway. "Ah, the passing of the baton perhaps? Let's do this now please, I have something in two, don't I?" he says and quickly disappears back into his office after snatching the bottle from my hands.

"You're up. The quicker you're in, the quicker I'm out," Jake tells me as he exits, leaving me alone.

I take a moment to straighten my tie again and slowly run my fingers against my eyebrows, and as I walk toward Nick's office I glance at De Niro one last time, his head down and hands in pockets.

Nick's cell phone begins ringing as I walk in and he motions for me to sit in an extremely comfortable, camel-colored chair, which I sink into. I lean forward, sitting as upright as possible, trying not to slouch; my father is always reminding me, "Losers slouch." Nick answers his phone and holds up a finger, letting me know it will just be a moment as he walks back into Jake's office, shutting the door behind him. Sitting alone, staring out at the skyline of Beverly Hills through the tinted-glass windowed wall of Nick's office, I can now hear the faint sounds of traffic on Wilshire, and I close my eyes, enjoying the moment for only a brief few breaths before Jake appears, telling me we need to reschedule because "Nick has a thing." I quickly walk out of his office, getting back to my runs.

Head down, hands in pockets.

23rd at Mastro's

Today's my twenty-third birthday, and I'm racing to Mastro's from work to meet my family for dinner. Listening to the new Ghostface Killah album, I come to a red light at Canon and Wilshire and see an older, blond-haired woman in a head-to-toe spandex outfit doing jumping jacks. She did thirty-three during my stop, and I'm impressed and transfixed and now cars are honking and I know I've seen this woman before somewhere, I'm sure of it.

Outside the aqua blue steak house, cigarette smoke from an extremely weathered-looking girl clouds my path. The doorman lets me in with a nod of recognition, and the smell of melted butter, vodka, and cologne consumes me. Surprisingly, I spot my parents right away, and I'm absolutely shocked they're not seated; I've never seen them wait for a table.

My father is anything but pleased. "Some Russian gangster is at our table."

"Just 'cause he's Russian doesn't mean he's a gangster," I tell him.

It's not that he's ignoring me; he's just preoccupied by the fact that we're actually waiting for a table alongside the groups of out-of-town salesmen and the homely couples celebrating anniversaries who have never eaten here before. He's baffled.

"Do they sell blinis? Are we in West Hollywood? I am fucking unaware." He snorts while grabbing his BlackBerry and slamming it against the side of his head, answering a call.

Mom comes to the rescue.

"Hi, my love, happy birthday! Tell him happy birthday, honey," she snaps.

Dad puts a hand over the phone for a second and says, "Happy birthday, Champ. Who loves you more than me?" Then he looks away, continuing the call.

And I'm thinking, *Um, Mom.*

"How was your day, dear?" she asks.

"Standard," I offer while walking toward the bar, yelling back at her, "Drink?"

Five minutes later we're being seated and walk past the Russians who were at our table. My father is almost growling at this point, ready for an encounter with someone whose only crime is taking too long with their coffee and butter cake. My mother and I quickly take our seats while I watch Dad stop to talk to Jeff Katzenberg, who's sitting in his usual booth toward the front of the downstairs dining room. Tonight Jeff is with his wife and Eddie Murphy, and they're all sharing orders of sautéed shrimp and scallops. Before taking his seat, my father also says hello to Ron and Kelly Meyer, who he often works with in only philanthropic ways; Doug Ellin and Stephen Levinson with a bunch of dudes I don't recognize; and right before hitting our table he stops to talk to an attractive redhead with dramatic bangs that rest only millimeters above mascara-lined, charcoal eyes. Fortunately, my mother doesn't notice how he happens to linger with her for just a few seconds longer than at any other table he stops at, but I do. I always do.

He takes his seat, jokingly asking no one in particular if it's "studio head night" before yelling out, "Scotch," which startles me. I'm not even sure if he saw our waiter, but seconds later a glass of Blue Label neat arrives and I rip a piece of pretzel bread from the basket in the center of the table, paint it with cold salted butter, and pop it in my mouth like a gum ball.

My older sister, Emily, and her husband, Keith, a successful real estate broker, arrive at the table throwing a Barneys gift card at me after falling into their chairs with the grace that only a Valium and bottle of Pinot Grigio consumed at home can offer.

"Twenty-three! Fuck, I am old," my sister squeals with her usual narcissistic charm.

"Grass on the playing field is getting a bit brown," Keith whispers to me, which Emily overhears and then throws an elbow at him.

Keith and I are laughing as a bottle of Pinot Noir is brought to the table and sniffed by my father. Glasses are filled as my younger sister, Cate, enters the room, eyes locked on her iPhone, engrossed in a text message, slowing for only a second to exchange smiles with the same woman my father was saying hello to earlier.

I watch them as Keith finishes his first glass and reaches for the bottle at the center of the table to pour another. "Sorry, everyone . . . Happy b-day, big bro!" Cate wraps her arms around my neck, squeezing me tight, which feels genuine.

"Who was that?" I quietly ask as a group of tuxedoed men set down salads in front of everyone.

"Who?" She looks back at the woman with bangs, who's now sitting across from a man with a bushy, graying beard and a brown tweed jacket.

"How do you still not have an iPhone?" she asks, attempting to divert the conversation.

I quickly look to my father, who's deep into a sniff of wine with his eyes closed before taking the tiniest sip and holding it in his mouth for what feels like a full minute prior to allowing it to escape down his throat.

"A toast," my mom blurts out, holding an almost empty glass in front of her. "Happy birthday, baby, the world is yours."

They all repeat, "The world is yours," lifting their glasses, which is quickly followed by "Cheers" all around and one or two *mazels*, and I nod with a smile, taking an indulgent gulp of Pinot.

A seafood tower overflowing with shrimp, oysters, crab legs, and lobster tails touches down in the middle of the table, replacing the steam from the bread basket with a tsunami of powder-white liquid nitrogen smoke that spills out of the metal protrusion and rushes along the bleached white tablecloth. I repeat my mother's toast—"the world is yours"—once more in my head, and I feel as if it may be true.

Later, Mom mentions higher fees at the country club and a petition to ban Persians.

"If L.A. Country Club can ban Jews, why can't we ban Persians?"

No one answers. She sips her wine, irritated. Emily and Keith tell us about their recent trip to Paris and how "cheap everything seemed."

While applying lip gloss, Cate asks if anyone has heard anything about the guy that went hiking in Runyon Canyon and killed every dog he saw with a golf club.

Emily asks, "Are you serious?"

Cate replies, "Dead."

Keith giggles.

Mom finishes her glass of wine and looks at my father, who is lost in thought, then turns toward me as I'm straining to get a better view of the woman with red hair, who is following the man in the brown tweed jacket out of the restaurant. "You okay, honey?" Mom asks.

"Yeah," I lie, finishing the rest of my wine while Dad wipes his mouth with a cocktail napkin, watching the woman exit the room as well.

Another bottle of Pinot arrives a minute before the steaks and sides, and the smell from the crab-and-truffle-cream gnocchi is overwhelming. I'm halfway through my bone-in fillet, and I'm utterly full and craving a cigarette but continue eating regardless. The bill comes, and I sneak a look: $1,135. Dad puts it on the house account and leaves two hundred-dollar bills and a fifty on the table.

Waiting at the valet, I kiss my mom and sisters good-bye and give my father and Keith a hug. A Rastafarian bum is dancing in the street in front of us begging for money, and I hand him my black bag of leftovers and warn him not to waste the truffle-and-crab gnocchi, explaining, "Be careful, it's overwhelming." He grabs the bag, takes a peek inside, and while continuing to dance tells me, "Thank you, Mr. Rockafella, you is the bess, Mr. Rockafella." Minutes later, my X5 pulls up, and I'm laughing so hard thinking about the Rastafarian that I forget to tip the valet, then speed home with a terrible pain in my stomach.

A Signing Meeting

impressed some nebbish fuck of an agent named Ben Bernstein yesterday when I organized the bagels by flavor for a company meeting. Apparently, this guy hates poppy seeds; he has a real stick up his ass about them, because they get stuck in between human teeth. He actually said "human teeth." Anyway, the fact that not a single one of those tiny, black demon embryos ended up all over this putz's sesame-seed bagel dazzled him, and now he loves me.

My glorious reward?

I get to sit in on some signing meeting he's having today for Bronx Jones, former heavyweight champion and current big deal du jour who just wrapped filming the *Kindergarten Cop* remake at Universal that Te-D (pronounced Teddy), a former client, is directing. Jones is taking meetings around town after firing the agent he's had for the last two years, who works out of an office in Sherman Oaks and actually got him the *Kindergarten Cop* gig, but life sucks for an agent at a tiny shop in the beautiful San Fernando Valley, so fuck him.

I wonder what Derek is doing right now. He's certainly not in a signing meeting; and neither is Kevin, Tyler, or Alisa, and when I told them I was asked to sit in on one, they pretended like it was no big deal, like they'd all get a chance to do the same in the future, and this makes me smile.

When an agency meets with a potential client, they schedule a signing meeting for a few key agents in the building to kiss ass and promise the world to the artist. If you can talk the talk and put on a decent enough show, most times, they'll sign. Hours after lunch, as I'm checking in a package from HBO for a young television agent that's leaking some sort of fluid, Ben Bernstein's assistant, this blond-haired doofus from Orange County who's wearing the thinnest tie I've ever seen, grabs me out of the mailroom, and seconds later I'm sitting intensely still in the corner of one of the nicer conference rooms in the building, looking out at all of North Beverly Hills and into West Hollywood.

The sun is beginning its usual descent and is penetrating the room with a warm, deep orange glow. The white marble table in the center of the room overflows with cheeses from the Cheese Store of Beverly Hills, including pecorino Toscano, cabra Romero, Emmentaler, Gorgonzola Dolcelatte, bleu de Bocage, and sottocenere al tartufo, a mild, black-truffle-infused cow's milk cheese that sits in an edible vegetable ash spiced with cinnamon, coriander, nutmeg, and fennel. Also on the table are homemade garlic pita chips and black olive focaccia from Spago, white bean puree from Mozza, fresh fruits and vegetables from Vicente Foods, a collection of Crumbs cupcakes that, as one agent pointed out, "look like a rainbow vomited," and every variety of Dr. Brown's soda in glass bottles. An hour from now, the meeting will be over, and there's a 90 percent chance not a single item will be touched before the cleaning crew comes in and throws everything away.

Ben, Larry Lazar, and two other agents I don't really

know—Jason Greenberg and Dan White—enter the room, and Ben walks right over to me, giving me an incredibly awkward handshake and half a hug while Larry lingers in confusion near the door for a minute before blurting out, "What's the mail-room doing here?"

"I invited him. . . . You should have seen what he did with the bagels yesterday," Ben says.

"Bagels?" bursts out of Larry, and a second later, Bronx is escorted into the room.

Enthusiastic hellos, handshakes, and hugs are exchanged.

Then a tornado of movement hits. The head of the agency, David Michaels, appears like a phantom, and he's a ball of nuclear energy. I'm so riled up I can barely contain my glee as I blindly take a seat and he starts his spiel:

"I heard something recently and I just want to know the truth."

There's a slight pause, which I use to creep toward the edge of my seat.

"Is this a jerk-off meeting?"

I love this man.

"Should I just pull down my pants, spit into my hand, and start beating myself to a bloody pulp with my eyes closed thinking about my sixth-grade girlfriend, Jenny Baumgarten's mouth?"

I feel faint.

"Because, I hear when you're done jerking us off over here, you're walking right down the street, meeting with those ass clowns who think being an agent is only about wearing two-thousand-dollar suits, eating at The Grill, and buying Damien Hirst paintings, and then signing with them."

David walks closer to Bronx, then eases into another gear.

"Now look, if this is true, mazel, my man, god fucking bless. But just tell me now, because if I'm gonna jerk off at work, and trust me, I jerk off at work at least twice a week, I'm gonna do it in my office, either at my desk watching the live feed I have from the women's bathroom in the lobby or leaning against my window watching model after model leave the salon across the street, and then I'll giggle as I watch some trainee come in and wipe down my glass."

My excitement immediately vanishes as I struggle to remember if I've ever cleaned David's windows. Bronx jumps into the ring. "Dave, we're all good, man. But, yeah, I'm taking other meetings. I'm excited at the prospect of signing with you boys, but to be totally honest with you, the only hesitation I have comes from what Te-D recently told me about his experience here."

David grinds his teeth as Bronx continues.

"Now, he was here for what, six years? He knows you guys well, so when he tells me not to sign here, I've got to at least entertain the thought, no?"

"No, you don't," David counters with a jab and then steps in for the haymaker. "You married, Bronx? Ever fuck the same woman for over ten years?"

Bronx says nothing.

"No? Well, let me tell you something . . . as a happily married man for the past twenty-one years, that shit gets old quick and you need to spice it up."

I would follow this man into the flames of hell.

"You need to let me dress you up in a Girl Scout outfit, knock on my door looking to sell me some Samoas and Thin Mints before lifting that brown fucking skirt and offering me a pussy patty like my wife did a week ago!"

Everyone is on the edge of their seats.

"What I'm trying to say is, sometimes *time* forces people apart, Bronx. But this is day *one* for you and me and my dick is rock hard and filled with white-hot Jewish venom that will go out and sell you to the town as the next biggest horse-cocked motherfucking movie star in the world. I'll have every studio head convinced by lunch tomorrow that you butt-fucked Will Smith and Leonardo DiCaprio into the fucking ether; because you're all that fucking matters and I'll stop at nothing to represent you."

Bronx is down for the count . . . we all are. He signed with the agency thirty minutes later.

DAVID MICHAELS

46 years old

Motion Picture Talent Agent/Chairman & CEO

- Earns $13 million a year plus holds a 37 percent ownership in the company, which is valued at $127 million

- Lives in a house in Brentwood with 9 bedrooms; 7.5 bathrooms; a screening room with a 300-inch screen and 25 reclining leather seats; an indoor basketball court that is an exact replica of the Lakers' court at Staples Center; 3 pools (one is an indoor lap pool connected to the master bedroom); tennis court; bowling alley with 2 lanes; a game room with 5 poker tables designed by the company that makes them for the Bellagio; and a full, live-in staff consisting of a chef who spent three years working at Babbo in New York and the past two years cooking for Richard Lovett, 3 maids, a dog "consultant," a chauffeur strictly for the children, and a butler who prefers to be called a concierge

- Cities in which he owns other homes and/or condominiums: Aspen, Florence, New York, Palm Springs, and Kaanapali

- Vehicles owned: silver G550 Mercedes SUV, white Cayenne Turbo S, black 911 Turbo Cabriolet, pearl white Tesla Roadster Model S, and a black Prius V, which is only driven by the staff for home errands and chauffeuring the children

- Married to his college girlfriend for the past 21 years and is suspected to have never cheated

- Father to 2 sons and a daughter, who all attend John Thomas Dye and are locks, no matter what their GPAs are, to go Crossroads, where David feels children are more "artfully schooled"

- Sits on the boards of Citadel, Oracle, American Cinematheque, and his temple, which he gives a few hundred thousand a year to, reserving him prime seats on the bimah for every High Holiday

The Weekend

The high from the Bronx Jones signing meeting evaporates when I'm asked at 7:47 p.m. on Friday by Stan to "stick around for a few." Defeated, I loosen my tie and release the top button of my shirt watching Ty and Kev gleefully wave and tell me "buh-bye" as they're joined by Alisa, who seems somewhat empathetic when mouthing something about calling me. But she's gone moments later, faint laughter echoing off lobby walls, my compadres on momentary leave, abandoning me . . . much to their enjoyment, it seems.

The only action in the mailroom is Stan talking to Perry Eisenberg (who has tears in his eyes) about the proper way to pick your teeth in public. A firm pat on the back is followed by Stan opening a drawer in his desk, reaching in and searching for something, then handing him a bunch of toothpicks before sending him off with a bit of advice, "Teeth, son, *teeth* can't be ignored." A knowing nod of the head follows as Eisenberg shuffles out of the room, saying something about it only being a poppy seed, but before I can tell him about poppy seeds being known to get stuck in human teeth, Stan floats in front of me, flipping a lit cigarette in his mouth.

"Love it when all you ladder-climbing fucks leave for the

night." He inhales with closed eyes and exhales smoke rings above our heads.

"So, what's up, Stan?"

He exhales again, stretching his upper body. "Cigarette?" He offers the pack to me.

"Reds?"

He happily nods.

"Gross."

"Pansy." He giggles, blowing another set of white rings above us.

"Stan?"

He swings a manila envelope into my chest. "You're about to pay admission to that signing meeting you attended yesterday."

"I already paid . . . the bagels?"

"Fuck those bagels. You think you're the first kid to come in here and organize a tray of Jewish donuts by flavor?"

I'm trying to figure out if Stan is Jewish to determine whether or not I should be offended, but when I decide I don't care, he's walking away from me, saying something about Bronx having dinner with some agents at the Chateau and I'm to bring the envelope to their table.

"Can you do that for me, shitstain?"

"What's in the envelope, Stan?"

He's halfway out the door, a maroon leather briefcase hanging from a worn strap off his shoulder, before turning back to face me, inhaling one last time on the Marlboro Red, smoke leaking out of his nostrils, telling me, "Nothing . . . but soon"—he holds the shrunk cigarette between his lips, checking his watch—"hopefully for your sake, our legal department will be finished drafting his agency contract and you'll stuff that envelope with it and race the fuck over to the Chateau like a good little trainee." Then he's gone, the cigarette hitting the ground outside as the door shuts, leaving me with one last mission for the week.

An hour later I'm waiting in the legal department offices while two young lawyers, not much older than myself, finalize the drafts, and I've read *Variety* and this week's *Hollywood Reporter* twice, been on Twitter and Facebook so many times my BlackBerry died, traveled outside to smoke every cigarette in the vicinity, and just as all hope for a decent night seemed to be swirling down the drain, one of the lawyers, who looks like he hasn't slept in a week, hands me the contract, watches me stuff it in the envelope, and drops his head on his desk with wide-open eyes, watching me exit the scene.

The valet line at the Chateau stretches from inside the hotel drop-off out onto Sunset, east of Crescent Heights. It's well past 11:00 p.m. once I'm inside the hotel, envelope in hand, searching for Bronx and the agents. I was told they'd be having dinner or drinks or, more specifically, they'd definitely be somewhere in the hotel. But all I see are the usual suspects (who I also see at Goal, and every Katsuya in the city), and celebrities aren't hiding addictions, they're flaunting them. And I'm one with the room, my Armani suit (a college graduation gift) and Jil Sander tie a proper camouflage for this battleground that's presenting Cameron Diaz and Drew Barrymore sipping mojitos; James Franco and Terry Richardson sharing sweet potato fries; and there are a few Lohan look-alikes wearing sunglasses, hiding in salads, shrouded in smoke from burning ashtrays, and I recognize an agent or two who ignore me, but Bronx is nowhere to be found.

Waiters and busboys buzz by as a mass of people surrounding the hostess grows at an appalling rate. A camera crew is filming Scott Disick and Kourtney Kardashian making out on the patio, and I accidentally walked into their shot searching for Bronx, so a young, shiny-faced producer asks me to sign a release and I ball the paper up and eat it as he watches, horrified.

Larry Lazar slaps me on the back, feels my jacket, and asks, "Shit, is this Armani?" I nod yes, and he snorts, draining a glass of vodka. "Typical," he says, brushing his thinning, mud-colored hair back with two fingers. He sets an empty glass on a table and instructs me to follow him. I obey without a word, closely shadowing Larry, watching him glide through smoke and all the beautiful skin, and he doesn't introduce me to the tall, androgynous Asian who he kisses on the cheek before entering the poolside bungalow—a two-story, two-bedroom space with black hardwood floors, a raging fireplace, and an outside deck with an obstructed view of Sunset where they're all sitting, the cast from the signing meeting, eating what looks to be monkey brains out of the heads of dead chimpanzees. But before I can question anything or get a better look to confirm the visual, David Michaels appears, snatches the manila envelope from my hands, and Larry twirls my body around and pushes me toward the door with only one word: *scram.*

The weekend unfolds routinely from there, but at no point do I stop analyzing what I believe I witnessed at the Chateau. I go to Runyon first thing Saturday morning with Kevin and Palisades; we race each other up the mountainside, ignore the view at the top, then jog backward down the paved road—we do this three times in a row while eagerly scanning the trails for the man who has been beating dogs to death with a golf club. Then lunch at Café Midi for egg whites and Arnold Palmers, followed by shopping at American Rag, Unis, and Undefeated. At home, later in the day after a trip to Yogurtland, where I tasted every flavor and left without buying anything, I skim a few scripts (all shit), watch a couple of short films (huge wastes of time), and jerk off to videos of girls with ridiculously large natural tits (a satisfactory experience). Dinner at Perso in Sunset Plaza with Alisa follows a short nap and a thorough shower, where I focus extra attention on my balls, which stink by day's end. We talk about the clients Brian Katz was able to take from the agency, dream first desks out of the mailroom (David Michaels's obviously), bisexuality among colleagues (more rampant than we'd like to admit), our sex life (I broach anal, which she quickly dismisses). "But here's what I do know . . . someone's getting a *little gift* tonight for this fab meal," she squeals, giving me drunk eyes, and I chuckle until the bill comes, displaying the price of Alisa's white truffle pasta—sixty dollars— which she barely touched and anything she did touch will only end up in a toilet later, spewed from her bulimic face. Oh well.

While we're waiting at the valet, staring out at the gridlock on Sunset, a cool gust of wind blows Alisa's hair out of its perfect place. She wraps her arms around my waist, looks up at me with a smile, and says, "Thanks." A limo driver gives the middle finger to kids running through the street, and the sound of car horns overrides everything. "Look at me," she says, my attention on the street scene. "Look at me," she pleads. I finally turn my head away from Sunset and toward her. "I really liked my pasta."

"Good." I tell her.

• • •

Sunday at Toast with Alisa, Palisades, and some girl he met and took home from a dinner party at the Mondrian last night. We're all smoking cigarettes, waiting the obligatory hour and a half to get a table, talking about *Volcano,* which Alisa and I watched last night after she blew me and swallowed (my "little gift"), and we stare at the Beverly Center in the distance, imagining rivers of lava in the streets. They're discussing a concert in Berkeley next weekend that everyone is taking off work to attend. Then Perry's girl (whose race is unknown) asks if I'm excited about the show, and I tell her to "gimme a break." Alisa mentions something about me "hating humans," and Perry laughs, flicking his cigarette into a Mustang convertible parked at a meter as our name is called.

After Hours

Most trainees are going to Trader Vic's at the Beverly Hilton pool tonight for drinks with kids from a few other agencies. It's something that happens roughly once a month, and it's basically a waste of time. We all know each other. We're aware of who the stars are among us and have perfected how to handle the zeros who will eventually evaporate. A few scorpion bowls, crispy duck tacos, and orders of beef cho-cho will be consumed. Film tracking for future releases will be discussed and analyzed, along with fantasies of promotions and familiar sob stories of twisted bosses and their manic, quick-triggered, caffeine- or menstruation-fueled, erratic behavior.

I'm pretending to be working on a project for an agent that "must be fucking done within the hour." This is what I tell Ty and Kev, and they buy it and are out the door soon after I promise to meet them at Trader Vic's, "in like twenty," but in like twenty all I'll be doing is trying to get ahead while they're drinking rum out of foot-long straws, hanging with kids from lesser agencies who think the only projects worth talking about are ones their clients are affiliated with.

After hours is a valuable time at an agency for someone trying to learn the business. It's the perfect time for someone with a bit of access to hunt down anything and everything happening within the building. After hours is the only time when I can try to uncover intel that could help me land the Nick Rizzo desk.

With the exception of a few assistants who stay late catching up on work they were too busy to complete during the workday, or assistants who are forced to stay in the office until their boss has finished dinner, drinks, or a screening to roll calls (Industry Fact: No one in Hollywood with any power places their own calls; they have their assistant dial for them, and it's called rolling), cleaning crews, and the rare instance of an actual agent burning the midnight oil, the agency is an absolute ghost town just after 7:31 p.m. every night. It's wide open for the taking. Since most file cabinets throughout the common areas of the building are left unlocked, I can easily make it look like I'm filing or taking notes or doing countless other believable, tedious things when all I'm really doing is scouring for any and all information I can get my soon-to-be-promoted hands all over.

By 8:05 p.m., with the exception of a vacuum cleaning a distant office, the place is vacant. It's Redford walking back into the office in *Three Days of the Condor* quiet, so I eagerly start poring over files, seizing all details. An enormous script sale to Paramount after a bidding war with four studios competing that, according to the notes, lasted a month. What a scale actor deal looks like on low, midlevel, and big-budget films. The specific language used in every scenario, what's handwritten and what's typed, who gets first-class travel and who pays for their own economy flights (a lot of writers), feature and Broadway option periods on novels and screenplays, profit participation and the difference between cash breakeven and first-dollar deals, and how box office bonuses and escalators work. It's all here waiting to be absorbed.

I recently read the Geffen and Ovitz biographies and learned how they would stay late when they were trainees at William Morris to study files and get ahead of their peers, and I'm surprised more of my colleagues aren't taking advantage. But maybe they do. Maybe when I'm off drinking or wasting my life at a screening for a film that will never get distribution and go straight to DVD, Ty and Kev and Alisa are here putting in overtime. But I don't think they are, and even if they ever did read those books, they would never think to use them as guides, to mirror the moves, to even for a moment consider walking in the footsteps of giants.

As I'm buried in a file of check receipts for celebrity client appearances at Bar and Bat Mitzvahs, weddings, and, in one case, a funeral, a creaking sound startles me, forcing my head up and out of the files. The far-off vacuum is still working harder than an out-of-work actress sucking up all the filth Hollywood has to offer, but the office remains empty. Even the few assistants who were still at their desks are now gone.

"Hello?" I call out softly, rotating my head in all directions, finding nothing.

A shiver flutters through my system as I return the file to the metal cabinet, still looking in all directions, before leaning back softly into the Herman Miller chair I wheeled away from a nearby assistant's cubicle. The red message light on my BlackBerry is blinking. I've been ignoring e-mails from Ty and Kev, who are wondering where I am and if everything is cool, and eventually, I have to respond by telling them I forgot about a family dinner at Tavern in Brentwood. Nervous they don't believe me, I build the lie and tell them how I don't love Tavern and wish we could just walk across the street to Toscana. Ty asks what I'm ordering, probing me, possibly sensing that I'm lying. I quickly type back that I can't find anything to order on the dinner menu—everyone knows it's limited, thus the lie is more believable—therefore I ordered a turkey burger from the lunch menu. I also send a tweet praising the turkey burger at Tavern and list Good Stuff, BLD, and 25 Degrees as also having excellent turkey burgers, to further drive the lie home. Kevin writes that he loves the turkey burger (everyone does, he's such a cliché) and asks if I would take a picture of it so he could: *take it to the bathroom and jerk to it.*

Another e-mail from Ty follows at an impossible speed: *HaHaHa SEND IT BRO!*

They're definitely probing now; I decide to stop all communication. My excuse will be the phone running out of batteries tomorrow when they ask with raised, waxed eyebrows why I never sent the picture of the burger.

The noise returns, closer now, forcing my head into a spin cycle, searching for the source. As the vacuum in the distance is silenced, my attention snaps to the north side of the building, eyes darting, searching for a janitor who never enters the field. A voice from the south pierces the silence; my head turns toward it to find Derek with a purple Brooks Brothers tie hanging below a cherubic face.

"Derek," I say, while spotting the red, blinking BlackBerry light on the periphery.

His lips commence movement, and I begin to feel the pulse in my forehead pumping blood at a sickening pace as he launches into a story about searching for his messenger bag, which, according to him, he must have lost while dropping off orchid arrangements to every office on the floor this afternoon. How it was a gift from his grandfather and I think he mentions that it means a lot to him and something about an hour search throughout the building.

"Bummer."

"Yeah . . . but no, I found it." He reaches down next to his leg and what looks like the same pin-striped pants he was wearing when I first met him, and lifts the black nylon Tumi with leather accents up. "See?"

"I do."

"Well," he says. Sensing my eagerness to end the interaction, "See ya."

I nod as he moves past me.

"Oh"—he turns back—"thanks again for showing me around the other day."

"Yeah, man, no problem."

"Okay, see ya."

"See ya, bro," I yell down the hall, giving him a thumb up, which quickly morphs into a middle finger.

"See ya," I repeat at a lower volume, watching him hug a corner and disappear by the elevators.

Back into the files.

Searching through client contracts, I seize on the language used to define hotel accommodations on press tours, premiere obligations for all above-the-line talent, an actress who has to stay under a certain weight or she loses money, and, depending on the schedule, how she could be replaced if the weight doesn't "come off," an actor who agreed not to come out of the closet until after a film cycles through all ancillary markets, a known gambling-addict director who needs all his money up-front (a friend of the family, I knew this already), the screenwriter who does two weeks of rewriting on a film for a higher one-week fee to up her quote, the client who pays

15 percent commission because they so desperately want to be represented, the client who pays zero commission because the agency so desperately wants to represent them, the geysers of commissions collected from clients with first-dollar-gross film deals and the mountains of wealth created from commissioning television shows in syndication, and it's an overload of names and numbers, of robotic semantics, of all the connective tissue of the business.

Time slips away. The last e-mail I received from the fellas was over an hour ago saying something about Trader Vic's being out of beef cho-cho, how that was unacceptable, so everyone went to the bar at Cut, and now they're stuffing themselves with mini Kobe sliders and Japanese bluefin toro tartare with Jean-Claude Van Damme, who's hanging out at the bar, and someone tried to sign him, but he offered to remove their face instead, so that ended. There are also numerous interrogating texts from Alisa, questioning my whereabouts, her lack of self-esteem oozing from her words, especially the last text, which reads: *don't you miss me?* I want to text her back no, but I can't, this would disrupt the lie about the phone running out of batteries and I'm almost positive she's fucking someone else, possibly even Kevin or Tyler, so I'm not overly concerned about hurting her feelings.

Certain I'm now completely alone, I move toward Rizzo's office and, after a final scan of the area, duck into the connecting assistants' office, where Nick files everything in a four-drawer, cherry-finish wooden cabinet that sits handsomely below the original *Taxi Driver* poster. And I attack it. The first drawer is overflowing with scripts that spill out of the stuffed cavity as I slide it open. I quickly pick up copies of *Pierre Pierre* by Edwin Cannistraci and Frederick Seton, *L.A. Confidential* by Brian

Helgeland and Curtis Hanson, *D.I.E.* by Simon Wilcox, and *Unbound Captives* by O. C. Humphrey, which is a pseudonym for the husband-and-wife writing team of Madeleine Stowe and Brian Benben, and stuff them back, slamming the first drawer shut.

The second drawer reveals bulky stacks of Rizzo's monthly expense reports dating back at least five years. Thousands of dollars spent at restaurants, nutritionists, bars, movie theaters, coffee shops, playhouses, bookstores, nightclubs, golf courses, websites, hotels, marijuana dispensaries, airlines, casinos, private car wash services, personal chefs, private tailors; there's no end to his spending, and I quickly calculate that he expenses more a month than I make in three months, which delivers a suffocating rush of envy throughout my body that I can only alleviate with slamming the contents away and moving on.

The third drawer is inhabited by at least fifty individual folders with either Rizzo's clients or associates' names on the file tabs—jackpot. Legal names, bank account numbers, favorite restaurants, agency agreements written on hotel bar napkins, lists of birthdays, favorite wines and scotch, pets' names, children's names, divorce agreements, private investigator contracts, car leases, home loans, lots of social security numbers, old and current passports, a sealed evidence bag with a rusty hammer in it (I'm hoping it's movie memorabilia), tons of party and screening invites, copies of driver's licenses, endless paperwork, a golden row of specifics, and my fingers can't move fast enough until I get to the last file in the drawer, labeled NICK. I'm inside it in an instant, but it's empty, causing me to flip the green paper file around with my fingers in disbelief at the lost opportunity to truly educate myself on the man that can get me out of the mailroom and on a path toward the goal.

Frustration builds as I leave Rizzo's office and move into the hallway, where the air is cooler. Leaning against a nearby wall, eyes closed, my head touching plaster, chewing a Xanax, a detail from the night that seemed benign at the time doubles back. I don't remember Derek ever using a messenger bag or carrying one around the office before tonight. If it meant so much to him, why had he not used it on his first day of work? Closing my eyes again, the memory of the interaction replays, the sound of creaking from the south side of the building, the side I'm standing in now. "The perfect time," I whisper to the silence of the third floor.

I dash back toward Rizzo's cherry red cabinet, yank the third drawer open, and rip the file labeled NICK out, staring at it as flashes of Derek emptying its contents into his messenger bag go off like a strobe light. Breathing heavy, I recall Derek's interest in the MP Lit Department from the mail run I took him on days ago, and I'm struggling to catch my breath as I return the file to its place and hit the light, dipping myself in darkness.

Just a Day

I think I may be Maverick in *Top Gun,* flying a fighter jet at a ridiculous speed, gliding through a turquoise, cloud-spotted sky, when I see Kevin and Tyler sitting tandem in a jet racing ahead of me, so I fly above them, flip the plane upside down, give them the middle finger, then roll out and settle in behind their jet, take aim and launch a missile. A mind-piercing alarm works its way into the Kenny Loggins sound track, and everything goes black as I find myself in bed at 5:55 a.m. and I'm pissed because I slept in.

I jump out of bed with a hard-on pushing my Lakers authentic game shorts out in front of me, flip on the local Fox news, where Jillian Barberie is doing a style report at Trashy Lingerie on La Cienega, and I could easily jerk off to the outfit she's wearing but I'm late for my trainer. I quickly get dressed, grab a blueberry-oatmeal Clif bar, which I finish on my way to Equinox to meet Reggie, my half-Asian, half-black fitness trainer, who starts me off at a jogging speed on the treadmill for ten minutes. Gavin Polone is running next to me, covered in sweat, reading the *New York Post* Sports section, and he makes me feel like a loser; he's probably been here for the past hour, and I can't stop trying to figure out his net worth. Over the next forty-five minutes, we work my arms, chest, back, and abs while Reggie tells me about some song he wrote about stepmothers and a music producer who wants to record it, and, according to Reggie, "This guy is like the next Crust," and when I ask who that is, he adds another fifty pounds onto the bar I'm bench-pressing and mimics me, "Who's Crust?" And while shaking his head in disgust he catches his reflection in a mirror and flexes his left bicep, which is mostly covered in a tattoo that says PAIN.

I'm drinking room-temperature water (Reggie never shuts up about how cold water is bad for the system) while walking past people riding stationary bikes to nowhere, reading scripts on iPads or the *Los Angeles Times* (but just the Sports, Arts, and Calendar sections). I flirt with a trainer named Stacey, which enrages Reggie, so he moves me back onto a treadmill, and sets it at its fastest speed and highest incline. He barks encouragement as I strain to breathe, slapping my hands every time they reach for the machine's railings. Stacey walks by us with an older male client wearing a faded, pink LA Gear shirt, giggling at me, and I attempt to ignore the fire in my legs by running down today's schedule in my head: I'm on post office pickup this week, meaning I'm responsible for retrieving the entire agency's mail, usually three huge carts' worth, which has to be signed for at the Beverly Hills Post Office on Maple Drive at 8:00 a.m., driven back to the office, and sorted before the first mail run of the day. Stan made a comment yesterday about today being "interesting" due to numerous trainees and assistants—Kev, Ty, and Alisa included—putting in for a day off for the concert in Berkeley, where Phish and the Fugees are playing that I have zero interest in attending. I have a lunch scheduled with my father at Matsuhisa that I assume he's going to reschedule, and I think I'm almost done running but not exactly sure because Reggie is covering the time on the machine just to fuck with me, and I might puke, but last time I puked at the gym Reggie made me run another mile, so I hold it in. I just don't have the time.

As I'm climbing to the top of the parking garage and exiting on North Camden, my phone registers three messages, all from Stan, all asking me to "pick up the fucking bagels today," which I thought Derek was supposed to be handling. I call Stan immediately, reminding him I'm on post office this week, and he quickly shuts me up, telling me about all the trainees who took today off. "These fuckers think we don't know about the concert in Berkeley. The agency booked the fucking groups for Christ's sake."

"Stan."

"Listen, I know where your head's going, just stop. I put Derek on a desk today. I had to."

"What desk, Stan?"

"David Michaels."

Stan continues as I'm reeling, running reds on Third Street, and I may have just run over a jogger or maybe it was just a pothole—I'm not sure. "They specifically needed someone to stuff envelopes for some charity benefit for goblin kids. It's a shit job," he tells me.

"The fuck is a goblin kid?" I ask.

There's no answer.

I'm pulling into my garage, my mouth dry, and it hurts when I try to swallow.

"Almost everyone I have needs to be covering desks today, so you're my man," he tells me.

I'm silent, panicking.

"Look," Stan continues, "any shitstain can fill in for nothing assistants, but I need the nastiest shitstain for a few special runs today." He means this as a compliment, and I'm somewhat flattered.

Riding up in the elevator through the guts of the Versailles, I run into a girl who lives in the building, whom I often run into smoking on the roof, and I believe she once told me about wanting to be a newscaster, but I don't know her name and we just nod at each other. She's wearing a wrinkled dress, her hair is a neat mess, the scent of vodka and cigarettes winning the olfactory battle with my post-workout sweat and B.O., which, by the way, is the only time in life I'll ever have a hint of it, and this is obviously a walk of shame situation, which gets me a little hard, especially since I didn't have time to jerk off earlier this morning. I stare at her intensely, enjoying the moment, imagining what positions she was put into last night or earlier this morning, how willing she was to please, and now I'm almost fully erect by the time she exits on her floor, and I have to reach into my underwear and pull my dick up, pinning it against my stomach and the elastic band in my shorts in case I run into anyone in the hallway. While showering, I imagine her a few floors below, hunched over on a tiled-shower floor, under a cleansing stream of hot water, regretting her recent escapades.

After I pick up five dozen assorted bagels with an emphasis on sesame, cinnamon raisin, and plain, and three flavors of cream cheese—plain, lox, and chives, all low fat—three and a half carts of mail and small packages at the Beverly Hills Post Office are lifted into my ride, and I'm gone as quickly as possible, pulling out onto Maple, rolling through a stop sign, and heading toward work. Minutes later I pull into the agency's garage, where Derek is waiting to help me unload everything. Pop the trunk, notice a load of fan mail has turned over, and I'm certain my carpet is now coated in disease. Derek smiles to himself while collecting the stray pieces, and he wheels half the trunk's contents into the elevator, holding it open, waiting for me. I breathe deep, trying to calm myself for the day ahead as the elevator doors close in front of my face with the rest of the morning load in an oversize cart in front of me.

"Late night at the office, huh?" he casually drops.

"For you as well," I counter, "a productive night *all* around," letting him know that I think I know what he may have done in Rizzo's office.

A moment of silence passes, and then David Michaels's executive assistant, Shane, a lifer assistant in her late thirties who's actually pretty hot, steps into the elevator with a UPS package in her hands. She looks me up and down and says, "What, no tie today?"

But by the time the final syllables of an excuse fly off my tongue, the elevator hits the lobby and she slips out through the doors like a phantom, floating toward the mailroom as Derek shrugs his shoulders and exits behind her.

We finish sorting the mail, getting the temps who are filling in for all the absent assistants familiar with how the building functions, and at 9:30 Derek disappears before I can confirm if he's carrying the Tumi messenger bag. The clock strikes ten and the army of temps mechanically shift out of the dungeon like a scene straight out of *Metropolis* for the first mail run of the day. Stan hovers over me, the information he's about to unload all but spilling out of his mouth. He smirks as he goes through the list of my responsibilities for the day.

And I'm off.

First up is a run to Barneys strapped with the company credit card to buy candles. I am to purchase fifty candles on the "cheaper side" for common areas inside the building and select assistant stations. For this I go with an assortment of Diptyque and Le Labo. I am to also purchase thirty "high-end" candles for all reception areas and select agent offices. I'm told by the sales guy wearing black Reebok Pumps and a pink sweater vest that the store received a shipment today of Jonathan Adler Muse Monumental candles, and, "They're only two hundred ninety-five dollars, and that's like a steal," so I take the entire shipment. Last, my orders say to *GET DAVID MICHAELS A NICER CANDLE THAN ANYTHING YOU'VE ALREADY BOUGHT*, so I choose a D.L. & Co Bust of Dierdre, which is a perfectly sculpted face of a young Irish girl who weeps wax out of her eyes when the candle burns.

While waiting at a counter in the first-floor beauty section, I run into a kid I went to high school with whose name I can't remember. He tells me he's in from New York. I think he went to Brown or Penn, but I'm not sure. This familiar stranger won't shut up about working in finance, how sick some trip to Russia was a few months back, and when I probe about the economy, he says, "Don't believe everything you read."

I'm still waiting for the hipster to bring out all the candles while the kid from high school is telling me how he's out here on vacation and a chick who could easily make a living as a model except for the fact that she's a bit short snuggles up with a Marc Jacobs bag in her hands, which she holds up for his inspection, whispering, "Please, daddy," into his ear, and he just nods, not even looking at her, pulling at the purse and slamming it down on the counter to the right of us. Something about the Beverly Hills Hotel for drinks later pops up as they're walking away, both sliding Ray-Bans on before stepping out onto the sun-soaked Wilshire corridor, and I watch them stroll away—she happily swinging a giant black Barneys bag as he lights a cigarette. The guy in the pink sweater vest startles me by dropping two huge cardboard boxes filled with candles on the counter. I quickly look back to the corridor, but they're gone, nothing left except the memory of running into a kid I went to high school with who's already a millionaire and on a vacation with a model staying at the Beverly Hills Hotel while I'm picking up candles, making $35,000 a year with overtime if I'm lucky. The thought of this begins to overwhelm me as I'm loading my car in the bowels of the parking garage with the Barneys employee, who says "one love" as he pumps the tongue of his Reeboks before walking away.

Kid Cudi's "Mr. Rager" surges from the ride's speakers as I'm circling my way up and out of the depths of Barneys with only a few more runs to make before heading back to the office. Fifteen pairs of Paul Smith socks from Saks are needed, which irks me because I could have gotten them from Barneys, so I call Stan to say, "Fuck you, Stan, I could have gotten these at Barneys," and he quickly informs me they're for David Michaels, and he specifically wants them from Saks. Stan tells me he'll transfer me to Michaels's office, and I hang up before the first ring. A vanilla buttercream cake with chocolate-chip filling from Hansen's for a third-floor birthday party next, followed by twenty-five hot dogs and sides of coleslaw and kasha varnishkes from Nate 'n Al for a reality TV lunch.

More stops before heading back include getting three thousand-dollar gift cards from Williams-Sonoma, a men's Himalayan suit from North Face, and ten orders of avocado egg rolls from the Cheesecake Factory, which will be paired with the hot dogs for that reality TV meeting. Apparently, the agency is trying to sign a heavy-hitter producer, and someone found out what he would want for his last meal if he were ever on death row, which, in my opinion, establishes quite the tone for the meeting. I then sprint up and over to Canon and hit Edelweiss, where I buy numerous bags and boxes of candy, including chocolate golf balls, gummi Coke bottles, mini Swedish fish, two pounds of dark and light chocolate marshmallows, and candy escargots—I have no idea what or who this is for.

I head back toward my car, arms weighted down with shopping bags, a slight layer of sweat forming at the top of my forehead, my Boss suit and shirt feeling slightly uncomfortable. I pray I don't run into anyone I know, especially what's-his-name from high school and the model I'll be jerking off to at some point in the coming days. I don't even slow down when I hit the intersection at Beverly and Brighton Way, crossing diagonally through the overexposed concrete walkway before descending into the public parking garage elevator, relieved I didn't bump into anyone.

I'm on the way to Best Buy for the last run before hitting the office to drop everything off, my father hasn't rescheduled lunch yet, and I need to be quick, the food is stinking up my ride, and it's getting hotter, which isn't a good thing for all the candy. I'm stopped at the light on Pico and Motor, the 20th Century-Fox studio lot to my right. There's a giant movie poster near the front gate, plastered on a monstrous billboard, featuring a young man whose eyes are covered by someone else's hands and the tagline on the bottom reads GUESS WHO? A symphony of horns prompts me to drive through the intersection, and I fight to shake the thought of going blind.

Inside Best Buy, *Master of the Flying Guillotine*—a movie about an Asian assassin who throws a box with a blade inside of it, which acts like a guillotine, onto his enemy's head, slicing the enemy's head off—is playing on numerous plasmas throughout the DVD section of the store, captivating every employee and a few customers. While waiting to be helped, I consider building one of these this weekend and using it on people at the Katsuya Hollywood valet stand.

I finally get an employee's attention, and he disappears without me saying a word, then quickly returns with a box filled with DVDs, reading off of a list, confirming its contents. The Criterion DVDs the agency needs purchased are *Throne of Blood, Eyes Without a Face, The Bad Sleep Well, The Rules of the Game, Contempt, The Most Dangerous Game,* and *Thieves' Highway.* I check my list to confirm. The employee then continues listing Blu-ray Criterions the agency needs. They are *Charade, Gimme Shelter, Playtime, Paths of Glory, Antichrist, Days of Heaven, Repulsion,* and *Hunger.* I check my list one final time, ask why *Grand Illusion* wasn't mentioned, he checks his list, then the box, and confirms it's there.

Back at the office, when I drop everything in the mailroom, the load is immediately attacked and dispersed throughout the building by today's temps. Stan slaps me on the back, and it stings, pissing me off, but he's all smiles as he hands me a sealed envelope along with another list of runs, telling me to "enjoy lunch, then get after it." As I'm walking out of the mailroom, Stan says, "Oh, one last thing." He inches closer to my face, his breath smelling like a pack of cigarettes butt-fucked a cup of coffee. "There's a check for two million dollars in that envelope, so don't fuck up."

Waiting for the elevator, I let the fact that a $2-million-dollar check is rubbing up against my leg sink in. It feels good. The elevator doors open to Derek and Shane in midconversation about some TV show, which I believe is *American Idol* from the contestants' names, and they're laughing and wonderfully animated.

I step in, swing around quickly, facing the doors, and hit the button for the last level of parking. Within seconds the doors open again, presenting the first level of parking. Shane's tight little frame slithers by without her taking her rapt blue eyes off Derek, who makes eye contact with me for only a brief moment, smiling, as he walks out with her, and I slap my hands over the doors, holding them in the open position, watching the two new friends jump into Shane's silver Mercedes coupe and vanish up and out of the garage.

Dropping my car off at the valet of Matsuhisa, rushing inside a few minutes late, trying to forget the sight of Shane and Derek all BFF, I feel my BlackBerry vibrating, an e-mail from my dad's assistant saying he'll be late (Industry Fact: If you're meeting someone for lunch and they're more important than you, even if it's your father, you'll be the one waiting). Locating the table, I order an Arnold Palmer and limestone lettuce with scallops from a passing waitress before I take a seat. Dad shows up twelve minutes later while I'm composing a tweet about the

Menendez brothers, and he yells at me to stop using Twitter and then says something about an accident on La Brea killing two Hasidic teenagers and finishes his sentence with "So that happened." Then he orders nameko miso soup, kakiage donburi, an assortment of sushi, and I'm hoping he's going to order sake, but he doesn't.

He tells me about the wife of an A-list director who recently passed away and the cover-up of her drug addiction and fascination with whoring herself out on Sunset east of Highland from time to time. Chuckling coincides with this part of the narrative while I nervously feel for the check in my pocket. His phone rings. He inspects it but doesn't answer, and tells me he's considering switching to an iPhone. I can't remember a time my father neglected a call in my presence. Then a conversation begins regarding the smaller-budget films that his studio is concentrating on these days. How they have more "upside." How "it's like the late sixties and early seventies all over again . . . minus all the genius."

Mike Ovitz walks by our table, stops to playfully punch my father in the shoulder blade, and jokes about us not being able to get a table at Hamasaku (an excellent sushi restaurant he owns) for lunch. I look Ovitz over, from his shining shoes to his sparkling, designer-spectacled eyes, and I'm struck by his size— I thought he'd be smaller. He tells us about having to get to a meeting with someone who buys his Lakers floor seats from him every season, but before leaving he turns to me and introduces himself. He tells me he hears I'm working at an agency, and, with a sad face, he leans in and says, "Image, son. Image. There's *nothing* else." And he winks at me before walking away, stopping at another table in the distance as Dad mumbles,

"Thank god we got rid of him," and the food is devoured, a hug is shared, the valet is tipped, and the day continues.

My car is scorched, and for some reason the steering wheel is greasy. I turn left onto La Cienega, heading north as Mobb Deep's "More Trife Life" plays while the air conditioner desperately attempts to cool everything. I pull the envelope out of my pocket and check Stan's list for the first time at a red light near the Beverly Center. Next to *"#1"* are instructions on where to go and who to deliver the check to: *SIERRA TOWERS & BARRY.* There's also a *"#2"* written under it: *CALL ME WHEN YOU'RE DONE WITH #1.*

As I'm rocketing up toward the twenty-sixth floor of Sierra Towers—a building I've never entered before, despite seeing it every day of my life—I carefully slide my thumb under the tape that seals the envelope and glance inside. The check is made out to Josh Blum. There are very few units on each floor of this pearl behemoth, and a thick white carpet that looks and feels brand new under my feet leads me toward the double doors of the condo.

I feel uneasy twenty-six floors high. I imagine exactly where in the sky I am—hovering over Sunset, above Soho House— and it knocks the wind out of me. I want the door to open quickly, a maid to answer so I can throw her the envelope and touch the street again. But the note from Stan doesn't say throw the check at some destitute Guatemalan girl just trying to make a living so her family back home can buy a chicken once a month. What it does say, very clearly right before *#2 CALL ME WHEN YOU'RE DONE WITH #1* is that I am to ask for Barry and only give him the check. A woman opens the door who's dressed in jeans, clean white sneakers, and a vintage Coca-Cola T-shirt, and she's white, so she's definitely not the maid. I ask for Barry, and she points toward another room while silently walking in the opposite direction.

The walls are filled with framed original movie posters, the smell of weed is strong and carried throughout the space by a cool breeze coming from one of the walls where a balcony is located, exposing the southeast landscape of the city below. I follow the movie posters—*Stripes, Midnight Cowboy, Young Frankenstein, Animal House*—while the smell of weed strengthens, to find three guys lounging on a couch, eyes red and half shut, watching *The Last Detail* on what must be at least a seventy-inch Panasonic plasma, and in the corner of the room I glimpse a hologram clock that projects the time—2:46 p.m.— and day—Tuesday—in light blue, floating in smoke.

I recognize one of the kids is an actor. He's had some bit parts in half of Josh's films, a few failed pilots, a webisode or two, the usual. I ask for Barry, but they're stoned into silence. "Barry," I say again slowly, waving the envelope at them, unable to shake anyone loose from the haze. "He's not here," a voice comes at me, but I was looking at the screen, admiring its resolution, so I'm not sure who said it. The actor then sits forward and I'm waiting on him to speak again, but he only grabs a bong off the wooden coffee table, takes a medium-size pull off it, coughs as he exhales, and leans back down again without moving his eyes from the screen.

"He's not here," the voice repeats, now behind me. I swing around to find Josh Blum standing in a pair of boxers and a shirt that says MARIJUANA in the McDonald's font over golden arches, and underneath the image it reads A BILLION STONED. He's holding a bowl of cereal up to his chin, spooning what looks to be Cocoa Puffs into his mouth, milk dripping from his lips and chin, before asking, "Who's this dumbfuck?" while spitting little bits of chocolate cereal in my direction.

"I'm from the agency. I have a check for you. For Barry," I correct myself.

"Oh, give it here." He reaches out, almost spilling his cereal.

"I was told to only deliver it to . . . Barry."

The Boss suit feels uncomfortable again.

He drops the bowl of Cocoa Puffs onto the coffee table; the stoners don't flinch, still zoned into Ashby on the Panasonic.

"You dumbfuck, give it here." His arm is now fully extended toward me.

"Are one of you guys, Barry?" I ask, hoping for an out, glancing outside, feeling queasy being eye level with certain houses in the hills that look so distant from the street. But the final scene of the film hypnotizes them. The characters are cooking hot dogs in the freezing cold, and, as it plays out, one of the stoners finally speaks. "I'm hungry." The woman who answered the door appears, asking everyone what they want to eat.

"She's your cook?" I ask.

Josh turns to her, but before he can get an order out of his mouth, she speaks. "Double-doubles?" and in unison all the stoners say "Yes" as one of them, the shortest and ugliest of the bunch, grabs the check out of my hand. "I'm Barry," he tells me, disappearing into a connecting office.

The guys laugh as Josh sits, pulling a long, thick cloud out of a bong, blowing it in my direction. "She makes double-doubles, can you believe that shit? She found the right buns, cheese, and meat. You'll have one."

"I like mine animal style," I tell him, and he barks back at me, "Fuck mustard."

I start moving for the front door.

"I'm kidding, I'm kidding," he tells me. "Chill for sec, smoke a bowl."

I hesitate.

"Am I not a client of the agency you work for?"

"You are," I tell him.

"Do I not bring in millions a year in commission for that agency?"

"You do," I answer again, straining to keep my eyes from the windows, wanting desperately to get into the hallway outside the unit.

"So, whatever I want, I fucking get, and right now I want you to smoke, chill out, and watch some motherfucking Hal Ashby. You know how many people want to smoke and watch flicks with me?" he asks while taking another hit. "Aren't you guys supposed to do whatever I say?" Josh adjusts his nuts in his boxers as one of his friends speaks up. "I bet CAA or WME would smoke with us."

"Shit yeah, they would," Josh says. "I bet if I put out lines of blow around the block they'd race each other snorting it up just to get a general with me; and all I'm asking you to do is take a teeny, tiny, little hit."

"Just a teeny, tiny, little hit," someone mimics Josh, who's smiling at me, leaning back into the couch, enjoying the high. "You know what I'll do, dumbfuck? I'll call my agent and see what he thinks about this."

He smiles at me. "Barry," he yells toward the office, "get Chris on the phone."

I pray he's bluffing, and, just as I'm about to leave, Josh blurts out, "Dumbfuck, someone's on the phone for you." And it's the way he extends the word *fuck* that sells it.

I've never spoken to Chris Warren before; we've only exchanged nods in the hallways and at company functions, but he's got a strong list of young stars, which means he's going to be around for a while and it would behoove me to stay on his good side. So I move back into the room and take the phone from Barry. I'm in the zone, prepared for the inevitable.

"Chris, what's up?"

"Who is this?"

"I'm a trainee, my name—"

"Listen to me clearly." He cuts me off sharply.

Pause.

"Are you listening?" he asks.

"Yes."

"It's very simple. If you want a future as an agent, you will listen and obey clients. If you want to be an agent, you will roll up your fucking sleeves, rip that fatty out of that fatty's hand, and you will fucking puff, bro. You will puff that magic fucking dragon until he tells you to stop. Shit, you suck his dick if he asks."

"Fine."

"What're you, a fucking fag?" He laughs. "Listen, man," he continues. "That lump of stoned shit in front of you pays my kids' tuition to Buckley and my wife's daily visits to Chanel. You puff or we have a problem."

He hangs up.

All eyes on me.

Smoke dancing in the air.

The end credits crawling up the Panasonic.

High noon at a little before 3:00 p.m. on a Tuesday, twenty-six floors above Sunset . . .

"Give me the bong," I declare, loosening my tie, unbuttoning the top of my Boss shirt before sitting down as Barry stuffs the stem with a fresh pinch of weed. Without hesitation I torch and clear the entire bowl in one hit, exhaling toward the ceiling. "You know, Ashby formed a production company in the seventies called D.F. Films. Stood for Dumb Fuck Films," I tell them, inhaling out of the device again, clearing all remaining smoke from the glass tube.

I smile at them, buttoning my shirt and straightening my tie, as a silence falls over the room.

Josh sits up, straight-faced, looking like he's going to say something, and vomits a splash of laughter, which I quickly fall prey to, feeling the effect, joining them all in a fit; stoned.

The double-double tastes surprisingly on point as another pinch of weed is offered while *Being There* now graces the Panasonic. Josh tells me about an idea he has to remake *Tango & Cash* and *The Toy,* which the friends respond to positively, so they break out laptops and start writing treatments for both ideas as another bong load is ripped clean out of a resin-stained glass vessel and released into the heavens of the condo. As I'm walking out, higher than the surrounding hills, needing to call Stan about *#2* on the list, Josh stops me and asks, "D.F. Films, that's a true story?" And all I'm thinking about is how easily these idiots are going to sell those remake ideas and how I've never been baked at work before, and I answer, "Google it," with a smile. And while exiting the unit, I hear Josh tell someone, "I like that dumbfuck."

• • •

Pulling out onto Sunset, heading west toward the office, still feeling twenty-six floors high, I'm leveled by paranoia during a phone call with Stan. He first tells me I sound strange and asks if everything is cool. I tell him I might have gotten food poisoning from sushi at lunch. I assume Stan is about to inform me about #2 on the list, but, for some reason, Derek enters my mind, thoughts of him excelling on David Michael's desk while I'm out driving around like I work for UPS. I keep repeating to myself that everything will be fine, that everything will work out for the best, that everything is meant to be, while Stan rambles on, and I see the woman with red bangs and mascara-lined charcoal eyes my father spoke to at Mastro's jogging toward me, but when I blink she's gone. The phone falls from my hands, forcing me to pull over, north of Sunset on Alpine. The call disconnects, and a text from Alisa comes in that reads: *Having fun? We are!* And the BlackBerry drops again as I fight to collect myself.

Back on the phone with Stan after a few moments to myself with the windows rolled down and the engine shut off. I am to pick up Lisa Howard from the Santa Monica Airport. She's an actress with a quote of $8 million a film, who has been working nonstop lately, bouncing from one terrible romantic comedy to the next, racking up incredibly nice commissions for the agency. So whatever she wants, she gets. I'm to pick her up and do as she says for the rest of the day, before dropping her off at the Peninsula hotel at 6:00 p.m. for a dinner meeting. She claims a driver once tried to rape and kidnap her; therefore, she never uses professional drivers when she's in L.A. I'm happy to do it; I'm just not quite sure what makes everyone think I won't rape and kidnap her.

Stan reiterates that I'm the perfect shitstain for the job (again, flattering), so I race down Sunset toward the 405, and the 10 West delivers me into Santa Monica. Later, while waiting for Lisa's plane to land at one of the airport's private hangars, I listen to Howard Stern interview David Arquette. Howard brings an eighty-year-old female midget porn star into the studio, and she lies down on the floor and masturbates for everyone; and I get the feeling Arquette is disturbed. Not because a geriatric midget porn star is masturbating but more so because she's doing it with her feet because she has no arms. The segment ends, so I shut the radio off, finally not feeling so stoned from the session at Josh's earlier. I tweet about waiting for an actress to land in a Learjet so I can kidnap her. According to all the replies, no one seems to care about actresses.

The plane lands, and the pilot escorts Lisa over to my ride as her luggage is placed in the trunk. I'm waiting for her to get in, but she's standing outside the door on a call, a Birkin bag swinging from her frail, spray-tanned shoulder, and she refuses to make eye contact with me, choosing to smoke cigarettes instead, her eyes fixed on the blue horizon.

She finally steps into my car, quickly introduces herself, and tells me that she just came in from a shoot in Chicago, where she's "never seen so many fat people." She lights a cigarette, exhales, then asks if it's cool to smoke.

"Only if I can have one."

She hesitates. "Only one left," she tells me as she bites a fingernail and blows a surge of smoke that barely finds its way out of the half-open, tinted window to her right.

Our first stop will be the Chris McMillan Salon on Burton Way. It's taking forever to get back to Beverly Hills because

Lisa won't allow me to take the freeway, she hates freeways and claims, "You don't fucking need them anyway." So I head east on Pico and make it a couple of blocks west of Sepulveda before Lisa looks up from texting and asks,

"Are we on fucking Pico?"

"Yeah."

"Well, get off it, no one takes Pico."

"It's faster this time of day," I tell her.

"It's ugly. I don't drive on Pico."

Heading north on Sawtelle, I ask if Olympic is better, and she tells me, "barely." I head east on Olympic, and when we reach Century City moments later I ask if she likes the movie *Die Hard.* She claims she's seen parts of it, noting that Bruce Willis is hot and how he's the only sexy bald man alive.

"Well, that's the building in *Die Hard,*" I tell her, pointing through my windshield toward the giant high-rise ahead of us.

She says nothing.

"The Nakatomi Tower," I say with a smile, still pointing down Olympic.

"Grow up," she tells me, her head slumped away from me.

More smoke is blown out of the half-cracked window, and too much of it is staying in the car, so I roll the window down as we head up Doheny. She screams, "No, keep the windows up." I apologize, and she tells me she's really not in the mood for interaction.

I drop Lisa off at Chris McMillan to get her hair colored, cut, and extensions added. While she's there, I run to get her a sprout sandwich from Urth Caffé, but she specifically requests I go to the one on Melrose, even though the one in Beverly Hills is closer, because, according to Lisa, the hummus at the Urth on Melrose is "less garlicky." She also wants a strawberry smoothie, but not one from Urth (where they're excellent by the way), she prefers them from the Beverly Hills Juice Club, who use frozen bananas and almonds as the base for their drinks—she's lactose intolerant, so this is best. Five packs of American Spirits and a slice of red velvet cake from Joan's are also required before heading back to the salon, where she tells me she thinks her iPhone broke. We go to the Apple Store at The Grove, and, after signing fifteen autographs, she buys a new 32 GB iPhone and a 64 GB iPad because she forgot hers in Chicago and misses it.

She finally talks to me two blocks from The Peninsula. "Why in the world would you want to be an agent?"

I want to tell her so I can fuck rich, famous actresses and then dump or divorce them when they can't get work anymore; but instead, for some reason, I tell her what feels like the truth.

"I want to be more powerful than my father, more respected than he ever was. And even though I'm his son, and he's provided me with everything . . . I was listening when he taught me early on that, life is a competition."

I drop my head to the right, staring at her while stopped at a red light on Wilshire.

"So, are you like a sicko or something?" she asks, rolling her eyes, and then she rips open a pack of American Spirits and lights a fresh one with the lit cig hanging from her lips as we pull into the guest drop-off area of the hotel. Lisa pops out of the car as bellmen descend on us, grabbing her bags out of the trunk. She vanishes without a word, a trail of smoke in her wake, and I think of my father again, back to the birthday party I had at Universal Studios, and what he said about actors.

I'm falling into a leather chair fifteen minutes later. It's quiet with little movement throughout the mailroom as I close my eyes, trying to ignore thoughts of Derek on a desk upstairs or Lisa blowing smoke in my car or Kevin, Perry, Tyler, and Alisa up north doing god knows what at a concert or Josh jamming Cocoa Puffs into his mouth or that kid from high school who's staying at the Beverly Hills Hotel with a model or seeing the redhead with bangs and mascara-lined, charcoal eyes. Stan gently lays a hand on my shoulder, an unlit cigarette hanging from his lips, telling me, "Thanks, shitstain."

Human Resources

I decide to invite Derek to Chipotle with us, but he declines, telling me he packed a lunch, and Kevin and Tyler have to walk away so as to not fall down laughing in his presence. They know you have to be careful in this town, that, although it's a long shot, Derek could be running the company one day or, more likely, be sitting on the opposite side of a future negotiation, and people never forget the humiliations.

"Cool, another time," I tell him and join in on the laughter once we're out of earshot as we travel downstairs toward the parking garage.

Within fifty-three minutes we've finished three barbacoa burritos, six carnitas soft tacos, two baskets of chips and guacamole, and discussed topics from how much money ICM has made on TV packages to Doughboys' breakfast menu highlights to Kobe Bryant's legacy to being pissed about missing out on buying certain media stocks to the best porn sites when using an iPad all while drinking so many Diet Cokes with lemon wedges that we each had to piss before heading back to the office.

I'm in a food coma when Stan tells me that Jennifer, the girl from Human Resources with big natural tits and an even bigger ass, who, from what I can tell from her appearances at company functions, only dates black dudes, sent an e-mail to the mailroom asking for me to meet her in the HR offices after lunch. I quickly run to the bathroom, wishing I hadn't gone to Chipotle, and comb my fingers through my hair, forming it perfectly in place, move closer to the mirror, checking my face and skin, which is surprisingly flawless despite the amount of saturated fat just consumed, and then back away, centering my tie, amazed that the usually lethal dose of Mexican food didn't throw me off-kilter or leave some hideous stain on my uniform. As I exit the lobby bathroom, I tell myself that, whatever opportunity they present, I'm going to take it just to get out of the mailroom.

I'm sitting with Jennifer, waiting for her to get off some phone call that I'm sure is supremely unimportant and noticing now for the first time her thin and unevenly waxed eyebrows, her generically bland clothes, crispy-curled, dyed blond hair, and slight southern drawl, which make me wonder why this girl is involved with the hiring at a company like this.

"So you've been here four months?" she asks, already knowing the answer as her phone slams into its cradle.

"Yes."

"And you want MP lit, I see?"

"Yes, I interviewed with Rizzo the other day, but it got cut short. He had a thing."

"Jake didn't set that up through HR; you have to officially set these things up," she tells me, no doubt enjoying the one time in her life she'd ever be in a one-up position on me.

"I understand, just sort of happened. I'd love to get back in to meet with him," I tell her, now hating her, wanting to slap her in the face with my dick.

"I think you'd be a perfect candidate for it," she responds.

I love her, I would never think of cock-slapping her.

"As you know, his assistant, Jake, is leaving, and I know Rizzo doesn't want to meet with anyone, so we want to get you back in there as soon as possible. You'll be the first one in, probably tomorrow, so be ready." I'm saying yes while getting up to leave, smiling, nodding my head, and thanking her, but all I'm thinking is, *I got this.*

An average stint in the mailroom lasts four to six months. You then work as an assistant to an agent or agents for two to three years on average. Some people have been assistants for five years, and some are promoted to agent in ten months. Like in any other industry, it's all timing and, more important, who you know. For instance, a year ago, this kid from Studio City who's a few years older than me is working as an assistant for a talent manager at a small firm that represents writers and a handful of actors who only really work in television. Managers are a lot like agents, except they're allowed to wear jeans every day and actually try to be friends with their clients. Anyway, this dude is working as an assistant, getting nowhere quick like the majority of people in this business, until one day his boss tells him he's being courted by one of the biggest agencies in town and he's considering ditching the management business, buying some suits, and making the jump to becoming an agent. Now, people take their assistants with them to new companies all the time. But this fucking guy tells the agency not only does he want mid to high six-figure salary guaranteed for three years, a company-leased Mercedes, and a lifetime membership to Equinox, but he also wants the agency to make his assistant an agent . . . and somehow, without any precedent, it happens. Here's how it went down: the assistant's best friend is Brent Styles, whose father, Arthur Styles, has been one of the biggest TV producers in the game for the last four decades. And guess what? Arthur is a client of the agency and would really love it if his son's friend was made agent and placed on his representation team. Boom, you're a fucking agent. That's one way it happens; one insanely fortuitous way it goes down, and the number of nights this story has robbed me of sleep continues to grow.

My father is almost as big as Arthur Styles. I mean, let's face facts, he may be younger and worth a few hundred million less, but he's making films, and that fossil Arthur is a glorified soap opera producer. Unfortunately for me, Dad isn't a client and, with the exception of putting in a few phone calls to get me this job, would never pull those kinds of strings. This kid was just a little luckier than me, which is fine because this shit is a marathon and I'm a skinny, Nigerian, marathon-running motherfucker trapped inside the body of a curly haired Hebrew. I'll do the time and see everyone at the end, years from now, all sweaty and struggling to breathe while I moon-walk across the finish line, smoking a Cohiba Behike, sipping Johnnie Walker Blue, getting the good booth at the Palm.

Rizzo Interview

My interview with Nick Rizzo is in fifteen minutes and I'm taking a painful, loose shit in the second-floor bathroom. I'm reading a story in *Variety* about a production company's acquisition of the life rights to one of the Columbine killers' best friend, some trench-coat-wearing geek who chickened out of going along with the two killers, and I think about all the kids that would have loved to kill me back in high school.

I also think about who would be good for the project once it's set up with a studio. Who would make it click? Would Soderbergh be interested in working with younger actors? Would Paul Thomas Anderson take a writer-for-hire gig and make it like licorice—dark and twisted? And if the studio didn't want to spend too much cash, which they probably wouldn't because really, truly, who the fuck wants to see this movie to begin with, then I'd try to place some second-tier writer on it who may have one to two decent unproduced scripts but really spends all his time at one of the coffee shops on the corner of Beverly and Robertson staring at a laptop while occasionally checking the UTA Job List for a real gig.

I'm wiping, washing my hands, straightening my hair, my tie, and practicing a few different smiles in the mirror, holding in another fart, scared to push it out and accidentally shit myself, which actually happened a few months ago at the ArcLight after I'd inhaled three orders of cotton candy foie gras at The Bazaar.

I'm sitting in Nick's office alone again, meditating to the sounds of traffic on Wilshire. He quickly enters, throwing his BlackBerry on the desk from at least five feet away, and stands in front of me, leaning against the huge wooden armoire, his arms folded, staring at me. My chair is positioned so that the sun blinds me and I can barely make out Nick's face.

"So, you want to work for me, why?"

"I—"

"No . . . you want to be an agent, why?"

"Well, I—"

"You know what? Forget it."

He just stares at me in silence for two minutes, looking me up and down. From my clean black Gucci loafers with shiny metal buckles, up to my navy blue pin-striped Ralph Lauren suit, bright white Calvin Klein button-down shirt, and finally to a dark purple Armani tie knotted in a wide full Windsor that hangs an inch or two above my YSL belt. Then he eyes my neatly combed, dark brown hair that's no longer curly since getting a $450 straightening treatment at Byron, and I look away, uneasy from the blinding sunlight and abandoned lines of questioning.

He slowly walks toward the door, shutting it quietly before turning around and making our first, true eye contact.

"How many pussies have you fucked?"

My mind goes blank.

"Quick! I like things quick. Lesson one, be quick or be gone!"

I recover, and he can see I'm about to say something and quiets me with a finger to his lips.

"So I'll ask you again, how many pussies have you fucked?"

"I've slept with seventeen girls," I tell him.

"Seventeen pussies?" he asks, not very excited by my answer.

"Yes."

"Seventeen pussies?" he repeats, thinking something to himself, slowly fingering and then rubbing his chin.

"Yes, seventeen," I tell him again.

"Any black pussies?"

"Yes," I tell him, not sure how this will affect his opinion of me.

A brief pause slips into a tense beat and he's lost in thought, thinking something awful, I'm sure.

"Did you just say something?"

"Just that I have fucked a black pussy," I tell him.

"What?"

"I have slept with a black girl."

"Oh, yeah . . . well, good for you."

I can't tell if this is sarcasm. We're just staring at each other. I'm on the verge of puking.

"How many black pussies?"

"Just the one," I admit.

"And nice, yes?"

"Definitely."

"You love the black pussy?" he asks.

"I *like* the black pussy."

"Yes!" He slams his hands together, clapping loud. "They like to get fucked," he tells me while shaking his head slowly, then laughing to himself.

"So you start tomorrow."

"I have the job?"

His smile disappears instantaneously, so remarkably fast that I'm actually taken aback by it, and he tells me, "Remember, be quick, okay? I don't like to repeat myself and I don't like my time wasted. Get it or get the fuck out of my life and, more importantly, out of my business. Do not fuck with my business. You start training with Jake tomorrow."

Nick quickly turns, picks up the BlackBerry, snatches his pin-striped jacket (I struggle to confirm the label but fail) off the coat rack behind his desk, and shuffles out of his office while asking Jake where his next meeting is. Jake tells him, and he's gone, leaving me alone in the room with a smile on my face remembering Joy Wells's smooth skin and the Britney Spears concert we shared at Staples Center followed by a night in my parents' pool house. My one and only black pussy, a special notch on my belt that just paid off.

While walking out of Nick's office I pass De Niro again, his head down and hands in his pockets, and I didn't get to use any of the information I obtained when looking through his files; the interview with Nick was almost too easy.

Just like Joy.

NICK RIZZO

54 years old

Motion Picture Literary Agent / Agency Partner

- Earns $8.5 million a year plus a company-leased BMW 750i

- Movies his clients have been involved with on the producing, writing, or directing end: *The Departed, War of the Worlds, Harry Potter* (most of them, I think, but who cares), *The Dark Knight, Scarface, Ocean's Eleven, Pineapple Express,* all four *Lethal Weapon*s, *Beverly Hills Cop I & II, The Godfather, Shrek* (all of them), and *Titanic*

- Has fired 9 assistants in the past three years, sent one to the hospital with what the report filed by Human Resources termed "odd cuts," tortured another one so badly that the assistant spent three weeks in bed without sleeping, and had a baby with a third whom he is fully "financing" in a house he owns on Mulholland that his present wife has no idea about. Were he at any other company in America he would have been fired for such behavior long ago. Instead, he's been promoted twice and has received three raises since joining the agency

- Currently on his fourth marriage, third agency, ninth diet (his weight has fluctuated up and down by 130 pounds in the past five years), second alcohol relapse, and first cocaine addiction . . . the perfect time to begin working for someone.

The Popcorn Bet

Jason Reitman is presenting *Boogie Nights* at the New Beverly Cinema tonight as one of his favorite films, and it's sold out, but I snagged two tickets the minute they went on sale and thought this would be a perfect date for Stacey, the trainer from Equinox. She has long, straight blond hair, a petite, rock-hard frame, and a very cute face—she may be better looking than Alisa who's out of town for the weekend at her family's home in Montecito. I'd love to trick Stacey into thinking I'm a decent guy, and maybe I'll get away with that, but it's doubtful; because tonight is only about one thing: the bet with Kevin.

It's a simple bet. We were watching *Diner* the other night and came to the realization that the scene where Mickey Rourke gets a girl to touch his dick, which he was hiding in a bag of popcorn, and convinces her that he isn't a total scumbag, which most likely led to him taking her home and at least getting a hand job, is probably the second most gangster move we've ever seen in any film. The most gangster move we've ever seen in a film is in James Toback's *Fingers,* when Harvey Keitel walks up to a chick he just met and fucks her standing up in a bathroom because she's dating a mobster he wants to disrespect. That's called rape, so we're skipping that one; but this popcorn shit is literally in the bag. Kevin owes me a dinner at WP24 if I get Stacey to touch my boner and still go home with me at the end of the night.

We're in our seats, a row in front of and two seats to the left of Kevin and Tyler, who are here to verify the bet, and what do you know—as it turned out, I was in the mood for a medium bag of popcorn. I think the large would have definitely made my dick look too small.

Soon the lights fade and Jason Reitman quickly introduces the film, "PTA made me want to start making films . . . one of the great L.A. movies . . . my dad blah, blah, blah," and everyone starts clapping as Jason takes his seat.

I'm giddy as the New Line Cinema logo floats into place, and I've decided to wait for the scene where Heather Graham does full frontal during Dirk's "interview" as the perfect moment where I could reasonably argue that my dick got hard and somehow found its way out of my pants and into the bag of popcorn. The thoughts I'm having while preparing to follow through on the bet range from wondering if Stacey spits or swallows to how painful paper cuts on my dick could be to who the Lakers play tomorrow night on TNT and whether or not it's gay for my penis to be in an enclosed space with Orville Redenbacher.

Here we go. Rollergirl is tongue-kissing Dirk, full frontal comes and goes, and I've been rubbing my dick against my thigh enough to pull this off no problem. Things move pretty easily from here. There's a perfect slit on the bottom of the bag, which I almost fully rip open, and after a bit of awkward jerking movement, which isn't lost on Stacey—she's glancing at me from time to time with curiosity, which I return with polite smiles—I secure it and a great sense of relief washes over. I proudly throw a kernel or two in my mouth and wash it down with a long sip of Diet Coke while turning around and smiling at Kev and Ty, who are bouncing up and down in their seats like ten-year-olds overdosing on Ritalin.

The relief doesn't last long. As I'm smiling at my friends, Stacey rips open a packet of salt and pours it into the bag, funneling the seasoning directly into my dick. I had gonorrhea once in college (which is no big deal, it goes away with one antibiotic) and it only stings when you pee, but this kind of hurt is constant. I jump out of my seat, the bag attached to my crotch like that dog in *There's Something About Mary*. Stacey never even reached into the bag. Kevin's and Tyler's laughter is the last noise I hear as I'm literally running to the bathroom in the lobby, where I pull down my jeans and boxers, lean into the sink's waterfall, and start praying my dick doesn't fall off.

Fifteen minutes later, with the pain subsiding, I return to my seat, and I'm positive Stacey thinks I was taking a shit. I hold up my BlackBerry, whispering to her, "My boss," but she just politely smiles and turns her head back to the screen, definitely not believing me. I pop a Xanax and chew it down as my anxiety pounds, mirroring Dirk on-screen, who's screaming with coke-caked nostrils, and the BlackBerry vibrates with an e-mail from Kevin which reads: *You Lose!* I turn around, shooting bloodshot daggers at them, and all I get in return are silent golf claps.

The last few reels of the film look out of focus, we skip the Reitman Q & A when Stacey says she's tired, and then it all plays out. Leaving the theater, dropping Stacey off at the Broadcast Center, a kiss on the cheek inside the car, her saying she'll see me at the gym, me saying something about sorry for having to take the phone call, her nodding and smiling again, new waves of anxiety and embarrassment coat me, then I'm home, naked, grabbing at a prescription bottle of weed, blowing smoke everywhere, my eyes water while moving into a shower so I can obsessively scrub my genitals and attempt to forget while enjoying the refreshing rush of hydrogen and oxygen that only an eight-hundred-dollar Lacava Waterblade showerhead can provide.

On a Desk

I t's my first day training with Jake on Nick's desk and I'm hungover and miserable and don't really remember what I did last night or what day it is. Time moves, with a flurry of calls, e-mails, screams, and one tremendous shit, during which I was able to read a third of this week's *Hollywood Reporter*. I never thought I'd make it to lunch, but according to the watch it's 12:55, and I'm utterly relieved. Kev was moved out of the mailroom for the day to fill in for an assistant who quit this morning after getting into a fistfight with an agent. He calls to tell me the agent and a young, extremely skinny guy with the letter *G* shaved into his head have been sleeping on couches behind closed doors for the past hour and he thinks they're on heroin, which wouldn't really shock anyone.

He tells me we should leave for lunch "right this fucking second, before they wake up."

"*If* they wake up," I remind him.

Kev laughs.

I give Jake the puppy dog eyes and he tells me to go. Three minutes later we're smoking Parliament Lights in my X5 with the windows rolled down and "No Church in the Wild" is playing as we pull onto Wilshire and head north up Robertson.

The line at Cuvée is out the door as crazy Robertson, a

perpetually shirtless homeless man with one of the better tans in the city, passes us, twirling through the Third Street intersection on a pair of roller skates. My apartment is a block away, and there's someone on the roof—I think it's the newscaster girl but really can't tell—smoking a cigarette, looking out at the city below, and all I'm thinking about is cold penne turkey Bolognese and a spicy shrimp Caesar. My attention shifts to the paparazzi outside Kitson snapping shots of some famous girls (Kim, Nicole, Nicky, Lindsay, Jessica—take your pick) shopping. More waiting, ordering, sitting, and being served while all that's discussed over lunch is the going rate for bareback blow jobs at massage parlors in West Hollywood, needing to make at least a few hundred thousand by the age of thirty "or it's pretty much all over for you," eating out hookers (pros and cons), golden parachutes (not a sex term), crack vs. freebase cocaine, Sacha Baron Cohen's new film needing/having "legs," the fact that it's twenty degrees too hot today, chances of heterosexuals getting AIDS without using protection (surprisingly not as high as one would think), and rating every girl who walks by us on Robertson using the "sister scale"—which is based on whether or not we'd kill our own sister to fuck them—fourteen girls in under an hour qualified.

Jake isn't around when I return to the office at ten after two. The connecting door to Nick's office is closed, so I take a seat behind the assistant's desk, check some e-mails, and listen to phone messages. The connecting door swings open, revealing Nick, who is ushering David Michaels's assistant Shane out of the office. He stops at the doorway in front of the desk, next to the *Taxi Driver* poster, watches her go, and then slowly turns around to face me.

"You know Shane?"

I tell him I do.

He takes a step or two toward my desk and extends a few fingers under my nose, causing me to flinch. "Michaels isn't the only one she's *assisting*," he tells me, now reaching for my nose again, telling me to "smell it, smell it."

Before I can tell him to fuck off, he rushes into his office, calling me a pussy under his breath but just loud enough for me to hear it. He screams out "Tom Rothman," and as I'm dialing Rothman's office I watch Nick take a seat at his desk, holding his soiled fingers up in front of his face. I lean over at a sharp angle, shout, "We're holding for Rothman," and catch Nick smelling his hand with his feet up on his desk, a black-and-white photograph of his new wife and young daughters posing on a beach, wearing all-white matching outfits, staring back at his closed eyes, replaying the latest depraved memory.

"Rothman, line one," hangs in the air for ten seconds before Nick opens his eyes to take the call.

Jake returns mouthing the word *sorry* as the call ends, and Nick is standing over us, incoherently muttering something to himself while he reaches for and pushes every script on a shelf above the desk (easily two hundred of them, organized alphabetically) onto the floor.

"You were both late after lunch, now stay late tonight and clean this shit up," he says.

Then he squats down in front of the cherrywood cabinet, pulls the third drawer open, and delivers a file to it before walking off to attend a company meet-and-greet for a new actor recently signed away from an Alaskan talent agency. They're hoping he's the first successful Eskimo in Hollywood; at least that's what Nick mumbles to us before he walks upstairs, picking his nose, straightening his tie, and soiling it with boogers.

I race around the desk, pulling the third drawer open as I drop to the carpet, and I see it—the Nick file, full of paper, back in place at the end of the row of files. Fireworks explode in my mind, sitting there, unable to blink or speak, and when Jake asks if I'm feeling well, I can only muster a slow-moving nod of the head while closing the drawer, attempting to make sense of things.

Later, Tyler calls inviting me to a premiere tonight, telling me Drew Diller is going as well and we can tag along in his limo (they grew up together in Malibu and remain friendly), and I'm almost pissed at him for thinking he had to ask. Jake waits for me to get off the phone, rises with at least twenty scripts in his hands, which he pushes into my chest and says, "Get these back on the shelf in the right order. I'll cover for you. You'll be working past eight every night for the next few years; this is the last premiere you'll have time for until you're promoted, so enjoy it."

"Should we really be touching the scripts before the end of the day?"

"The guy can't remember how many times he's been married, who's running Universal, or the last person he spoke with; no chance he remembers this. Go. Have fun."

I thank him as the thought of working past 8:00 p.m. for the foreseeable future lingers, bumming me out, but whatever . . . I'll just go to after-parties until I'm promoted.

A Premiere

In a white Range Rover limo on the way to the premiere of Tarantino's new flick *The Vega Brothers* with Kev, Ty, Drew Diller (no relation to Barry), and Drew's hottest new client, Caitlyn Crew, whom he discovered on the Venice Beach Boardwalk selling two-dollar bracelets made of seaweed. As luck had it, Tarantino once bought one and happened to be wearing it the day of Caitlyn's audition. She spotted it, the strangeness of it all was too strong to deny, so he hired her on the spot to costar in the movie. Drew is the youngest agent in the building, we went to high school together (he was two grades above me), and he acts like we're best friends, most likely because of who my father is, which makes me think he's a joke. Although, I'm loving him tonight because Drew also brought Jen Klein, who also went to Brentwood, along as his date, which provides much entertainment for me because Drew has no idea whatsoever that Jen and I once fucked at a Crossroads graduation party in the men's locker room of the Jonathan Club. She looks decent tonight, not much different from a few years ago. After we say hello, I'm certain of two things: one, that although she was drunk, she remembers our night together (who could forget two Jews fucking in a gentile beach club), and two, she hasn't told Drew about our tryst.

DREW DILLER

25 years old

Motion Picture Talent Agent

- Earns $85,000 a year and occupies the smallest office in the building, which features no windows

- Drives a maroon Cayenne Turbo that his grandmother bought him when he was promoted. When she dies he'll inherit $12.5 million and has already received $75,000 every birthday since he was 13

- Lives in a 3-bedroom, 2.5-bathroom home in Sunset Plaza next door to Dick Donner and Lauren Shuler Donner, down the street from Johnny Knoxsville and next door to Blake Griffin, who rumor has it once threatened to beat Drew up for not cleaning up dog shit on the sidewalk in front of his house

- Jen Klein is the 108th female Drew has fucked, and, according to him, he can tell you what the insides of all their pussies look like. Number 1 of 108 was a girl named Dana Sloan, whom he dated during his freshman year at Brentwood. She disappeared after last being seen with him eating mozzarella marinara at Maria's after school. He lost his virginity to her, and a day later, when he was with his family having brunch at the Four Seasons, she vanished off the face of Los Angeles. Months later, on July Fourth of that year, they thought they had found her when authorities pulled a thoroughly burnt corpse out of the Malibu lagoon, but the teeth were completely removed from the body and they couldn't get a positive ID. According to Drew, "That was a rough summer."

Odd Future's "Oldie" is blaring out of the custom JBL speakers as we turn off Wilshire onto Gayley, and it's only 7:05 p.m., which means we're very early considering these things always start at least a half hour late and we're only two minutes from the Fox Village Theater. Showing up early to a premiere is lame, so we pick up a bottle of Grey Goose at the liquor store near In-N-Out and finish the bottle in ten minutes, chasing shots of it with Heineken.

Caitlyn sprinkles coke on some weed that she stuffs into purple, grape-flavored rolling paper she's delicately holding with the tips of her fingers. I watch her, turned on as she licks the paper gently before twisting it closed and lighting it. I catch Jen watching me watch Caitlyn and stare her down until she is forced to look away toward Drew, who is sniffing lines of coke off an issue of *Vanity Fair* and missing the whole exchange as we turn onto Broxton behind a line of chauffered vehicles.

Two limos are still in front of us waiting to drop off their passengers, and three Persian teens smoking a hookah at an outdoor café stare into the tinted windows, trying to make us out. The limo moves up one spot as everyone readies themselves to exit. Drew checks his nose in one of the girl's makeup mirrors and wipes some sweat off his brow. I straighten my black tie and brush some lost coke off my dark pants. Ty pops an Altoid in his mouth. Kev smoothes out his eyebrows while I catch Jen watching me again as I watch Caitlyn uncross her legs, flashing her yellow-thong-covered crotch as she moves toward the back of the limo and finishes her joint that's dropped into a half-finished can of Heineken before sliding on ridiculously oversize black Tom Ford sunglasses as our limo is now in first position pulling up to the red carpet entrance.

The sounds of camera flashes popping and screaming fans

mix together, raising my coke-fueled heart rate as an enormous security guard in an all-black suit and sunglasses opens one of the doors. Caitlyn slides out, but before fully exiting she looks back at us in the limo, slowly pushes her glasses down, focuses her now wrecked eyes on Drew, and tells him that he's fired before quickly exiting and slamming the door shut.

The red carpet is a blur of security guards dressed in Tarantino-styled black-and-white suits, crazed publicists pushing their way through the hectic scene of Harvey smiling with Quentin, Bob not smiling with Lawrence Bender, Sam Jackson wearing a fatigue Kangol holding hands with Toni Howard, Kanye West posing with Jamie Foxx, Mike Simpson and Ari Emanuel with what look like assistants lingering behind them, Peter Bart, Joe Francis, J. J. Abrams, Amy Heckerling, Rick Reuben wearing a tie-dyed fur coat, Jason Barrett with LL Cool J, Brian Sher with T.I., Ramses IsHak and Mike Sheresky on either side of Ice Cube, who is wearing an all-black James Worthy Lakers jersey, Cara Lewis with Common, Andrea Nelson with Beyoncé, P. T. Anderson and Maya Rudolph talking with John C. Reilly, Selma Blair sporting a shaved head posing for the cameras, and more fans than I can count are screaming so loud as I pass behind John Travolta and Michael Madsen with my head down that for a minute I think I may be someone important before finally reaching the end, where I snap a picture of my new pair of Prada loafers on the red carpet to tweet with the following message: *Tarantino Time . . .*

Inside the Fox's packed lobby I'm grabbing for free popcorn and a bottle of water before sitting down behind Brent Bolthouse and some model and in front of J. C. Spink and a girl wearing huge yellow sunglasses who I can only describe as looking unkempt. I'm explaining to Kev and Ty how inventive this film's concept is, but they don't give a fuck, they can't keep their attention off the scene.

"*Reservoir Dogs* meets *Pulp Fiction* . . . that doesn't give you a boner?" I ask.

"She gives me a boner," Kevin says while motioning to Bolthouse's girl, who I pray didn't just hear that, we'd only be banned from half the parties thrown in Los Angeles.

"Hey, bro, if the thought of two guys in a movie is giving you a boner, that's cool," Tyler adds, pounding Kevin's fist, lusting over Bolthouse's girl as well.

"By the way, how is your boner? Still stinging?" They laugh, high-fiving each other and start a "Loser" chant. I think I hate them.

8:05 p.m. The movie hasn't started yet, and it's the usual pre-premiere theater scene. Brett Ratner is jumping around in the aisle hugging Woody Harrelson and Chris Tucker while Nicky and Paris Hilton sit nearby yelling at Brandon Davis, who keeps throwing popcorn kernels in their publicist's face, one deliberate kernel at a time. Garry Shandling locks down the aisle seat across from me and glances around; we make brief eye contact. He then turns to Bill Maher, who is holding hands with a Bai Ling look-alike, and I can overhear him asking why so many "no names" are allowed into premieres these days.

The room is starting to reach capacity.

Other people I recognize in the theater include Robert Newman holding hands with his wife; Terence Winter sitting next to Matthew Weiner; Richard Weitz trying on his brother's glasses; Scott Caan showing Anthony Mandler something on his iPhone; Pam Abdy sipping a soda; Chris Silbermann scanning the room in search of someone; Nathan Kahane cleaning a stain off his Chuck Taylor slips; Ryan Kavanaugh whispering something into Tucker Tooley's ear; Anne Thompson furiously scribbling, watching Ron Best quietly chat with his number one client, arguably the most successful actor here tonight, Luke (Industry Fact: You're a big deal if everyone knows you by your first name); RZA holding Eli Roth in some sort of kung fu grip; Michael and Eva Chow smiling at John Burnham, who is juggling three sodas and a two bags of popcorn; Gay Andrew sitting with a group of assistants throwing popcorn in the air and catching it in each other's mouths; Randi Michel sitting with three black dudes I don't recognize; Adriana Alberghetti and Chris Donnelly standing with Matthew Michael Carnahan, who is easily the tallest person here; and at least twenty-five assistants from WME, one of whom Kevin knows from Bikram yoga in the Palisades.

"Perry told me she can eat her own pussy," he tells us.

"I don't think I've ever seen that before," Kevin admits.

I agree, noting, "It's impressive."

Drew and Jen Klein finally appear, forcing the three of us to get up and move two spots down, giving them the first two seats off the aisle. Moments after getting settled, I track Drew's eyes toward the front of the theater, where I find Caitlyn Crew talking with Rich Coen and Sam Kagan, two agents not affiliated in any way with Caitlyn (as far as Drew knows) before tonight, who now own 10 percent of that cute little, bracelet-making ass. Drew looks defeated. Beneath a transparent facade of brewing anger and explosive ego lies a thick mass of hate and self-doubt that seems to be glowing under the theater's dull fluorescents. Losing clients is an element of the gig that you've got to accept to stay sane, but this is Drew's first loss, the first chink in the armor, and from the looks of it, he isn't handling it well. He's sweating bitterness while watching Caitlyn and her new agents as they ramble on in what appears to be a fabulously amicable conversation within the roped-off, reserved collection of rows in the center of the theater.

I take his moment of fleeting attention to whisper into Jen's ear, "You miss me?"

"You fucking wish," she whispers back, playfully twirling a lock of hair that hangs over her right shoulder.

"I think the after-party is at the Jonathan Club, should be a fun night," I tell her.

"Oh yeah, you think they'll be serving miniature cocktail hot dogs again? I hope not, they left me wanting more last time."

"Fuck you."

"Oh please, you . . ." She's definitely calling me some awful name right about now, but I can't hear her anymore; I can't hear or see anything, except for someone who looks just like Derek walking past us and into the roped-off area past Caitlyn and her new agents with a couple of older dudes wearing Brioni pin-striped suits with no ties who I don't know by name but recognize from around town at events and especially at Cut; these guys fucking love Cut. I ask Kevin and Tyler if they just saw Derek, and they each say no and continue busily typing on their iPhones and giggling.

"Fucking look," I demand. "Thirteen rows down, dead center."

"I mean, I definitely see a black guy in there, but is it Derek . . . I can't say," Kevin replies.

"I can't either," Tyler says before abandoning my investigation for more texting.

I'm pretty sure it's Derek. I have no idea who invited him, why he has better seats than me, or why he's with those fucks who love Cut. Kevin notices me steaming and leans over. "Take it easy, man, I don't think it's him. And even if it is, who cares? You're the one who got Rizzo's desk, right?"

Who cares?

I bite a Xanax in half and wash it down with the last sip from my bottle of water.

Who cares?

The room goes silent as Harvey Weinstein walks inside with his arm around Kevin Smith, and he looks happy as they playfully rub each other's bald spots. They're followed by a very pale-looking Bob Weinstein, who is screaming at his president of production, who's screaming at an assistant, who, looking wasted, carefully hands an enormous box of popcorn and Milk Duds to a woman sitting with a young boy who is busy talking on a gold iPhone. Jay-Z and Beyoncé are standing in the center aisle wearing matching red outfits—his a suit, hers a flapper dress—searching for their seats, entering a reserved row where Zach Braff and Donald Faison have to stand up to let them by.

Everyone shuts up quick as the lights begin to dim except for a bright spot in front of the theater, which is quickly filled by Quentin, who is wearing a black kimono, and he's talking a mile a minute, thanking the Weinsteins, his producer, Lawrence; his agent, Mike; the cast; and pretty much everyone else in the room except for me, Kevin, and Tyler. Seconds later, John Travolta and Michael Madsen join Quentin at the front of the theater and they're all hugging and celebrating and Jen mentions that Travolta looks "interesting" tonight. The spotlight vanishes, the giant purple curtain creeps open, and an anonymous voice in the crowd yells "Fuck yeah!" as the projector fires out the first glowing image.

Heavy applause accompanies the end credits while everyone is shuffling out of the packed theater at a snail's pace, and we hear this spaz in front of us already on his phone, excitedly telling someone that "he did it again, man!" And he really did do it again, but you don't talk like that, so Kev spits a disgusting, snot-filled, yellow wad into his hand and pats this idiot on the back agreeing with him, wiping the foulness all over his jacket, which causes Ty and me to laugh. Kevin's been doing this a lot lately.

Broxton is blocked off for the after-party from CPK down to the Janss Dome. Waiters are dressed in Tarantino black suits and ties, serving Bloody Marys and candy cigarettes—the ones you can blow powdered sugar out of—which seems like a complete waste because almost everyone is standing around smoking real cigarettes. Bright red lights flood the scene, and a violent strobe light is beating on Samantha Ronson on a stage set up in the outdoor parking lot. I'm talking with Nicole Holofcener, who's a family friend—it's speculated that Nicole based Joan Cusack's character in *Friends with Money* on my older sister—and she loves hearing my stories about the industry. I'm telling her about one of Nick's clients who recently met with a producer who showed the client pictures of herself wearing nothing but a strap-on dildo while standing on the 405 freeway in broad daylight.

"I think that's on the Internet," Nicole tells me as she scans the party carefully.

Derek, or someone who looks just like him, passes through the line to the bar, walking toward me, chatting with the guys in Brioni pinstripes who love Cut and three incredibly good-looking chicks, one of whom I believe is Heidi Montag, but I'm not sure. Derek or the guy who looks like him makes eye contact with me and briefly smiles before quickly looking away, abruptly shifting direction, and evaporating into a crowd near the five-dollar milk shake stand.

At that very moment Kevin and Tyler somehow find me, and I'm thrilled I won't have to stand here alone any longer. They're wired, little particles exploding out of their mouths, telling me how they were just in the limo in the alley behind Sepi's and caught Drew standing alone, crying and slapping himself in the face. We smoke, down beer, laugh and burp and make fun of people in the crowd, and spit on the ground and hit on young, random girls (Industry Fact: WME hires the hottest female assistants) and blow cigarette smoke rings and my vision deteriorates and Kevin's breath stinks and I can't remember if it's Wednesday or Thursday night and I decide to ignore the second "Derek" sighting.

Jen Klein appears. She's looking lost, asking us if we know where Drew is, which causes us to erupt, and Kevin starts slapping himself in the face and mock crying and we're laughing really hard, ignoring her, so she walks away, rubbing her arms from a chill in the night air.

Two beers, three cigarettes, and a royale slider with cheese later, Wilmer Valderrama somehow finds his way onstage. He's gripping a microphone, rapping along to the Kanye West sound track. The Hilton sisters and Brandon Davis are nearby staring at him in disbelief, trading whispers, and laughing, with phones now glued to their ears while Sam Jackson sits next to them smoking a cigar, slowly shaking his head from left to right.

The performance continues as Wilmer tries to get the crowd involved, and soon the entire party has come to a halt, with everyone staring at him wide-eyed. Thank god the song finally ends and Samantha pushes her way back in front of her equipment, firmly taking the microphone back while Fez flashes some sort of weird hand sign that I can only describe as a very odd mix between the "West Side" and "Peace" hand symbols while nodding his head and smiling to the crowd. Danny Masterson immediately runs up to him flashing the same hand sign and they hug and I quickly look away to find Sam Jackson with his mouth slightly open, his cigar barely clinging to his lips, still slowly shaking his head from left to right. Gay Andrew and his crew walk by us, and one of them says, "I wouldn't rim his ass with your tongue."

We drunkenly stomp into Jerry's Deli and order more beer, bagel chips, chicken fingers with sides of ranch dressing, and a Belgium waffle ice cream sundae. Two chubby Asian girls, most likely UCLA students, are sitting in the booth across from us wearing pajamas, surrounded by books and a half-eaten pepperoni pizza, taking turns glancing at us and kicking each other under the table while sipping strawberry milk shakes between giggles. Tired and drunk, I lift myself up out of the booth and head to the bathroom.

The smell while pissing into the ice-filled urinal and the thought of how utterly devastating those Asian girls' lives will most likely be in the future cripples me. I consider eating the half Xanax I have left just as my BlackBerry begins buzzing against my leg, and since my dick is hanging over the urinal without any hand support (thank you very much), I casually answer it. Alisa's voice invades my head. She just left The Dime, wants to fuck, and is heading to my place, "so be there fucking pronto," she instructs.

"I'm with Kevin, you sure you wouldn't rather fuck him instead?" I snort while belching and maneuvering my dick back into my Hugo Boss boxers.

"Oh pooh, just be there fucking pronto, you monster," she slurs while abruptly ending our call.

I return to the table, falling down hard into the rose red booth as Kev is licking his lips at the two Asian girls, telling us, "I might have to fuck fat tonight," and from what I know of Kevin, he's not kidding, he really does love to "fuck fat," and I think I remember biting into a chicken finger before quickly fading out . . .

. . . I slowly fade back in . . .

. . . I don't remember leaving Jerry's, getting into a cab, picking my car up at the agency, or even meeting up with Alisa, but I'm conscious now and it's clear that we're fucking in my bedroom. But not like we usually fuck. She's not present; she just rides my dick hard with her eyes closed. I think she fucked Kevin that night after drinks at Cut when I was searching through files or maybe even Tyler. It's very possible she fucked them both; I wouldn't put it past any of them.

She's thrusting harder onto me now, maybe hoping for a few more inches that aren't there, but probably were there with whichever friend of mine she was fucking last night while I was at home covering two god-awful scripts for Rizzo. I'm nowhere near ejaculation as she's screaming, "I'm cumming, I'm cumming!"

Thoughts of Derek's appearance tonight and the "popcorn incident" are hijacking my orgasm. I'm pretty sure Alisa is faking anyway, and I hope she's not going to ask to sleep over after this, because I can't sleep when she's here.

"I'm cumming!" she yells again, embarrassing me with thoughts of my neighbors listening to us. I consider sticking my finger in her ass, which I know she hates.

I can't stop thinking about who Alisa fucked the other night. I fucked one of Kevin's ex-girlfriends, Emma, a few months ago, but I don't think he knows about it, and even though Tyler does know about it, he swore to me he'd keep it a secret. But I'm not sure I can trust Tyler because he may know that I fucked that Jeremy Zimmer assistant he dated a few times but could never close. I don't think Alisa would fuck Tyler; he's definitely not good looking enough. At least, I'm pretty sure Kevin and Tyler didn't tag-team her.

"I'm cumming!" She won't shut up and now all I'm thinking about is, *How the fuck is this girl getting off for the third time? Am I that good?* I stick my finger in her ass, which is a mistake, because now she's repeating the word *yes* over and over again, louder with each repetitive chant, and she's asking me to cum inside of her, "cum, cum, cum, cum," she's demanding, and now I'm positive my neighbors are listening to everything and I'm still nowhere near finishing, and only one thing is clear: whoever she's fucking got her into anal; which isn't the worst thing.

I'm sure it was Kevin who fucked Alisa, because now I have to assume that Tyler found out about the Jeremy Zimmer assistant, got angry like a little bitch, and told Kevin about Emma, who, just as a side note, is a fairly large slut, so he shouldn't have been so vindictive. In the long run it was probably worth it, though, Emma has a fantastically tanned body, perfectly formed B-cups with tiny nipples (the best kind), five tattoos—three of which are on her back—and a pussy that honestly smells like a freshly made Magnolia cupcake, which, beyond being ridiculous and completely true, is all I find myself thinking about at the moment. If Alisa's pussy smelled like Emma's I would have pulled out and finished on her ass five minutes ago. But it smells like nothing so we keep fucking until I'm dripping sweat on her hips, which I'm grabbing on to and thrusting into my groin and the thought of Emma enters my mind one last time and sustains long enough for me to explode inside of Alisa, who is now curled up on her side, breathing heavy as a slight smile forms on her face.

"Don't worry, I started taking the pill," she tells me.

What, like I can't afford an abortion?

Then she asks if she can sleep over while pulling on the covers, and I ignore the question. She falls asleep almost instantly, but I'm wide awake and anxiety-ridden, slowly losing the ability to breathe regularly as I desperately search my room for Xanax. Later, I leave her snoring in bed, walk into the front room, start playing Grand Theft Auto, and quickly locate and beat a prostitute on the street to a bloody mess with a bat, my eyelids finally feeling heavy as she dies and disappears from the world.

Celebration

My sisters present me with a mug that says LEGAL DRUGS at Craig's in the back corner booth that my father is excited about sitting in because he heard George Clooney recently sat here.

As I'm looking at the gift, Cate says, "Congrats, slut."

"Cate!" Mom almost splashes wine in her eyes, mid-sip.

"Sorry," she says. "Congrats on not delivering mail anymore."

Emily, who's here without Keith, mouths, "Bitch," to our younger sister.

Mom finishes her glass of wine and says, "Yes, he's answering phones now."

Cate laughs.

Emily rolls her eyes, ripping a piece of warm focaccia from the basket in front of us as Dad returns from the bar, where he was speaking to Craig and "a few ex-colleagues," he tells us, unprompted.

Craig, who we've known for a long time—he used to be the head maître d' at Dan Tana's—walks over to the table, congratulates me, and asks if he can get any of us drinks "on him," to celebrate. The girls order gimlets, Dad and I get scotch, and once the drinks arrive, Craig downs a shot as we take our first sips.

"I've dealt with Rizzo," Dad tells me. "Be careful."

"Be careful, how?" I ask.

"Honey, you're scaring your son," Mom tells him.

"Yes, honey, don't scare him," Cate says.

I stare at Cate, sipping scotch. She's drunk.

"What has gotten into you?" Mom questions Cate, who's busy texting.

Dad attempts to diffuse the situation. "Speaking of honey, how's this honey truffle chicken tonight?" he asks, placing a forkful in his mouth.

Emily gives him a thumb up.

Our waiter, an average-looking girl with a nice ass, walks by, and Dad checks her out as he finishes chewing chicken and swallows with a satisfied grunt.

Mom asks where Keith is tonight. We're told he's showing a house to his most important client, a singer who buys and sells at least three homes a year.

"Jesus," Dad says.

"Yeah, she's the reason I don't use your credit card anymore," Emily admits.

Dad likes this and raises his glass in Emily's direction with a smile.

Later, over chocolate-chip challah-bread pudding, Cate mentions she may get bangs tomorrow at Byron. Then she alters her hair, brushing it down the front of her face, and asks, "You like this?" staring at Dad, who's on his BlackBerry and doesn't notice, but I do. I always do.

Rizzo

'm wide awake at 6:15 a.m., an erratic pulse beating through me, conquering any sleepiness in anticipation of my first day on Rizzo's desk without Jake. In the office an hour later, sipping from my new mug, shocked by how decent the office coffee tastes this morning, and I'm off and running. I familiarize myself with Nick's calendar for the day: breakfast at the Four Seasons with Guymon Casady (a manager Nick shares a few clients with), an MP lit meeting (where agents from the Motion Picture Department who represent writers and directors meet to discuss projects and "open" jobs around town), lunch at E. Baldi with a studio executive who's only a VP (she must be hot or else he'd never be meeting with anyone so junior), then he's in the office for the rest of the day until later tonight, where I see he has a block of time starting at 7:30 p.m. scheduled under the title "Dark"; which I assume is either a new restaurant I haven't heard of (unlikely) or the title of a new film being screened (probable) or a planned suicide (we'll see).

The words "He in?" startle me from the pages of *Variety* forty minutes later. David Michaels's assistant Shane is staring in my direction but not making eye contact, and I can only muster a shake of the head, no.

It begins a moment or two later with the ringing of line one, the phone number, one of twenty I was told by Jake to memorize: Rizzo's cell.

"Who?" the voice blurts out.

"Hi, Nick, it's—"

"No damnit, who?" He cuts me off.

"It's—"

"God, fuck."

Silence.

"Nick?"

"Who the *fuck* are you going to call for me first? *Who?*"

I quickly scroll through the phone sheet, looking for the most important names, and then speak.

"Woody."

"No, who else?"

"Ted?"

He laughs. "God no. Who else?"

Searching with the mouse's arrow, skimming names.

"Don."

"Don called and you give me Woody and Ted first?"

Silence.

"Nick?"

More silence, then . . .

"Get Don *now?*"

"Getting Don," I tell him.

Soon they're talking about Multi Grain Cheerios and a seventeen-year-old actress, and I take Don off the to-call status on the sheet—piece of cake. Don abruptly ends the call soon afterward; we call and leave word for Ted and Woody as Nick pulls into the Four Seasons and I hear him tell the valet to "wear these gloves" as he arrives at his breakfast (Jake warned me he hates when people touch his things).

While Nick is at breakfast, calls from his wife (I introduce myself, she seems nice), Graham King, Michael Sugar, David Michaels (Shane asks, "He's still not in?" *Fuck, I forgot to tell him, Shane stopped in*), Woody, and Ted. Other calls come in from two different writers looking to submit screenplays, a few calls featuring heavy breathing and nothing else, and E. Baldi looking to confirm lunch (apparently Rizzo is known to make reservations and not show up, which these days won't fly there because it's become so popular, and I confirm without checking with the studio executive because no way someone this junior to Rizzo reschedules).

Eventually, I have to turn the computer speakers off because so many e-mails are coming in and I can't find the option to turn sounds off in Outlook and when I'm returning an e-mail to the studio executive's assistant about lunch (of course she'll be there), Nick storms in, past my desk, into his office, then immediately storms back in front of my desk to scan the area, grab *Variety,* and leave as quickly as he appeared.

Minutes later the phone rings.

"Did you read my *Variety*?" he asks, his voice echoing.

"I did."

"Do not touch my"—his voice strains—"*Variety.*"

He's calling me from the bathroom down the hall while taking a dump and asks me who called. I run down the list, we try to leave word for Graham King and David Michaels (in that order, hopefully he never finds out I forgot to tell him about the call), the toilet flushes, the call ends, Rizzo reappears, and there's just no way he had time to wash his hands. As soon as he sits down I remind him of the MP lit meeting and he's up and out of his office, throwing *Variety* on my desk, telling me to e-mail him if Graham or Don calls.

Alisa wheels a mail cart past the office door, sneaking a look inside while dropping a script at an office across the hall.

"That was fun the other night."

"Was it?"

"What?"

"It was," I tell her, a smile forming on her pretty face as she wheels by, trailed by Derek, who steals a glance at my new perch, mouthing "nice," extending the word as he glides by.

Rizzo enters, mumbling something about "a waste of time." His wife calls again, which he declines to take, because he quickly reaches Graham on his BlackBerry to talk about a film shooting in Bulgaria and the Israelis who want to cofinance it, and he laughs really hard before saying something in Yiddish as he ends the call.

"Who am I eating today?" he asks.

"Sarah Roth, Fox."

"Oh, new meat for lunch," he excitedly announces while throwing his jacket on and exiting the office.

"Should I get your wife?"

He smiles at me while heading out of the office. "I'll get her."

A few assistants order California Chicken Cafe, which is healthy and, more important, easy, as I don't want to leave the desk today for any reason. The phones are silent throughout the building during the lunch hour (Industry Fact: No one is reachable from 1:00 to 2:00 p.m. during the workweek), allowing my mind to wander I think about what movies I want to see this weekend and how running into Stacey at the gym is such a hassle, which then reminds me of pain in my dick and Kevin and Ty clapping in my face. Alisa looked good today and I guess that was fun the other night and maybe we should get more serious, and I should definitely talk to Derek and ask who the guys in the Brioni suits were at the Tarantino premiere and what he was doing in the building that night a month ago and if he's got a thing for Alisa or if he thinks she's got a thing for him.

An intern is in my face setting down a low-calorie Caesar salad with whole wheat pita bread asking for nine dollars, interrupting a string of e-mails I was returning regarding client schedules. Nick enters, hears my order of a low-calorie salad, calls me a cunt and something else, and the intern giggles as Nick walks into his office. The phone rings. It's Don again, Nick jumps on, and the intern reminds me, "Nine bucks, man." Then he says "cunt" to himself, laughing again.

"You a freshman?" I ask.

"Yeah, UCLA," he answers, swallowing the giggles.

"Good, good . . . so by the time you graduate, I'll be an agent and you'll be back here in the mailroom or on a desk and guess who the big, dumb, wet cunt will be then?"

He doesn't speak.

"Go ahead, guess."

He looks down, shoulders slumped.

Rizzo reenters the scene, looking at us. "Two cunts walk into a talent agency . . . Stop me if you've heard this one." He chuckles and exits into the hallway.

I mouth, "You're dead, cunt," to the intern. He hurries out of the office, and the day's momentum shifts into another gear. Calls to and from Don again (I haven't quite figured out who this is yet); David Linde (producer of a film for one of Nick's Mexican directors); Nicole LaPorte (she's doing a piece on the upcoming awards season and needs quotes); Nick's wife (she calls again, the fourth time today—he doesn't take the call);

Shane in David Michaels's office (I'm asked to jump off the call so they can speak privately); Cassian Elwes (he wants to produce a director client's first screenplay); Scott Rudin (we leave word and don't hear back); Peter Cramer (studio executive in charge of a few client projects); Jeanie Buss (Nick has been begging for Lakers floor seats); Amy Pascal (she's flying to India and only checking e-mail); Robert Offer (some contract language issue only a lawyer could understand); and Jeff Kwatinetz (surfing reports are shared).

Word spreads quickly that Deadline is running a story about one of Rizzo's clients having just finished a script—it's a contemporary take on Joseph Conrad's *Heart of Darkness* done as a comedy, and, according to the article, Kevin James is attached for the Kurtz role, which is true. E-mails are unleashed on us and the phones light up all at once—the town is hungry for a look. Rizzo cracks every knuckle he's got, screams, "Heart of darkness, baby!" and the chaos begins. And here's what they don't tell you when you first start, green as a dollar bill out of the mailroom—it gets crazier than you can ever imagine. The calls, the e-mails, the script submissions, the needy, immature boss screaming ten things at once, it all flattens you like a ten-pound weight dropped off a skyscraper, squashing your insides, and a lot of kids can't handle it. For others, such as myself, it acts as fuel—the action—it charges the system, dilates the eyes, bringing everything into focus. So when a tornado hits in the middle of an already hectic day, I barely miss a beat. Everyone wants to see the script, we field as many calls and e-mails and even one fax (a producer in Bali who doesn't have any cell or wireless service) as we can, and Nick allows only a chosen few to see the material tonight, the "top-tier fucks," as he puts it, the "real-money fucks" he tells me while throwing his jacket on in front of my desk, pulling his shirt cuffs out from under the arms of the jacket.

"See ya," he says, exiting.

See ya? My eyes track toward the clock in the hallway, connecting Nick's office to mine. 7:18 p.m., I have no clue where the day went. I work twenty more minutes, answering a few e-mails that continue to trickle in, waiting for Nick to call, but he doesn't. Before leaving, I check the calendar for tomorrow (more of the same), then click back to today, to see Nick's current appointment: Dark.

Gift Giving

The first few weeks on Rizzo's desk were highlighted by three incidents. My third or fourth day on the job I walked into Nick's office and caught him eating a booger. I'm surprised I wasn't fired on the spot, but I totally miscalculated his personality, he didn't care and continued chewing snot. The second highlight occurred soon after the first nose-dirt meal in the form of an even more embarrassing buffet. Returning from lunch one Thursday, stopping in the kitchen for a glass of ice, I run into Nick, his head buried in the refrigerator, eating food left by assistants, some of it days old. The third, and most recent experience featured a phone call at 2:30 a.m. waking me after a grueling fourteen-hour Monday to come to Rizzo's house and unclog a toilet for him. The call went something like this:

Me: Hello?
Rizzo: Get over here!
Me: Dad?
Rizzo: Jesus, thankfully not.

Silence. I start falling back to sleep.

Rizzo: Get over here!

Me: Rizzo?

Rizzo: Jesus, and you're supposed to be the star
    trainee? My toilet is clogged, brutal meal at Fogo de
    Chão . . . Get *over* here!

But beyond all that, things have been good, I'm treading nicely, and the holidays are approaching, which means it's gift-giving time. It's also the time of gift receiving, and nowhere is this more evident than inside the agency. Gift baskets from Bristol Farms, high-end chocolates (one office has an open box of white-chocolate-covered sardines for people to try), bottles of wine, cases of champagne, bags of brioche pretzels, mounds of City Bakery brownies, barrels of key-lime-flavored popcorn, and stacks of iTunes and Target gift cards, and the hallways are so cluttered, mailroom trainees are having trouble wheeling their carts and have to do everything by hand.

I dodged a trainee-killing bullet getting out of the mailroom before the holiday season kicked into gear. It's all I hear from the crew these days. How the workdays are getting longer. How they're constantly running up and down the building delivering this or picking up that, and Alisa cried recently at lunch after they were informed they would have to be on call over the upcoming two-week break for mail sorting and any special deliveries and she bravely declares that there's no way she's missing Four Seasons Hualalai, how it's a family tradition, and she wipes away a tear and sips a bottle of Pressed Juicery, sulking—which I enjoy.

For me, the duties are Rizzo's holiday cards and gifts. The cards are a breeze; we send them electronically and they're totally generic and totally green, which is totally Hollywood, and the entire Rolodex gets blasted in under two minutes. Gifts on the other hand will be more time consuming. All clients will receive a copy of *Oh, the Places You'll Go!* with an inscription that reads: ". . . because of me! Happy Holidays, Nicky." More important clients also receive a bottle of Krug Clos du Mesnil to toast the New Year, which Nick either personally delivers to their home or he schedules a meal or drinks to present the bottle. Select studio executives and lawyers who work with Nick's clients or ones he just needs to butter up are given Palm gift certificates, which not only accumulates a tremendous amount of points on his 837 Palm membership account (which is key because the Palm refuses to put a cartoon of his face on the wall, so he needs to purchase the honor with fifteen thousand points—he's getting close) but also is easily hidden on his expense report. While at the Palm, signing for a thousand dollars in gift cards next to a martini-soaked actor from the original *90210* at 1:45 in the afternoon, I commence the holiday greasing of maître d's with Cedric ($200); then drive to Dan Tana's and leave envelopes for Christian ($200) and Zach ($150); then to Craig's (we leave a bottle of the Krug for Craig and $150 for Tommy); The Grill for Pamela ($200); and Tower for Dmitri ($200). There's also a list of select agents and managers who Nick shares clients with and/or simply needs to acknowledge as a matter of politics, but I'm to hold off on any purchases, wait for gifts to roll in to Nick, and he will then note which gifts he wants me to regift and to whom. I'm also to go to The Grove and buy gift certificates for most of the Rizzos' staff, including gardeners, the pool man, housekeepers, the nanny, both trainers, and the tennis instructor, and everyone gets $200 to spend anywhere at The Grove, and he also mentions, "Get yourself one for a hundred dollars."

Half as important as the pool man—it feels good.

Last, I coordinate a lunch Nick buys for the mailroom every year—five pizzas from Mulberry, Caesar salads, a bunch of sodas, and cupcakes from Hansen's. I'm down in the mailroom running some details for the lunch by Stan, who is still referring to me as a shitstain, and I spot Derek and Alisa entering the room together, immediately grabbing two gift baskets from Dean and Deluca, and heading back out to deliver them upstairs. While following them, I get an e-mail from Nick, who just had lunch at The Peninsula, telling me to clear the next couple of hours from his schedule. Every time he has a lunch at The Peninsula—at least once a week—it's an extralong lunch, so he's got to be fucking someone (Industry Fact: Mistresses get fucked at either The Peninsula or The Langham). It's at this time, while I'm discreetly trailing Alisa and Derek, noting their laughter and glances at one another when the other isn't looking, that two things dawn on me: I no longer feel connected to anyone in the building except for maybe Rizzo (frightening), and the only people in Rizzo's life I wasn't ordered to get gifts for are his wife and children and it's very possible he plans to do nothing for them.

Holiday Party

'm smoking a Parliament Light in a Beverly Hills cab heading north on Doheny to pick Alisa up for the company holiday part at Sunset Tower Hotel. I've texted her twice since getting in the cab and she's not responding, most likely due to a horrendous fit she's throwing because she can't find anything to wear in a closet overflowing with $200,000 worth of clothes and shoes. We haven't seen much of each other since the night of *The Vega Brothers* premiere and I've been so busy, I can't even really recall the last time we spoke other than last night, when I was horny and drunk-dialed her for phone sex and she asked if we could go to the holiday party together, and since I wanted her to participate, I said yes. The cab pulls over in front of her building near the top of Doheny, where it really begins to climb toward the Strip, and I'm waiting, losing my patience, smoking another cigarette, and finishing a red plastic cup of Jack and Diet Coke. I see two agents from a competitor exiting the building, laughing, looking back into the lobby as Alisa exits, waving at them before abruptly dropping her smile and swiveling her little bobble head toward the street, catching me in the cab flicking her off.

The line of vehicles jutting out of the Tower drop-off is about ten deep, creating a tail-like formation of Mercedes, BMWs, taxis, and limousines off the body of the hotel, and I'm literally twitching for more to drink. I tell the cabbie, "Right here is good," as I pull a crumpled twenty out of my jeans and toss it into the front seat while stepping out and onto Sunset. Two bikers sporting Oakleys, sleeveless flannel shirts, and cigarettes tucked behind their ears in front of the Best Western stare at Alisa, and one flicks his tongue at her—she seems into it.

We glide into the private entrance for the Tower's Terrace level, and, while riding the elevator with a few colleagues I've never spoken to and therefore totally ignore, I realize I have absolutely nothing to say to Alisa, and I'm pretty certain she feels the same. She looks good, though, so I decide to compliment her, and she smiles and says, "Something I picked up from Curve, you like it, babes?" The elevator continues its slow ascent, and as the doors open, I say, "Curve . . . on Robertson? I think Derek picked up genital warts from one of the salesgirls there," as I dash toward the bar without looking back.

My tunnel vision guides me to the free alcohol and helps me ignore everyone along the way. All that matters is getting a drink, but the line looks hectic and my anxiety rises, which I quickly counter by casually chewing a Xanax as if it were gum. Alisa appears at my side, looking all around while talking to me.

"What's your problem?" she asks.

"I want to pull a Jeremy."

"Huh?"

"Kill everyone I see . . . paint the walls red and black," I say.

"Jeremy? Did he work at APA?"

I give up. "I don't have a problem," I tell her with an uncomfortable smile.

"Oh, Pooh, you're such a drama queen, just relax, pop a Xani and grow up," she tells me, her head pivoting in every direction, mouthing "Hi, honey!" and "Love your outfit!" to almost anyone.

"Call me Pooh again, *darling,* and I'll take you into the bathroom and treat your tonsils like a piñata with my dick!"

"Promise?" She turns toward me, looking directly into my eyes for the first time tonight. "Because I'd like that . . . Pooh."

Then she vanishes.

I'm double-fisting Jack and Cokes, wondering what bathroom stall or dark corner of the room Rizzo is hanging out in, until Jason Greenberg enters my line of vision and grows larger by the second as he strolls in my direction.

"You're the bagel kid, right?"

I just stare at him . . .

"The bagel kid . . . Bernstein told me all about you," he says as he raises his beer toward the railing overlooking a southern, sparkling view of the city, where Bernstein stands, smoking cigars with Bronx Jones.

"Ben hates poppy seeds," I explain.

"Well, they get stuck in human teeth," he says.

"They do, they do."

"So, you're Rizzo's new guy, yeah?"

"Yup."

"How long were you in the mailroom?"

"Few months."

"Impressive."

"Yup."

"I got out in two," he tells me.

"Impressive," I respond.

Mental note: Look into this; it must be a lie.

"Yup," he says.

I have no idea what's going on here and move to get up.

"Wait."

I turn back.

"The Chateau . . . what you saw that night . . . with Bronx . . ." He's leading me.

"I didn't see a thing," I tell him, assuming I'm being tested.

"Good, good," he responds, taking a small sip of a Budweiser, then belching.

I finish my second Jack and am about to tell him I need to grab another drink, but he continues, "Fuck, man, lotta pussy here . . . hot pussy."

"Lotta muff," I add, bored, chewing ice, taking in the scene and catching Alisa walking by with Kev and Ty, possibly holding hands with Kev, which I'm straining to confirm but don't have the right angle.

"Like her," Jason continues. "I'd cheat with her." His eyes are glued on Alisa. "That's the kind of girl you want to cheat with . . . a girl has got to be young, has got to be tight. A girl has to be so fucking hot that you *have* to cheat, like you've got no choice, ya know?"

He pauses as I continue to mine any remnants of alcohol left in my glass. "There're these girls in the office . . . and they're cute and they're throwing their cat every which way, but, it's not always worth it. No . . . she's got to be special to cheat with . . . because it's a special thing, cheating on your wife," he tells me.

Now he's taking a long pull on his beer, eyes drilled into Alisa, who's dancing with a bunch of assistants to "I Gotta Feeling" by the Black Eyed Peas. I'm staring at her, too. She's dancing with Kev, tastefully rubbing her ass into his crotch with her eyes closed and a slight smile forming on her flawless face, and as the song ends I'm like a patient slowly coming out of a coma and Jason is nowhere to be seen. I don't remember walking to the bar to get another drink, but here I am, sitting down with a full glass of Jack, and I feel good.

JASON GREENBERG

36 years old

MP & TV Talent Agent

- Earns $275,000 a year with bonuses
- One of three agents in the entire agency who actually live in the Valley (at least it's south of Ventura Blvd.)
- Owns 5 Hugo Boss suits in different colors and only wears Paul Smith ties and socks
- Only drinks beer and even then only Budweiser, Amstel, Coors, Heineken, or Fat Tire
- Was a huge nerd in high school—his nickname was Green Goblin
- Lost his virginity the summer after his senior year of college—he was 22
- Met his wife, an actress named Laila, on a business trip to New York. They dated long distance two years, then she moved to L.A., where she didn't know anyone but felt it would be helpful, especially for her career
- They've been trying and failing to conceive a child for nearly 2.5 years—something she'd like to resent him for but can't; her womb is broken

I'm surrounded by people: Kevin, Alisa, and Tyler are sitting to my left on a white leather couch, while Gay Andrew, Derek, Perry Eisenberg, and Perry from the Palisades complete the circle. They're all smiling, drinking, eating soft lobster tacos and tiny bacon, onion, and goat cheese pizzas, talking about some director's assistant who started dating a costar on a film and how lucky he is, and how another kid who left the agency nine months ago to be a PA on a film in upstate New York became close friends with the director and is now running his production company. "Who's a luckier fuck?" Ty rhetorically ponders.

A young Mexican waiter walks by, and Kev leans over to ask him why they're not serving the truffle-oil French fries tonight and the dude just shrugs his shoulders with a confused look. Ty screams, "Well, find out. . . . We want truffle oil!" Everyone bursts into fits, especially Derek, like they're all in on some joke that I don't understand, and I consider laughing along with them but decide to forget about it and finish my Jack in one gulp instead.

A waitress passes out small bowls of moules frites, but Tower uses their regular fries with this dish, so Ty screams out again, "Truffle oil goddamnit, we waaant it," demanding to no one in particular, "we want it now!" Everyone is stuffing face with forkfuls of Santa Barbara mussels and arguably the best French fries in town, and while chewing, my mouth full of sautéed seafood and deep-fried potato, I finally join in on the symphony of drunken cackles.

"You ever see a testicle outside a scrotum?" Palisades asks.

"Fuck you," Ty snorts back, throwing a fry in Perry's direction.

Palisades holds up a fork with a lonely gray mussel dangling off it. "I'm serious . . . my cousin had his scrotum ripped open in Deer Valley last winter in a skiing accident . . . said his testicle looked just like a mussel out of the shell."

As he's saying this, he moves the fork over to Andrew, who tilts his head back and opens his mouth. "You like mussels, Alisa?" Perry asks, letting the mussel fall into Andrew's mouth. He chomps on it happily.

"Mmm, not only looks like scrotum but tastes like it too . . . de-lish!" Andrew says, probably not joking.

"You would know." Kevin laughs.

"You guys are too gross," Alisa playfully hisses while getting up and heading toward the bar, where Greenberg is standing, talking to David Michaels. He's honed in on her tits immediately as she makes her way toward them, and I take notice that they both take notice and I don't like it. As if on cue, David Michaels exits with a glass bottle of Evian in hand, and Greenberg politely makes room for Alisa. She slides by him, and they dive into conversation about god knows what, but the subtext is crystal clear from across the room.

My Xanax is either losing effect or just truly mixing to the next level with all the alcohol, or maybe seeing Derek so chummy with everyone is what's causing everything to slow. I can only see the two of them, at the bar, in conversation, smiling at each other and flirting. Then Nick appears, striding impossibly slow across the room with David Michaels, pointing at me, and David nods before disappearing into a cluster of dancing assistants. Then I see it—Alisa running her fingers through her hair, pushing the blond locks over her right shoulder with her head slightly tilted to the left. I know that move. She wants to fuck Greenberg, and for some reason, I care.

Derek snaps me back into reality, "You all right?" He's looking over at Greenberg and Alisa, then back at me, maybe piecing it together, but doesn't say anything. I decide to reengage with life and my colleagues, except for Derek; he is no longer present.

"I'm telling you, bro, it's gonna work."

"Fuck you, Perry, fuck *that*," Ty lashes out.

"I'm telling you, guy, it's no joke," Perry confirms, and everyone nervously giggles with intrigue.

"What?"

"Tell him," Ty says.

"Fucking tell him," Kev adds.

"We pretend to be gay at work."

The two Perrys smile, nodding their heads, and pound their fists against each other while everyone else laughs.

"They're serious, dude!" Ty confirms.

"Gay?"

Palisades explains, "There are a lot of gay agents with power . . . *promotion* power. If they happen to assume we're one of them and promote us sooner than you guys because of that, then we'll be the ones laughing."

"It's a homotion," Eisenberg adds.

I can't figure out if they're fucking with us.

"Sometimes you gotta seem like you get pumped to get bumped, baby!" Perry excitedly nods in agreement right as Spencer Levy walks by with Mitch Berg—both of them are extremely gay agents. They nod and smile at the Perrys, who nod back; Eisenberg even waves a limp-wristed hand at them.

Kinda makes me wonder if they could be onto something.

We're all silenced for a moment.

Everyone takes a swig of their drink, allowing the concept to marinate.

"You guys are fucking sickos," Ty finally blurts out.

"How's it any different than every gentile agent in the building going to High Holiday services at Jew temples all across the city?"

"They may have a point," I sheepishly admit while sipping from a bottle of Amstel Light, wondering if I would have the stomach to do it.

"If this was a thing, Andrew would already be an agent," Kevin points out.

"Aha! Good point," Ty celebrates.

"I don't do blow jobs," Andrew admits.

"So what happens when you're promoted?" Ty asks. "Or how the fuck do you think you'll be promoted in the first place without having to chug cock? Are you really willing to chug?"

"I mean, I guess whatever it takes to get ahead, you know. . . . Shit, it's better than having to sit through a fucking Torah reading," Perry from the Palisades tells us while Eisenberg simply agrees with a nodding of the head.

"It is?" I ask. But no one answers.

A moment passes before Kev and Ty blurt out "Fags" in unison.

"Whatever, man, you wish you guys thought of the homotion," Palisades tells us.

Leaving the bathroom after an epic piss, I accidentally bump into a woman, knocking us both off course. She's older and incredibly attractive. Not too tall or thin, with what look to be fake C-cups under a hip almond-colored blouse. Dirty blond hair with a slight curl hangs just below her chest, little makeup paints her face, and her full, red lips now smile at me. Once we regain our balance, our eyes connect, and I know immediately, I need her.

"I'm such a klutz," she tells me.

"No, totally my fault, I was looking at . . ." But I just trail off looking at her. ". . . you."

She bites her lower lip, which drives me crazy. I notice an iPhone on the floor, reach down, pick it up, and show it to her. She takes it, our fingers touching while our eyes are still locked. She says "Thanks," smiling, but we're soon interrupted.

"The Bagel Boy!" Greenberg blurts out, sliding in between us, swinging an arm around the woman. "I see you've met my wife."

"Laila," she tells me, offering her hand.

"My name's not actually Bagel Boy," I tell her, ignoring Jason's presence while absorbing our first real physical contact: a handshake that I may jerk off to later tonight.

"I figured that."

"I am Jewish, though, so, I guess that might be considered an acceptable nickname."

She laughs.

Intense eye contact continues, which Jason probably notices because he immediately whisks her away, and while he waves to someone in the crowd with his arm still around her, she sneaks a look back, flashing a smile and a helpless shrug.

"Shots" rings out from a recognizable voice. Chilled tequila rushes through and revitalizes me. Later, drunken faces swirl around the room, yet I'm still somewhat in control. In fact, I'm so lucid, I'm so undeniably on my game, that I'm able to scribble my number onto a Tower napkin and, when passing by Laila, force it into her hand without slowing down or anyone noticing. I look back. She opens it, smiles, and tucks it into her ivory leather Givenchy handbag. Mission accomplished. Now I can finally start drinking.

• • •

Two hours have passed, and any agent worth his weight has departed, leaving a mob of assistants and low- to midlevel agents (mostly covering agents who don't really represent anyone, they just gather information from the studios) in attendance. I'm babbling at this point and stopped counting shots of chilled Don Julio at seven. Kevin and Derek have disappeared, Palisades has his tongue in some chick from Accounting's mouth, jeopardizing the whole "homotion" thing, Eisenberg is sitting on the floor staring out at the city while guzzling a beer, and Alisa is barely alive, slumped over at a table. Tyler leans into me while smoking near the railing of the terrace, the city a glowing ink blanket at our feet, and says, "Carney's, motherfucker!"

Crossing Sunset is a blur; I'm trying to hold Alisa upright, basically dragging her like in *Weekend at Bernie's* across the Strip to the parked yellow train. Pounding a large Diet Coke, I find myself in the presence of two soft chicken tacos overflowing with shredded cheddar cheese, an order of chili cheese fries with two forks protruding from its mass, three butterflied hot dogs with mustard and grilled onions, a double chili cheeseburger, and an untouched grilled chicken sandwich on a wheat bun that sits in front of Alisa, who's sleeping with her head resting against a windowpane that has the word CRETIN carved into it. Ty's going on about an active serial killer in L.A. who's been scooping his victims' eyes out of their heads before stabbing them countless times in the heart. "So cool," he says, chomping on a hot dog, then forcing a forkful of chili-drenched fries into his mouth.

"Fuck truffle oil, bro. I'm inventing chili oil."

"I believe that already exists," I tell him.

"Yeah? . . . Well, fuck it," he says while shrugging his shoulders, licking his fingers clean, taking a long sip of soda, and belching. Now he's just staring at me, thoughts racing in his demented head before blurting out, "Body Shop," but Alisa doesn't budge, so I pick up her chicken sandwich and take a bite.

We flag down a cab after standing in a neon blue haze in front of the Standard hotel, and I lightly smack Alisa's face to wake her up enough for the three-minute drive home. I throw some cash through the passenger window, telling the driver, "The quicker you get her home the bigger the tip, comprende?" The fact is, this guy could butt-fuck her unconscious lump of a body and ditch it in an alley, which I've recently read has been happening around town when drunk girls take cabs by themselves, but I'm betting that doesn't happen. At the very least the odds are in her favor.

We're skipping toward the pink neon lights of the strip club. Inside we immediately locate Kevin (the least shocking part of the night), who's leading a six-foot-tall black stripper with long blond hair into the back room. I down two Red Bulls in one swig each, walk toward a little blond girl with natural tits named Kacey, who's wearing a fuchsia-colored bikini and bright yellow high heels, grab her hand, tell her, "I want you," and let her lead me into the back room.

During a lap dance, she slaps my crotch, upset that I'm not hard. "Don Julio," I tell her, running my hands through my hair.

"Wow, Rolex Oyster Perpetual, I love these," she says, while riding me like a horse, mesmerized by the watch my father gave me for my twenty-first birthday.

"It's just a watch," I tell her as she rides more vigorously, eyes still glued to my wrist.

She's certainly giving it her all, but after three songs and seventy bucks, there's no movement, a victim of liquor dick, so I leave without saying a word to anyone. I finish two cigarettes waiting for a cab outside, and on the way home I notice a strange text: *Hey Bagel Boy . . . let's hang sometime.*

Laila

Thursday night following the holiday party, Rizzo jumped on a red-eye flight to New York, leaving me with nothing to do or read or watch for the first time in weeks. There's an office function at Pink Taco, but I don't want to see anyone from work, so I get really high instead. A text from Jason Greenberg's wife, Laila, hits my phone while I'm drifting, watching a *SportsCenter* special on the worst sports injuries of all time, which features an abundance of bone.

Jason's in Chicago—wanna play :)

I'm tired but intrigued, and that smiley face got me horny, so I text her back.

Sure . . . where are you?

Ten seconds later.

Home—already playing—leaving the door unlocked.

I'm in my car seven minutes later after a quick trim of my pubic hair and a shower that consists of a thorough soaping of my dick, balls, taint, ass, and armpits. Blasting "Lady" by Chromatics with my tinted windows halfway down, I'm cradled in a protective opaque shell as the X5 scales Laurel Canyon toward the valley with the night air blowing cold against my freshly shampooed, damp hair. Crossing over Mulholland and descending into Studio City, I'm grateful that I made a few runs to the Greenberg residence during my mailroom stint. Thanks to Jason's need for a certain script at noon on a Saturday a few months back, there's absolutely nothing stopping me from defiling his wife.

I quietly enter the house, shut the door behind me like I'm robbing the place, and turn toward the living room, where I see her in a cute little robe that hangs open, exposing her naked form. After letting the robe fall off and onto the floor, she begins cupping one of her breasts while tracing the other side of her body seductively with her fingers. She drops to her knees, and I'm immediately upon her, taking my dick out of my Nike sweatpants. She aggressively spits in her hand, starts stroking my shaft, and then swallows me for the next five minutes as I stand in the middle of the room with my stoned eyes closed, head tilted back, and dick choking this absolute whore of a woman's throat.

I haven't jerked off today, and I'm going to cum any second, and I love nothing more than cumming in a girl's mouth. It's just so much more satisfying than blasting a vagina or a hand, but unfortunately she pulls me out of her mouth, strokes twice, and I instantly blow my Yiddish DNA all over her $12,000 34 Cs.

I immediately fall to the floor, cock pointing straight up, and tell her to hop on, and she does and she feels amazing for the next twelve minutes, during which time she cums twice and it feels like her pussy is grabbing my dick and squeezing it, which is a very decent thing. I finally cum again, and she slides off me as we're both breathing heavy, lying on our backs covered in sweat, cum still on her tits, and the air-conditioning clicks on just in time. I roll over and reach for my pants, pull out a cigarette, catching my breath, and while lighting up I'm amazed that I'm still somewhat hard.

She slowly moves to the kitchen and starts slicing fresh pineapple while I move to the couch, pulling my pants up, and start rolling a joint with the weed I bought earlier today, ironically named Trainwreck. After smoking half the joint by myself, I gesture to her, and she shakes her head no without looking away from an episode of *The Tonight Show*. I wake up facedown on the couch a few hours later, and she's staring at me while sitting on a windowsill, smoking a cigarette, wearing my white V-neck with her legs spread but not in a sexy way. We continue to lock eyes in total silence as she finishes her smoke, pulls my shirt off, throwing it back at me, and it dawns on me that she hasn't said a single word the entire night; so I leave.

Two-Week Break

When you're an assistant getting crushed every day of your life, you're only really thinking about one thing all year long: the holiday break. All the agencies in town take a two-week paid vacation, bringing the industry to a grinding halt from the latke-flipping days of mid-December to the hungover Monday following New Year's. During this time I wax my feet, shoulders (only a few stray hairs), eyebrows, and ass crack at a salon my sister tells me about where the owner, an older Danish chick with giant fake tits who stinks of cigarettes, doesn't shut up about a soap opera star's dick she just waxed. "His dick?" I ask. "Yeah, his dick," she replies while yanking a wax-smeared strip from above my right eye in a freakishly quick motion.

I text Emily: *Nice chick.*

She replies: *The Best! Love you, off to Aspen!*

Then I tweet about getting waxed and at least six people call me a fag.

A few of us go to an art show on La Brea for a new artist named Havoc, where half the crowd is wearing masks, drinking out of wine bottles, and there's no speaking allowed, just sign language, which only occurs to me later in the night at

Mel's Drive-In when a waitress asks me to stop smoking in-doors with her voice. Later, I buy a subscription to a website featuring videos of older men watching their mature white wives getting fucked by younger black dudes at ghetto bus stops.

I e-mail Kevin and Tyler: *The rumors are true, Derek has a second job, check out this site.*

Kevin doesn't respond.

Perry writes: *Not funny.*

Then, ten minutes later Perry writes: *What's your user name and password for this site?*

My parents and I share strips of bacon with the tomato and onion salad, a porterhouse, German potatoes, and creamed spinach at Wolfgang's, and when I suggest ordering dessert (either the key lime or ice cream sundae), they laugh, order another scotch and wine, and ask for the check. Then I tweet out a list of my favorite steaks in Los Angeles, which gets a lot of attention and one reply about Outback being someone's fa-vorite, and I almost swallow my tongue.

I spend a day at Malibu Country Mart shopping for surf-boards (but I couldn't find any) and eat a cashew chicken salad sandwich that I puke up hours later at The Whitley, after downing an entire can of watermelon Four Loko that a friend stocked up on before the FDA outlawed it.

Perry e-mails me later in the night: *Did you puke?*

I write back: *Four Loko is very real.*

Someone gives me a script to read about a white, chubby loser who sleeps with his father's wife on a vacation to Thai-land—it's *Precious* meets *The Hangover Part II*—and it's quite good, I'll meet the writer for coffee in the new year and see if I can get any agents interested in signing him. I also see a movie at the Village in Westwood with my boy Cohen (who recently got back from a rehab in Tuscany), then have dinner at CPK, and we discuss Persians taking over the city and whether or not there's a movie in that concept.

"Isn't that what *The Taking of Beverly Hills* is about?"

I answer, "No."

Dinner at Cecconi's with the family next to an eighty-year-old agent from another agency feeding lobster tagliolini to a twenty-three-year-old Israeli model with a unibrow.

Mom stares, mouthing "gross" to us.

Dad asks, "What, the unibrow?"

Alisa and I go to a Glass Candy show at a warehouse downtown next to a river where homeless people are washing their clothes, and she mentions Derek a few times and how he lent her Oscar screeners the other day. When I ask her if she knew what Derek was doing over the break, she responds, "Like I care?"

Laila texts me: *I hate the break, no time without HIM.*

I write back: *Shame.*

Walk around the Westside Pavilion eating a corn dog, thinking about my childhood, then buy three pairs of sneakers with no laces. See a movie at the Nuart, which is the last time I'll see a movie at the Nuart. Smoke a blunt the size of my thumb and go to an outdoor bowling alley in Culver City with Kev and Ty at night wearing the new Ralph Lauren aviators I got for Hanukkah.

Laila texts me: *He's going to the gym, I have an hour. Wanna?*

I write back: *On way to airport. Shame.*

We fly first class to Cabo, and I'm sitting next to Cate, who now has bangs. I tell her she looks just like "the woman," making quotation marks with my fingers.

"What woman?" She makes quotation marks back at me.

"From Mastro's? With the bangs?"

"I wish I had a clue what you were talking about," she says, putting Beats by Dre in-ear headphones on before dozing off.

I eat a lot of guacamole and shrimp in my room at Las Ventanas while getting massages and lying out on the balcony overlooking the ocean. I also lie on my back in the sand to see how long I can stare into the sun without looking away.

Later that night I tweet: *Going blind in Cabo.*

Laila texts me: *Just saw tweet, jerking it that much? Lols!!!*

I don't explain, then we sext while she's in bed next to Jason.

At Squid Roe I buy coke from some dude named Tommy and share it with a stripper who gives me a disturbingly dry hand job. Then it rains the next day, so I read a script about a Jewish family in 1939 that takes in a runaway who turns out to be Hitler Youth, so they kill him—it's *The Blind Side* meets *Inglourious Basterds*—and I hear David O. Russell wants to direct it.

I ignore four texts from Alisa and consider calling her back for phone sex, but it sounds too exhausting, so I end up jerking off to porn on my iPad, which is a mistake when drunk, but luckily the iPad screen is easy to clean. I have trouble falling asleep, thinking of Alisa and what she's doing and who she's seeing—if it's Kev or Ty or Derek—and I wonder if Laila fucked Jason after sexting with me the other night.

New Year's Eve dinner with the family at Edith's, where Cate drinks numerous margaritas and barfs a pink clump of chips on the table mid-countdown, then black out in a strip club sniffing Vicodin with the dry hand job chick because

Tommy ran out of coke, wake up on the beach in front of the hotel New Year's Day, pack my bags, and fly home chewing Advil, sipping orange Fanta, praying I didn't pick up an STD that can't easily be treated, and, while taking a seat in the airport, waiting to board my flight, I tweet: *That was fun.*

The Girl with the Hairy Arms

It's 9:57 a.m. on the first Monday back after the break and I'm desperately fighting to get in sync with the workday. There was an emergency meeting called for 10:00 a.m. to discuss signing strategies for Luke, who just made *Forbes*'s top-ten paid actors list for the second year in a row, who has never carried an agent, preferring to just use a manager (Ron "Fucking" Best as Rizzo likes to say). Rumor has it he's finally ready to add another component to his team and we've been making phone calls since 8:00 a.m. trying to collect data—Rizzo has been obsessed with signing Luke since he first appeared on an episode of *Friends* when he was sixteen—and in three minutes I'll be able to go to the bathroom when he flies upstairs to the conference room. I'm leaking gas (my stomach hasn't been right since Mexico), which is grossing out the thin-nosed, pale, non-Hebrew with a great body but hairy arms who sits right outside my office.

I fart loud enough for her to hear.

"Ew . . . you're fucking gross," she whispers loudly as she clicks on the Mute button while rolling calls with her absent boss.

I quickly click my Mute button.

"Brisket for Shabbat last night," I tell her with a grin. "You know how it is."

"Shabbat was not last night, you dick."

"How the fuck would you know?"

"Hello? I fuck Jews." She clicks back on with her boss and connects another call.

I start imagining how hairy she must be everywhere else if she can grow that kind of concentrated mass on her arms. I wonder if she can feel the hairs separating when she sits down to pee. If her bush carries into her ass, forming tumbleweeds of hair between her butt cheeks, which I've seen on girls before, but mostly just in the early years, when grooming hadn't preoccupied them yet. Now I'm becoming obsessed with her, really looking her over for the first time. I can tell she doesn't come from money, that she was probably raised middle class and doesn't dedicate the attention to grooming that most girls I know prioritize over everything else. She probably shaves instead of waxes, and there's certainly no way in hell this girl can afford laser treatments. She definitely shaves, and most likely just the outlining areas if anything at all, and I'm disgusted and turned on at the same time imagining her naked.

An empty water bottle flies through the air, hitting me in the head. Nick is standing over my desk putting his jacket on and says, "I swear to fucking god another agency must have sent you here to *ruin* my business."

I start to say something, but he just cuts me off. "Her tits don't want to be fucked with your eyes."

He leans down, getting right in my face. "Fill up my water bottle before I have to go upstairs and nail this Luke thing. . . . Why do you think I gave it to you?"

Rubbing my head while quickly moving to the water dispenser, where I fill the Fiji bottle, unbelievably tempted to spit in it, but fuck that *Swimming with Sharks* bullshit—I'm not that stupid. I could get caught somehow and it'd be absolutely over, everyone would be talking about it, which really wouldn't matter that much, because Dad would bail me out and hook up another job, but still, why do this now when I could fuck him up a thousand times over in the future without a chance in hell of getting caught? I could do so much worse. I could forget to tell him a client called a few times then add it late to the call sheet with an adjusted time to cover my ass. I could not return an e-mail here and there to a publicist or a lawyer at a crucial time. Decline to remind him about a meeting or two he should follow up on. I could piss off clients in so many ways where it wouldn't exactly be my fault and might even seem like I'm clumsily covering for him, and it would all come crashing down on his rich, lunatic ass. Were he at all smart, he would never throw that fucking water bottle in my direction again.

Fucking Assistants

get up from my desk at 12:55 for lunch and meet Kev, Gay Andrew, and Ty in the lobby before heading to Mulberry. We're on South Beverly within three minutes, and Beverly High must have just gotten out, 'cause there are so many Persian kids around that I feel like a soldier who got separated from his platoon in the Middle East. We rush toward the counter, and I order two slices of the lasagna pizza, a side salad, and a Sprite Zero. Kevin and Tyler order the exact same thing, which I've been noticing a lot lately and I don't know how to feel about it. Andrew complains about being on Atkins while removing croutons from a salad. Topics of conversation throughout lunch consist of the following: whether or not I've gone out with Stacey the trainer since the "salt thing" (I tell them no, and that luckily she doesn't work at the gym anymore, which I think is a lie), Lindsay Lohan's career trajectory and tits (real or fake), Kate Bosworth's weight, the newest Koppelman and Levien script, and the Luke rumor about signing with an agent being just that: a rumor.

I finish my meal and am still starving. So I order a slice of Sicilian cheese and another Sprite Zero, bark at a girl standing too close to me, and sit back down in time to hear Kevin ask Tyler if he'd pass the Parmesan cheese and to please not rub it on his balls this time. More conversation floats around the table as I finish the slice of Sicilian: the new RJD2 album, assistants who snort Adderall, the "most fuckable" *Jersey Shore* cast member (we argue over Sammi and JWOWW while Andrew is certain it's Vinny), and CAA vs. WME, which somehow always seems to find its way into conversation. We have some time, and the fellas want to get high because Stan is home sick, so Ty rolls a six-inch-long but not very thick joint in my backseat, and I drive up and down Charleville, secondhand-smoking what Kev keeps referring to as "That San Andreas shit," listening to Howard Stern interview Casey Anthony.

Back inside, I run into David Michaels and his assistant Shane exiting my office. Nick is sitting behind his desk, grinning, rubbing his chin, staring out onto Wilshire. When he catches sight of me, he stands up quickly and says, "Get me someone on the phone . . . get me anyone right now." As I'm searching the phone sheet, about to make a selection, a call from David Michaels's office comes in.

"Michaels, line one!"

Nick immediately tells me to "Close my door, and put him through." He then stands up and gazes out the windowed wall. "Oh, and drop the fuck off the call."

I rush back to my desk. "David on one, I'm dropping off," I tell him before slamming his door shut.

But of course I click back onto the call.

David: Are you fucking her?

Rizzo: What the fuck kind of question is that, David? You know I'm a married man.

David: Oh please, cut the bullshit. Are you fucking her?

Rizzo: Are you?

Pause.

David: You do not fuck my assistant, it's totally
  unprofessional.

Rizzo: You are, aren't you?

Pause.

David: Do not fuck with me, Nick . . . do not *fuck*
  me.

Rizzo: I'm not fucking you, David, I'm fucking your
  assistant . . . now FUCK OFF!

Nick slams the phone down and I'm able to jump off the
line before him.

Jesus.

Golden Globes

We're outside Andrew's condo on La Peer, having just watched the Globes, which I live-tweeted to a stirring response (a few celebrities starting following me on Twitter), and Perry from the Palisades asks whether or not I'd fuck Snooki and I tell him to kill himself while lighting a Parliament Light and ducking into a cab headed for an after-party at Chateau Marmont. Then, I'm gagging in a room blowing a chunk of cocaine from a pile of white powder that fills half the sink in the half bath in the hallway of the suite. I haven't seen Kev or Ty or anyone else in at least twenty minutes. An extremely cute, petite brunette girl with a black eye, wearing a white shirt with no bra, sits on the toilet behind me with a red thong wrapped around her ankles.

"Someone, like, closed the drain and filled the sink," she says, giggles, and sniffs while wiping her nose with a wad of paper that she drops into the toilet between her legs.

I give her an enthusiastic "fuck yeah," while clearing my left nostril with a short, quick snort, staring at her through the mirror as I check my face for white residue. After realizing that she may be taking a shit, I quickly exit and thank god that this party is in a decent room with a balcony. If I couldn't walk outside and breathe some fresh air, I would have been in trouble.

I'm leaning on the railing of the balcony, drooling, watching my spit hit people below while praying no one notices me desperately trying to recover from the rush. Taking tiny sips of Jack and Diet Coke, staring east out onto Sunset wondering if Hyde exists anymore, then looking west at the line to the Body Shop and I'm reminded of the stripper who liked my watch, and I wonder while adjusting the band on my wrist if she's working tonight.

Later, I'm talking to some girl who works at 3 Arts who claims I tried to stick my foot in her at Tao last weekend in Vegas. I deny this vehemently while trying to remember if it's true, while also lighting numerous Parliament Lights for a bunch of older kids who are lost in a coke-hazed conversation about *Silver Spoons, Diff'rent Strokes,* and *Punky Brewster.* I haven't been speaking because the coke is too strong and I've never seen any of the shows they're talking about, and the girl from 3 Arts playfully crawls onto my lap and whispers into my ear, "I would have let you," causing my dick to stiffen, which she immediately feels and jumps off me giggling and calling me a monster while blowing kisses at everyone as she walks backward into the room, which is now illuminated by lots of tall white candles.

Another hour breezes by as I stumble back into the bathroom where the brunette girl may have been taking a shit and find zero coke left in the sink and I get a text from Laila that reads: *I want to do it again . . . he doesn't know a thing.* I pocket the BlackBerry, then run into Derek and Kevin, who are both blacked out and mumbling about some after-after-party at The Dime. I quote Swingers, "Good, this place is dead anyways," and they laugh and we're off and I get home much later—around 4:30 a.m.—and decide to text Reggie and cancel our session at the gym. He immediately texts back: *I'm charging you, loser*, and I fall asleep watching *SportsCenter*.

Drop Off This One

'm still in a haze, but there's a good mood in the office because the agency had eight Golden Globe wins last night. The producer and director of the Best Picture Drama are in the office, thanking all the assistants and staff for their support. They're also letting anyone pose with the Globe, which would be nicer if it were an Oscar rather than something awarded by a collection of unknown, celebrity-obsessed foreign journalists who have been rumored to take bribes, but it's still nice.

I'm rolling calls with Rizzo when a call from David Michaels comes in, and before I can even answer it, Nick screams out, "Drop the fuck off this one," as he answers the call, slamming the door to his office shut. The sounds of yelling and objects being thrown against walls are muffled through the door. A minute later, Nick storms past me without saying a word. Minutes after his exit, David pokes his head into my office and asks, "He in?" To which I say, "No, missed him by two minutes. I can try him on his cell if you'd like?"

"No. Wouldn't work anyway, I've had it shut off."

That can only mean one thing.

"You're the kid from the Bronx Jones signing meeting, yes?"

"Yes, sir."

"The Bagel Boy, right?"

"Yes."

"Right, you were good in there. Always best not to say anything in that situation. You looked the part, which is almost everything."

I tell him "thank you," shaking my head, thrilled with the moment, but still uneasy.

"Nick isn't with the agency anymore . . . You want to come work for me?"

"Absolutely."

"Smart answer," he says, while turning out of the office.

The Beginning

Managing the office is Shane, who David nicknamed Sugar—because he's a fan of boxing, but more so because she always has full jars of Skittles and almond M&M's on her desk. Shane spends most of her time inside David's office, placing and answering the hundreds of calls a day that bombard our world. She's hardened from years of working at a feverish pace, frozen in the form of a lifer assistant. But her clout in the building and cache to the outside world came from her role as a keeper of the gate, and her hush-hush, low six-figure salary (unheard of for agency assistants).

There's also Joyce, another lifer assistant, another keeper of the gate with a "Shush, don't tell anyone salary." Joyce has been with David since the beginning of his career and she handles all e-mails that come in to the desk, all the scheduling (not only David's but clients' as well), and all incoming and outgoing mail. A few days into the new gig, Shane explains that Joyce doesn't speak, so don't bother unnecessarily engaging, and this gives me comfort.

In the beginning, I plug any holes that leak. A call Shane can't answer or e-mail Joyce doesn't reply to, but the hours are mostly consumed with running packages (hard submissions, FedEx, gifts, et cetera) down to the mailroom, supervising the detailing of David's cars in the parking garage because there have been "incidents" in the past and "everything must be monitored," and greeting anyone meeting with David with cold bottles of Evian—glass, not plastic, because "liquids in glass bottles taste better." In the beginning I couldn't pass anything off to the mailroom; everything has to be just so, under a watchful eye. The well-done sautéed mushroom and egg white omelet with dry whole wheat toast from The Farm. The triple-shot, sugar-free vanilla iced soy latte with two Splendas and one raw sugar "vigorously stirred" from Starbucks. Effrey's dry-cleaning pickups and how shirts are to be hung behind the driver seat and pants and suits are to be hung behind the passenger seat of David's car. The exact placement of all six DayNa Decker white tubercose candles throughout our office quarters and knowing which ones should be lit. The grilled swordfish from The Ivy, which "better be well done and cooked dry." The watermarked copies of the most important scripts of the day that better not leak or "kiss your pretty 90210 ass good-bye." Accompanying David's private manicurist into the office once a week and not letting other agents use her—which they always try to do. The sealed envelopes dropped off at every hotel in the city under names like Travis Bickle, Ivan Drago, and Hans Gruber. The pickup of sealed envelopes from fully clothed men lying in chaise lounges by the pools of those same hotels. The voyages to Geoffrey's when David doesn't feel like driving—and "drive smooth, 'cause he gets carsick easily, and if he gets sick, trust me, you'll be sick, too." Escorting clients out of giant black tinted SUVs, up private elevators, into David's office. The phone calls to the office at 11:47 p.m.—Shane on the line feigning shock. "Oh, you're still there? You could have gone home hours ago, silly."

While I'm on a run down to the mailroom for something, Alisa and Kevin sing the lyrics "Mr. Big Stuff, who do you think you are . . ." and I force a smile before heading back upstairs citing something phony that demands my attention. My life is now all or nothing with a single focus—the end goal—which means, among many other things, the consideration of my peers is at the bottom of my list. The boss is everything. The clients are key. Other agencies are to be surveilled.

In what seems like only days after my starting for David Michaels but really is a few weeks, Kev and Derek are both promoted out of the mailroom and onto desks—Kev in TV Talent working for some dude who just came over from ICM and Derek in MP lit working for Larry Lazar. Alisa and Gay Andrew fall onto Reality TV desks, while Eisenberg leaves for CAA, which shocks me—maybe he does have it in him. Ty, who I've fallen out of contact with (my doing, not his), struggled to find a desk or what most people think was the passion to find a desk, so he leaves the agency to pursue business school. Sometimes I think about them (especially Derek) in their new lives, and I don't know if it's because I've been so busy lately or if it's because I haven't been going out as much, but they don't seem to exist these days.

My Place

Laila texts me—*It's been too long* and something about Jason visiting a client in Pittsburgh and how she'd love to see my apartment—just as David Michaels is stepping onto a red-eye. Shane tells Joyce and me to leave, saying, "Go ahead, he's sucking on Ambien anyways," so I text Laila back: *My place, 9pm.*

I stop at Katsuya Izakaya on Third to pick up some baked crab hand rolls, spicy tuna cut rolls (with soy paper because seaweed is too fishy), and miso-baked eggplant. Their sushi grades aren't the best in the city, but they're acceptable, and I'm not willing to drop any kind of real money by picking up Matsuhisa. The place is jumping, packed with tourists; good-looking but trashy kids, dressed like they're going out for a night in Vegas. Familiar faces are spotted and ignored, some dude in a suit with a cigarette tucked behind his ear gives me a high five as he's leaving, and after I sign for the food and motion toward the door, the entire staff screams "good-bye" or "thank you"—I'm not sure, I don't understand Japanese.

I quickly lay the food out on the dining room table once I'm home, light a couple of candles, jump in the shower, then spend a good ten minutes soaping my pubic hair (I probably should have trimmed before showering), ass, dick, and balls, which leads to obsessively checking myself for testicular cancer. While I'm stepping into Polo sweats and a black V-neck, Laila's call from the lobby triggers memories of Alisa. I buzz her up, thoughts of both women—their lips and tongues intertwined with mine—override my mind, but it quickly stops with a knocking on the door.

"Enter, enter," I tell her. She looks turned on, wide eyed, running her hand across the red Armand Diradourian blanket folded on my couch.

"I'm really starting to figure out my place in the world." She's talking while picking roasted almonds off the miso eggplant (the only thing she eats tonight with the exception of, I hope, me). She's going on about this new acting workshop that's having therapeutic effect. I nod my head, telling her how wonderful it all is, while really feeling bad that it's taken her over thirty years to figure anything out.

"It's not about acting, it's about learning how to act, you know?" She's rambling on about time running out on her career and the shelf life of actresses, and I throw away all the food (the crab wasn't right tonight—too much mayo), fill our glasses (hers with wine, mine with Jack), put on *Say Anything* (her suggestion), and casually dim a few lights before settling in next to her on the couch. I lean in to kiss her moments later, and, without taking her eyes off the screen, she raises a finger to my lips, moving her head away from mine, telling me to "wait for it."

Ione Skye breaks John Cusack's heart, and Laila is in a trance, riveted by the scene.

"You've seen this before, yes?"

"Yeah," she answers, refusing to look away from the screen, "she's so damaged."

I need another drink and move to the kitchen for a refill. "I'm into damage," I tell her, returning to the couch.

She finally looks away as Cusack raises the stereo over his head, pulling her black tights down, exposing some of her thigh and ass, which feature dozens of healed, thin marks. Fascinated, I reach out, gently touching the concentration of wounds on her inner thigh that I somehow missed our first time together. She doesn't flinch. A delicate rub becomes something else while I'm pulling her tights off and kissing. "I'm into it," I tell her, my hand grazing the cuts again.

"You wanna?" she asks, sucking and biting my neck while sitting on top of me. We're face-to-face, grinding. "You wanna?" she asks again, staring through me.

She carefully selects a knife in the kitchen. I finish my drink, ice and all, watching her feel the weight of the blade in her hand. Running a finger against the edge slowly. Playfully dragging it across her palm before choosing a fresh section of her inner thigh to pierce. Her breathing deepens and eyes close as the metal connects. After aggressively sipping another glass of Jack, finishing almost all of it, I grab the knife from her. She pulls my sleeve up, over my shoulder, and rubs under my arm, stretching the skin, leading me into action. Curious now, I slightly dig into the skin, drawing a line no longer than an inch, causing a trickle of blood.

"I don't feel it."

"Neither do I," she admits, taking the knife from me, drawing a new wound on her leg.

"I used to."

Later, I'm fucking her doggy style over my couch, her head resting on the red throw she was admiring before, while Jon Stewart smiles smugly at us. Drunk, lost in it all, I slap her ass, then reach between her legs to rub her, staining my hand in blood, and right as I pull out and finish on her back, I can't help but think, *This is the closest I've ever come to fucking a girl on her period.*

Sunday Night at Madeo

Ugh, Sunday nights" are the only words uttered when I arrive at my family's regular Sunday night table at Madeo. I'm not certain if it came from my mother or younger sister's lips, but when the same voice says, "We haven't seen you in forever," I know it's Mom because Cate would never say that. Chunks of Parmesan and black pitted olives are already on the table, as well as a bottle of Chianti (my mother's favorite Reserve), which I reach for, but a nearby waiter beats me to it, promptly filling the only empty glass on the table.

"And how is everyone this fine L.A. evening?" I ask, popping a piece of cheese in my mouth, rinsing it down with wine. "Whatever," Cate answers while texting, her head pointing down, a lavender spaghetti-strap tank top exposing too much cleavage. Mom winks at me as she empties her glass, pours another, then leans over to kiss me—"in that order," I'll tell a future therapist.

Dad is twisted around talking to Scott Stuber in one of the booths that line the southern wall. I slowly sip the Chianti and chat with Cate, who just finished her junior year at Brentwood, about my college experience; how I didn't sleep for days before leaving home, how isolated I felt, and, toward the end of the discussion, I finish the first glass of Chianti, the same nearby waiter pours another for me, and Cate says, "You went to USC, dude." My father finally turns back around, facing us for the first time since I arrived, and joins in. "Fight on!"

All the regulars are here tonight. The families and couples with standing Sunday night reservations, many of them, like us, gathering together for one meal a week. It's waving or nodding or winking at the kids of the studio head, the lawyer, and the sitcom star; and friendly waves from waiters and even some bus-boys. I'm hungry tonight, so I order the Bolognese to start and the chicken pizzaiola. Dad gets the lobster al forno (his usual), and the girls get the branzino, which, I notice, is being served to at least one person at every table in the restaurant.

"Thirty thousand for in vitro shots?" Dad asks.

"Thirty?" Cate says, giving her full attention to the conversation for the first time tonight, her iPhone finally abandoned.

"Three-oh," Mom says, eyeing her empty wineglass.

"Did I pay for that?" Dad asks, shocked. Mom waves him off, staring at the nearby bottle of Chianti.

The discussion continues about my older sister's failed attempts to get knocked up (which was not a problem in high school) and the bout with depression that has kept her home, in bed, for the past week.

Cate picks up her phone, mumbling "poor thing" as her fingers drum the device again.

"There's always adoption," I say, as my father snorts in agreement while diving into an order of organic heirloom tomatoes and burrata, "flown in from Naples this morning," according to the waiter. I'm then told in hushed tones she refuses to adopt, that "it must be hers," and I can just hear Emily crying,

"It must be mine!" like she used to when we were younger, squealing about a lunch with Shaq she demanded at the annual Pediatric AIDS silent auction or the French bulldog she was obsessed with at the Beverly Center pet store who ran away days after my father finally caved in and brought it home.

We're on to entrees when Dad asks how my weekend was and I can tell him the truth about the five scripts David Michaels needed covered; the Saturday morning trip to David's house to realphabetize his family's endless first edition book collection after a small earthquake broke the shelving, sending them all to the floor; or the gay guy I called a cock smoker at Equinox, who asked me out while he was slightly erect in the changing room; or how I barfed on a wall in the bathroom at Dominick's after eating a giant meatball and drinking six mojitos; or about the married woman who's into watching me get sliced up; but instead I tell him, "Fine."

A flurry of flashing lights from the glass window wall near the staircase brings a sudden hush over the room as Al Pacino strolls in, saying "Bona sera" to everyone before being shown the middle booth against the wall, parallel to our table. Dad immediately gets up to say hello, then quickly returns, calling Al a "shrimp who isn't worth anything foreign anymore."

"Whatever that means," Cate says, before adding some insult about Al's hair that my mom finds funny, but I miss it because I'm reading a text from Laila, asking me if I can meet up later.

"Keep not eating, Cate," Dad says.

Mom gasps.

I laugh at the brazen attack while Cate continues texting, shaking her head.

Mom mentions a new charity, then something about an incident at The Ivy involving her hairdresser and a *Dancing with the*

Stars contestant, which leads to more reality TV discussion—mainly, how she recently auditioned for *The Real Housewives of Beverly Hills* and the audition went miserably because she blanked in the interview when asked to name all of Spago's maître d's and their head valet.

"Who eats at Spago anymore?" she demands to know a bit too loudly, self-consciously sneaking a peek around the room to catch a few of the faces staring back at her in shock. "Huh? Who?" she whispers to all of us. "Tell me!"

Outside, surrounded by paparazzi not photographing us, Dad pays for my valet, places his arm around my neck, and asks, "So, everything's fine? Michaels isn't being too tough on you?"

"No, it's fine."

"Yeah? 'Cause these young guys, they can be real monsters to assistants."

I want to laugh, thinking of the assistant Dad had a few years ago who left the business to live alone in Palm Desert, but flip the sincere switch so he'll back off. "Really, it's all good. It's tough, but I'm handling it."

He releases me from his grip, inspecting the paparazzi as our cars roll in front of us, and I wonder if he ever assisted an agency head, if his career started out as promising as mine, but I don't ask him.

"David Michaels's Office . . ."

David Michaels's office . . ." is the phrase most used by us every day, and it's not so much the words but the way they're delivered that matters. This is the preferred greeting when answering phones. The words should be rendered in a friendly, businesslike manner, taking into consideration the decibel, tone, and cadence of speech.

"David Michaels's office . . ."

No "Hello." No "Hi." It's *This is who you've reached,* now speak.

The majority of calls come in from legit industry players and clients. The spit-flinging Harvey Weinstein; the composed Brad Grey; the eloquent Stacey Snyder; the movie star on set who hates his private chef's sushi skills; the writer who's being forced to turn in an outline to the studio for free; the bored, aging actress who can't get jobs like she used to; and it never stops. Intraoffice calls are also heavy. Young agents trying to reach David so he'll stop by a signing meeting to close a new client; midlevel agents looking to impress David with a nugget of information they learned from their daily calls with studio executives; big-time agents who share clients with David; the head of HR confirming a reference on a résumé (David has a lot of friends with kids who want to intern for the company);

and the Corporate Communications Department is always calling with agency or client-related breaking news stories or to ask how the agency wants to comment on this takeover or that lawsuit or the death, divorce, or departure of a client. Then there's the little guys: the VPs or DODs at studios or production companies who dare to call about clients on their projects; the journalists in town (with the exception of Nikki Finke or Sharon Waxman—who David actually talks to on a weekly basis); and, on rare occasions, desperate agents at other agencies looking for jobs or to screw over former clients or colleagues by outing them in any way possible. The rest of the calls come from the crazies. And you know almost immediately the call is a complete waste of time. A manager in Kansas wanting David to help package a film; the fifty-year-old actor in Alberta looking for representation; the endless stream of unsolicited script submissions classified as "must reads" in the handwritten cover letters; the older women claiming to be friends or ex-spouses of clients who are looking to contact the client (most likely stalkers); and the absolute worst of all the calls, actual friends of clients who all have their hands out for something ridiculous, and no one knows for sure how well connected they are, so they're all treated equally, which, in comparison to the other crazies, is like royalty. "A lot of people say *Entourage* was bullshit, but Turtle getting a meeting with Ari at Spago was no joke," Shane told me my first day on the desk.

The calls are the pulse of the office. The constant ringing can overwhelm you like an anxiety attack (which even happened to Shane once, causing her to disappear for a quick trip to the Cedars-Sinai emergency room), but they also keep us alive. One day the phones will stop ringing for David, his days only consisting of a slow, thorough reading of *Variety* and *The New*

York Times, rotting away in some nothing office he's actually paying for, waiting for any kind of contact or correspondence from the handful of his peers still alive. No one retires from the business, the business retires you.

David has a good twenty years left. Twenty more years of steady calls from 6:00 a.m. to 11:00 p.m., seven days a week. Twenty more years of e-mails coming in at such a furious rate that your assistants have assistants who are in charge of reading, summarizing, and ranking messages in order of importance. Twenty more years of constant meetings and a constant flow of visitors and minions and colleagues, all wanting something from you. Twenty more years of flashes directed at you when posing with clients on red carpets. Twenty more years of getting the good table at E. Baldi, The Grill, Craft, and Spago for lunch.

Twenty more years till it's all over.

A Lakers Game

It's mid-May, which means the Lakers are in the play-offs, and we have floor seats on the baseline, behind the basket, which aren't as good as being on the sideline, but our feet rest on hardwood, so it's pretty good. Dad shares the seats with a producer friend who's currently in rehab for a severe foot fetish, which he's embarrassed about, so he's telling everyone he's in rehab for alcohol addiction. The assistant who messengered the tickets to my father forgot the parking pass, which is actually a valet service, so we could have parked in one of the nearby $20 lots across the street from Staples Center, but instead choose to pay $150 to valet with everyone else who has premium seats.

Falling into our padded folding chairs halfway through the first quarter of play during a TV time-out, we're officially the last people in the building to take our seats—everyone is here. Starting clockwise, sitting on the floor, enclosing the court in a flashy, human fence are Irving Azoff holding two phones, chatting with a pretzel-eating Christina Aguilera; George Lopez posing with a fan for a picture; Dyan Cannon sharing popcorn with Magic Johnson; Kanye West and a girl who looks like she was sent from the future; the Lakers' bench (the players are all standing up, looking at the big screen above the court, which is displaying shots of women dancing in the stands, who, coincidentally, all have dick-sucking lips); WME's seats (a.k.a. the best seats in sports) are right next to the Lakers' bench and are occupied by Ari Emanuel, Jonah Hill, Patrick Whitesell, and his wife, Lauren Sanchez; Norm Pattiz (billionaire and minority owner of the Lakers) standing up, banging a rolled-up piece of paper against his hand; then David Geffen and a much younger (by at least thirty years) blond dude wearing thick black frame glasses with no lenses. On the other side of the scorer's booth sit Lou Adler and his son, Cisco; the always present Jack Nicholson and his one-time Miss Golden Globe daughter, Lorraine; Sam Gores with Tracey Jacobs (they must be friends, no one would try to woo an agent from another agency this publicly); an Asian woman who has literally been to every home game I've ever seen; and the visiting bench, who are all huddled together so tightly they remind me of penguins trying to stay warm from that depressing documentary. Penny Marshall's seats are on the corner of the next baseline, and she's looking, as my father puts it, "unwell"; Chris Warren, the agent who balled me out for not doing drugs with a client, is sitting next to that client, Josh Blum, in the agency's seats (David rarely uses the tickets), and I tell my dad I once delivered a check for two million to Josh, and he asks, "Is that all?" James Goldstein is in the house next, wearing a lime green crocodile suit and matching cowboy hat, sitting beside a model drinking soda using red licorice as a straw, and when I point him out, Dad mumbles something about money making the world go around. The rest of the baseline is made up of no ones, and curves around to an absolute murderers' row of bank accounts, starting with Jimmy Iovine sitting with Mary J. Blige, her husband, Ryan Seacrest, and Simon

Fuller; Ron Best and Luke pointing at someone across the court and laughing (I tell Dad we're trying to sign him and he says, "Good luck"); and Leonardo DiCaprio covering his mouth, saying something to Tobey Maguire. Avi Lerner and Sly Stallone stand up clapping as the game is almost under way, gulping beers next to the Katzenberg family—Jeff, his wife, son, and daughter sit in the four seats leading up to the half-court line—who are all cheering and eating McDonald's. At half-court, Vanessa Hudgens, the actor she's dating, and a Saudi prince are huddled together in conversation, sitting next to Joel Silver and his wife (an extremely attractive blonde who reminds me of Laila), enjoying food from a grocery bag. When I point out Joel's gold and purple oversize clothing, Dad asks if I'm here to watch the game "or all the bullshit," but he stops short of berating me when he sees the Silvers across from us and simply says, "Jesus, Joel." Further down the sideline is some "schmatte" millionaire and his five kids, who are all dressed in an excessive amount of Lakers gear; Adam Levine in a leather jacket with no shirt on underneath, but he has so many tattoos it really doesn't matter; and Denzel Washington sitting next to David Beckham, who are laughing in front of the Lakers girls, who are finishing a routine, desperately wanting to be seen. Back to our baseline, where Chris Silbermann and Mark Gordon sit next to us; and a few photographers are sitting on the floor, in front of all the baseline floor seats, inching closer as the action comes hurtling toward our end of the court, and when one touches me, I growl at him, and he backs away, missing a ferocious two-handed dunk by Kobe Bryant, who is lit up like Kim Kardashian leaving a nightclub.

The plan was to get off work early and eat at the Palm a

block away before the game, but that was just nice talk about a father-son night out—it was never going to happen. There wasn't a chance of us both getting out of our respective offices with enough time to spare; so the plan was quickly scrapped, and the second quarter just started and I'm starving. I quickly rummage through the red gift bag sitting under every courtside seat, but the bottle of water, pens, and coupon for a few thousand dollars off space tourism offer no nutritional value. I order chicken fingers and caramel popcorn drizzled with white and dark chocolate. When a waiter approaches, I ask Dad if he wants anything, he looks at me like I'm crazy, says, "God no," then quickly reconsiders and asks for a soft pretzel with no salt.

There isn't enough ranch dressing or ketchup to saturate the chalk-like chicken finger I'm desperately chewing minutes later, so I eat the pretzel Dad ordered, because he's refusing it.

"I ordered carbs?" he asks.

"You did."

"Weird." Then he gets up and screams at a referee after a questionable call.

Seconds before halftime, after sliding the half-eaten food under my chair, an e-mail comes in from Laila saying she just saw me on TV eating a pretzel, and I'm embarrassed, but happy about being seen in good seats on TV, and she mentions a party she's going to be at next week which I was also planning on attending.

Her: *So I'll c u there?*
Me: *Will Jason B there?*
Her: *Uh . . .*
Me: *See you guys there.*

Curious about my texting, Dad asks, "Michaels's panties in a bunch?" I consider saying yes, then mull over the concept of revealing the truth about my thirty-year-old conquest but say nothing as the horn sounds at the end of the first half. Players exit the court, everyone gets up to stretch as the halftime entertainment reaches center court and begins juggling chihuahuas, so everyone heads for the Chairman's Room; an exclusive bar on the floor level of Staples Center open only to guests with courtside seats. The polished wood walls feature a few small plasmas running sports highlights and feeds to the court, and there are a few pieces of furniture scattered throughout the space, but not nearly enough for the crowd that packs into the room for fifteen minutes every game, waiting for drinks at the bar, munching on bowls of popcorn, nuts, and pretzels. While my father is in the bathroom or cheating on my mom with the redhead with bangs and mascara-lined, charcoal eyes or whatever he's doing, I run into a friend from high school who's the daughter of a director. She's talking to Vanessa Hudgens and I heard she was friends with her, which looks to be true, and, when her mother enters with my father (she was a client of his "in another lifetime" we're told), they find Jack Nicholson in the crowd (he starred in the director's last film), and Jack introduces himself to everyone, sending shock waves of excitement through the group. Jack places a cigarette in his mouth and heads for a connecting smoking room where Leonardo DiCaprio and Tobey Maguire are smoking cigars next to a giant wooden humidor. Josh Blum appears, walking so close to Chris Warren it looks like they're holding hands. Chris and I say hello; he's much nicer these days, now that I'm working for David, and tries to remind Josh of who I am. "The kid who delivered that check," Chris says. "Of course . . . I love this dumbfuck," Josh announces, smiling wide, slapping my shoulder. They shuffle away; past my father, who gives Josh a pat on the back and a shit-eating grin. When he reaches me moments later, he says, "Josh, comedy genius, right?"

"Genius?" I reply.

"Oh, you're just mad you're not as rich as him."

"*You're* not as rich as him."

Dad thinks about it, asks, "Is that true?" then disappears again, mentioning he'll meet me at the seats. I shake my head, grabbing for popcorn on the bar, but the bowls are empty, and smoke from the nearby room with the giant humidor invades as the horn in the stadium sounds, emptying the room.

In the tunnel outside the Chairman's Room I bump into Ethan and Brian Gottlieb, twin brothers who grew up in Bel Air and went to SC with me. I didn't go to high school with them, but they were always around at parties and other happenings, blending in, known as the "convertible twins" because they drove matching BMW 300s. And although they aren't identical, there's a strong resemblance in the way they dress (mostly Ralph Lauren and Prada), their haircuts (tightly cropped faux hawks from the same stylist), cologne (only Gendarme), and the manner in which they speak (incredibly direct with occasional twitches in their upper lips).

"Look what the Bentley dragged in," Ethan says while slamming his right hand against my back.

Brian guffaws, then reaches for me with both arms, bear-hugging me.

"My dude!" one of them yells.

"The Gottliebs . . . What's happening, gentlemen?"

"I didn't see you guys on the floor, where you sitting?"

"Few rows back, but Father does a lot of work with AEG, so we have Chairman's Room passes."

"Father, huh?"

Who says Father?

I'm bored, but continue with them.

"How's Stark?" I ask them.

"Best graduate film program in the country, that's how it is," Ethan replies, checking out some model's ass in white shorts, heading into the tunnel.

"It's nice," Brian adds, watching the girl in the white shorts as well.

"How's the agency? Heard you landed a whale."

"Moby fucking dickhead from what I hear." Brian speaks over his brother, still eyeing the model.

"He's cool . . . it's cool," I tell them, irritated.

Then we're alone, isolated in the tunnel.

"You know, we've got a killer script."

"Yeah?" I ask, dying to get back to my seat, back to the hardwood.

"Charlie fucking Manson."

"I'm not sure if he was an actual killer," I tell them.

"No," Brian says. "But it's so good, it will make you kill someone. We're attached to produce."

I'm interested. "Yeah, what is it?"

Brian pitches the script: "An American soldier in Afghanistan is blown to bits and paralyzed from the waist down. He returns home to his disgruntled scientist father, who builds him a bionic body with endless weaponry and impenetrable strength, to return to the Middle East, seeking revenge."

"It's *Captain America* meets *RoboCop*," Ethan says.

"The only thing people love more than a hero is a *handi-capped* hero," Brian tells me.

"Physically challenged, that's what they prefer to be called," Ethan reminds us.

"They fucking love challenged heroes . . . Oscar voters especially," Brian adds, then continues. "I'll e-mail it to you, you'll love it."

"Charlie fucking Manson" is said again.

Wheels begin to turn. I tell them not to e-mail the script but to bring a hard copy to Nate 'n Al tomorrow for an early breakfast and we'll discuss the project in more detail. By this point, I'm almost certain a few time-outs have come and gone. And I'm right, because half of the third quarter has vanished.

Back at the seats, Dad is on his phone, talking to someone about how much money Ron Meyer has made in the last two decades, and in between the third and fourth quarters, a fan makes a half-court shot, winning $147,000. While we're standing up, cheering (this is the most excited the crowd has been all game), I make eye contact with the Gottliebs, who are a few rows up and to the right of us. Ethan makes a gesture to call him later with his fingers against his head (thumb and pinkie sticking out); I do the same. Dad asks, "Who is that?" and as the clapping and cheering around us intensifies with the start of the fourth quarter, I answer, "Charlie Manson."

The Gottliebs

I couldn't meet the Gottliebs for breakfast (David called an emergency meeting at 8:00 a.m. for all his staff—home and office—to discuss cleanliness), so we meet at Sharky's for lunch a few days later. We order salmon burritos on whole wheat tortillas, a spinach quesadilla for the table (we request a whole wheat tortilla be used for this as well), and we all decide that chips, which are made from flour tortillas, are totally unacceptable. At the table, waiting for our number to be called, the brothers complain about Sharky's not having whole wheat tortilla chips, and I tell them no restaurants in L.A. offer them.

"You telling me that's not a great idea?"

"No, I'm not."

"You don't think that's platinum?" Brian comes to the defense of his sibling.

"It's platinum, set it up, make a killing selling chips, mazel."

"That's right, it's platinum," Ethan repeats.

Brian drops his drink on the table, points a finger at me, and says, "Platinum," one last time.

"Anyways . . . Your script." I steer the conversation toward the main event, taking a big sip of Diet Coke before continuing. "I'm into it."

"No shit you're into it, the *town* is into it, buddy."

"What does that mean? Have you shown it around?" I jump at them.

"No, it's just a saying, relax."

"That's not a saying."

"It's just a saying, guy . . . chill out," Brian pulls the script out of a black Prada messenger bag and tosses it at me.

"Platinum," Ethan repeats as the script hits the table.

"I'll let you know," I tell them.

The remainder of the meal is fueled by talk of the rumored merger of two lesser agencies. Brian says, "Yeah, I heard they're going to rename the company LOL." We all grin and nod our heads at this. Ethan tells us about a friend who hasn't left his Wonderland home in over a month, how "he's done a few hits of pure MDMA every day. . . . I think it's a *Leaving Las Vegas* situation."

"'Leaving Los Angeles' has a nice ring to it," Brian says.

"No it doesn't," I tell him.

The burritos hit the table, and for fun we see who can finish his meal in the fewest bites. Brian wins with two and a half, but when a woman watching us from the tabletops across the way starts gagging, Brian laughs so hard he chokes, spitting out his food, and is disqualified.

Shane is breathing fire when I return. "Hey, it's Lunch Break Boy! He's finally graced us with his presence. I think you're done going out to lunch forever. What do you think, Joyce?" Joyce is typing an e-mail, refusing to look up from her screen. Shane continues, "Yeah, I think that's just about it for you." At first I thought she was just on her period or maybe she was upset that her youth is so far behind her, or that she has no real career growth and people will be referring to her as an assistant for the rest of her life. But apparently her 'tude is forgivable.

"It was hell," she told me. "He shit blood all over us."

I ask Joyce, "He shit blood?" And she scrunches her eyes, nodding her head.

Shane motions frantically, enjoying the retelling of the horror story while shoveling a small La Scala chop salad in her face. It was something about a short film by a Scandinavian or Indian director, "I don't know, the details were shrouded." She tells me he was certain it was last seen on one of the assistants' desks, and not his own, where it obviously ended up being. An important client was coming in who we all heard was taking meetings at other agencies because he "needed a change of scenery" or "wanted some new blood infused," which are all really decent ways of telling an agent to fuck off. David thought the client could adapt the short film into a killer feature-length project.

This is all Shane is willing to tell me.

The door to David's inner office swings open, revealing him with Simon Wilcox, who looks disturbed. I mouth "Simon Wilcox?" to Shane, the importance of not letting a guy who has written on films with total grosses of over $4 billion just get up and leave the agency. Shane gestures back a blow job in my direction, beating her tongue against the inside of her mouth before answering the ringing phone, "David Michaels's office . . . No . . . Sir, I said no. . . . Do me a favor, get a life."

"Simon, if you don't like this, that's fine, we'll find you another one," David tells him, emerging into the outer room, where Shane, Joyce, and I are pretending to be busy.

"I need something," he pleads. "Something . . . I haven't had an original thought in months. I can't fucking think."

David throws a reassuring arm around his neck. "We'll find

you something. I want you to come in tomorrow for lunch. I'm gonna bring in Apple Pan, you want Apple Pan?"

"Yeah, a hickory burger," Simon whines back.

David swings his head toward me. "A hickory burger for Mr. Wilcox—"

"Two," Simon interrupts, "and chocolate cream pie."

"Ice cream or fries with that, Simon?" David asks, his arms now folded against his chest.

Simon takes a moment before answering, "Yes."

"Two hickory burgers, fries, chocolate cream pie à la mode, and we'll sit down and give you as many ideas as you need to find the one golden ticket to make a fortune with, 'kay?"

"I am challenged! I am fucking challenged!"

"Don't be silly," David tells him. Simon shoots a look our way, but we're buried in computer monitors and phones, so he looks back to David.

"Challenged!" he screams out, near tears.

"You will receive so many ideas tomorrow, the only *challenge* you're going to have is deciding what summer tent pole, billion-dollar grosser you're *not* going to be writing because you *will* be writing an even bigger one," David tells him. "Trust me . . . go get some rest. We'll see you tomorrow."

David escorts Simon out of the office, to the elevator, and quickly returns, shaking his head.

"Joyce, send an e-mail to all of MP lit: Client needs source material pitches by tomorrow at lunch. Two nights at the Post Ranch Inn for whoever brings me the winner."

"Got it," she confirms, the first words she has spoken today.

"Shane, get me Bernard, now please."

"Getting Bernard," Shane calls out as David returns to his

office, stopping in front of the glass wall overlooking Beverly Hills.

Shane gives me the stink-eye as I move into David's office, then screams out, "Left word for Bernard."

"Sir."

He spins around at my words.

"I may have something."

Party Weekend

The definition of *ass-to-mouth* is the main topic of conversation at Malo over beef and pickle tacos and spicy cucumber margaritas and countless rounds of Modelo Especials served in frozen cans by a waitress with the right side of her head shaved, highlighting a bold tattoo in block lettering over her right ear, which reads HIP. Alisa and I haven't seen each other outside the office in months, so when she asks if she can roll with us the night of Derek's birthday party, I hesitate, but Perry and Kev invite her anyway. Palisades is with a girl named Mia, an assistant who recently left the agency to become an agent at a joke of an agency specializing in launching the careers of child actors, and then losing them to the more significant competition in town. We all agree it wouldn't be out of the question to consider her move as a demotion.

"A post-anal blow job," Perry declares as Mia bites into a lobster taco.

"It's true," says Kev, "very true and very dope."

We're all laughing except for Mia, who spits out a wad of lobster and corn tortilla, then exits for the bathroom.

"You must be into her," I joke.

Perry sips his margarita, chewing salt-flavored ice, staring me down. "How could you tell?" Alisa and I make quick eye contact and share a brief smile. Then we discuss the big spec sale of the day—a comedy written by a pair of reality TV producers about a monk who switches bodies with a George Clooney type actor—that Perry claims sold in under an hour for low seven figures.

Mia returns talking to someone on her iPhone, seemingly unfazed, and for the next ten minutes she's screaming to whoever is on the other end of the call about how to handle the fact that their biggest client, a twelve-year-old Spanish soccer prodigy turned actor, just admitted on *Jimmy Kimmel* to losing his virginity to a fan twice his age. While the freak-out is occurring, a round of chilled Don Julio shots are passed around and downed.

"I got this one."

Kev and I think Perry means he'll pay for this round of shots, but later it's revealed he meant the entire meal, and when Alisa and Mia thank him, Perry responds, "Two eighty, no biggie," which Kev follows with "I'll get the valet." How kind of him; it's three bucks, the cheapest valet in the city.

Fridays at The Whitley are still popular, but it isn't the most elite night on the club's weekly calendar. Exerting little effort, we bypass the line and head inside toward the back of the space, where Derek has arranged a table through a friend of a relative who knows one of the promoters, who pretty much knows everyone in Los Angeles except Derek. I'm amused with the scene tonight. "Not exactly the look," Kevin agrees, his head twisted back, watching me follow him through a sea of mediocre faces from Huntington Beach and Pasadena, who are all blind to the fact they could never get in on a better night, or have the knowledge to come on a night where it is "the look." And they all appear to be for the taking—which is cool—drunk on spiked cranberry juice, stinking of cigarettes, flashing roughly shaved, sunburnt, meaty legs, grossly protruding out of H&M miniskirts, moving in strange circles to a Chaka Khan/ Tupac mash-up that's booming through the space.

A quick tale of my impressive career standing is shared with the hottest civilian in the vicinity, this little Westwood brunette with saucer eyes and fire lips, who hangs on every word. I was responsible for inspiring the biggest writer in town on his new script; but today's other tasks, such as unclogging a toilet filled with used tampons and feces, were not relayed. The life sounds sexy and hip, and her eagerness to hear more, to extract even the most mundane detail, is a turn-on. But then Alisa appears, smiling again, after an extended bathroom jaunt, her presence blocking me from claiming the Westwood victim. Ignoring Alisa, I watch Kevin lightly grind with a short, tan blonde. Leaning against the sticky, wet surface of the bar, Kev stands centered among the party, a strange female rubbing her spandex-wrapped ass on the front of his raw denim jeans.

"You all right?" Alisa asks me.

I offer nothing.

"Hello?"

I continue watching Kev until she playfully elbows my chest, begging for my attention, as Perry and Mia appear, leading us back to Derek's table, where one of the guys who loves Cut and Brioni is pouring vodka for Eisenberg and Andrew, a small group of Paradigm, APA, and Gersh assistants, a few girls—one whose father owns either Ron Herman or Fred Segal, I can never remember—and a handful of black kids who are all wearing purple, pink, or yellow cardigans, and as soon as we arrive, a chorus of "Happy Birthday" is sung while a platter of freshly baked cookies with lit candles stuck in them is placed on a table.

When I reach for the bottle of Ketel One, my head dips down close to Derek, who smiles, thanking me for coming. He looks away, missing my generous pour of vodka into a small glass that's still warm from a recent washing. The man wearing a Brioni suit with no tie pulls the bottle from my hand, saying, "You must be a glass-half-full kind of guy."

I cheers him, smiling, unsure if he's attempting to be ironic, and notice Derek watching us.

"We haven't met," I say, extending my hand, needing to know who he is, enjoying Derek seeing us together.

But he tells me, "I know you, we all do." Then he walks to Derek, says something I can't hear over the music, and they both smirk, nodding their heads as I finish the cup of vodka, wanting to leave.

"Empire State of Mind" is mixed into the final verse of "Jump" by Kris Kross, and Alisa says, "I've missed you," before tapping her overflowing cocktail against my empty cup. The night plays out in generic fashion from here: more drinking, a few cigarettes outside, Kevin almost getting into a fight, a few key bumps in the bathroom, watching Perry and Mia tongue-kiss on a couch, blurred vision of passing cars on Sunset outside the club, furiously clawing Alisa in a cab and I may have attempted to force a hand job which I think she refused, but then we fuck back at the apartment with little energy on either of our parts, but I'm not sure, we were both out of our minds.

Brunch at the Beverly Hills Hotel in the morning is our only option because Nate 'n Al is closed for the filming of one of the

Kardashian shows and we hear the wait at Toast is exceeding three hours. There's a group of guests doing yoga on the ice-cream-cone-shaped grass lawn near the cabanas, and they all look up at us in disgust when I burp out a burning chest full of beef and pickle tacos soaked in liquor. Alisa screams, "Gross," slapping me in the stomach. The instructor, an old man with a cleanly shaved head and gray beard down to his crotch snaps at us to move on. It's too hot and we look like shit, so we decide to eat inside at the Fountain coffee shop under the stairs leading to the Polo Lounge instead of outside at the pool. After a twenty-minute wait standing by the door, pretending to read the *L.A. Times* Sports section, keeping conversation to a minimum, two stools open up at the counter, and we take our seats and order: grilled cheese with bacon and a Diet Coke for me and scrambled egg whites and an English muffin for her.

"That was . . . interesting last night," she tells me. "You were—" Denise, the waitress, interrupts Alisa, placing waters in front of us, which I attack, demanding a quick refill.

"I was what?" I ask, chewing ice.

"You were . . . so . . . nice," she says, smiling at me.

I don't know what she's talking about, but I return the smile with one of my own.

"It was fun," she tells me.

I have no memory of what she's referencing. She's looking at me with soft eyes, and her skin is perfect—an olive complexion, heightened by her recently dyed blond hair. James Gandolfini walks in wearing a hotel robe, baseball cap, and slippers, sipping a beer, going mostly unnoticed. Food is served and quietly eaten, and I consider asking her to go to Lance's party with me tonight but ultimately decide not to, thinking of Laila.

Lance grew up in L.A. and he was at every party in high

school, but no one is sure where he went (not Brentwood, SaMo, Crossroads, Pali, Harvard-Westlake, Buckley, or Beverly) and he always seems to evade the question. It never became a thing because he was rich and had the dope house North of Sunset in Beverly Hills and his parents were never home and he has never not driven a BMW 5 or 7 series or not had drugs on him and he's always hanging out with one or two gangbangers and he still lives North of Sunset, but now in the hills, high above the La Cienega intersection, and he's a producer; at least, that's what he tells people.

"Los Angeles" is spelled out in coke on a six-foot dark coffee wood-frame floor mirror sitting in the middle of a pool table as a Johnny Jewel instrumental blasts over a scene of kids with lit cigarettes between their lips or fingers, babbling about box-office reports, Nikki Finke, and studio heads (I heard my father's name as I walked in followed by a laugh, which is funny, but people are talking about him, they know him, and this makes me jealous).

Lance is a "hip pocket" client of the agency (Industry Fact: When a young agent wants to sign someone before they have full signing power, they can hip-pocket a client and unofficially represent them), and he's somehow attached to produce a few Blacklist scripts, so a lot of my colleagues are present. Kevin, Derek, both Perrys, and a few other assistants, including the girl with the hairy arms, are in the living room across from the pool table in front of a glass wall displaying a twinkling, 180-degree view from downtown to the high-rises of Westwood, and some guy behind me yells, "Don't fear the raper," chasing a girl with strawberry blond hair in circles till she finally gives up, falling to the floor in tears of what I believe and hope are laughter.

As I approach my colleagues, someone hands me a bottle of Johnnie Walker Blue with crushed balls of ice clinking around inside it. I interrupt an impromptu dance contest between Derek and Palisades, both of them presenting their best running man to the new Kaskade single, which has taken over the gathering. I offer a "Bravo!" raising the bottle an arm's length into the air and pouring a clumsy shot in my mouth, which doesn't go down easy, nauseating me.

"Nice moves." I tell them, nodding my head to the rhythm of the sound track.

Kevin laughs, adding, "Yeah, it's like Dance Dance Revolution up in here."

"I wonder if anyone has those film rights," I say.

"Sounds like a classic in the making," Derek says, easily removing the bottle from my hand, taking an impossibly long sip.

"Smooth," he brags to the group, spitting a few shrunken pieces of ice out at me like a Gatling.

Derek rushes my space; we're nose to nose as the electric sound track fades to silence, and the lights go black, and he whispers, "Boo," then smiles and walks off, prompting the light and sound to return, leaving me holding the bottle of scotch again.

My eyes scan across the interior of the house, past the Marilyn Monroe Mr. Brainwash and the Sony plasma and a Warhol print (it couldn't possibly be an original, could it?), toward a chestnut leather couch where the girl who was crying is now making out with the grim raper guy under another large plasma; this one, at least seventy inches, playing a Blu-ray disc of *Woodstock*. And there's Laila, sitting with her husband in the midst of what looks like an emotional conversation, which quickly concludes with Jason exiting for the coke-covered pool table, where a girl finishes an entire letter *S* in one slithering sniff.

Laila disappears. I desperately scan the scene again as Kevin, Derek, and Perry all chug beers with a group of girls cheering them on. I catch Alisa for the first time, next to the *Lost* pinball machine, talking with Jason, who shares a few clients with Alisa's boss, and images from the holiday party, them talking together at the bar, come back to me, so I don't say hello.

Then Laila appears again, exiting the house alone through the front door.

"Where's hubby?" I ask, sneaking up from behind, lighting a cigarette for her. She nervously looks back inside for him as a white Denali slowly drifts in front of us. "Don't worry, he's blowing coke," I tell her.

"With Alisa?" she asks.

"That too." I light my cigarette. "Do you care?"

"I don't know, do you?" She smiles at me, inhaling smoke.

"Doesn't really matter," she continues, "we're over."

Uncertain if she's talking about them or us, I flick the cigarette onto the sidewalk near the now idling white truck.

"Nothing matters," I tell her.

"It wasn't always like this."

I'm looking into her eyes as she desperately tries to avert my gaze, focused instead on the cigarette she's draining down to the filter.

"You may be right," she quietly admits, looking into the house again, the cigarette finally falling to the concrete below.

"Maybe we should stop this . . . us," she says.

"There is no *us*."

She finally looks at me, pained, but aware of the truth. She shakes it off, pops another cigarette in her mouth, and confirms the thought. "I know."

"I still need to see you," I tell her.

She looks at me slightly horrified, only able to inhale smoke, nicotine soothing her. Silence builds as we stand staring at each other. She's upset. The Denali circled the block and is now rolling back in front of us again, the windows down, a rap beat seeping out, slowly building in volume as the truck nears. Masta Ace is now blasting out of every window. The driver, an older white man wearing a backward retro Cleveland Indians hat, stares past us, into the house, waiting for something, music at full blast.

Lance appears with a few kids, including a Mexican wearing a Raiders jersey I noticed inside but tried not to make eye contact with. They swarm the truck, grabbing the driver, pulling him from his seat through the window with incredible speed, and start stomping him, sending a geyser of blood, spit, and teeth into the air, causing Laila to rush back to the house, finding Jason in the doorway, who's been watching everything.

Kev, Eisenberg, and Derek push past Laila and Jason, joining me on the curb to witness the violence. They're jumping up and down, forcing their bodies higher into the air, howling for the driver's guts, squealing for the gore, cackling as the driver loses consciousness. I look away—past the blood-soaked lawn, the gleefully dilated eyes of my friends, and the chubby girl who forced herself into a size small dress, barfing next to a tree—to find Jason holding Laila, her face buried in his chest, frozen in the doorway, and he's ignoring everything except for me, staring into my eyes.

On My Way

The day starts out like any other morning since I landed on David Michaels's desk. Up at 5:30 to work out with Reggie, who's in a bad mood because his new single "didn't grab ears," and I'm to pay for this with a fifteen-minute sprint at a tremendous speed with a ten-pound weight in each hand. Forty-five minutes of core workouts as Reggie keeps repeating "don't puke" follow, and I'm dressed and in the office an hour later, ready for the day. Joyce is already on the phone making travel arrangements with the company's personal American Express Platinum travel agent for a set visit to Toronto for David, next winter's family vacation to the Four Seasons' Maui (she reserves pool cabanas as well, David is on an elite list of guests where this is allowed), and a last-minute booking for this year's Sundance Film Festival, which, although it's still half a year away, is basically totally booked, so in desperation, Joyce tells the travel agent, "He'll probably just buy a place."

After dropping off a certain client's script at half the desks in the building (a pile of them were left on my chair with a note that read: *Get these to the following offices by 9:00 a.m. or else*), Shane follows me in, drops a black Marc Jacobs duffel bag, starts her computer without making eye contact, and says, "Chai tea latte." Seconds pass before I realize she wants me to go to Coffee Bean and get her one, and before I exit, Joyce begs, "Me too please," with the phone hanging from her neck, then returns to the call with the travel agent, saying, "I will find you if this doesn't happen."

Later, we're sipping lattes and *Variety* is delivered with the following front-page headline: WILL & WILCOX. The accompanying story details Will Smith's attachment to the new Simon Wilcox pitch that was purchased after a three-studio weekend bidding war. Peter Berg, Jon Favreau, and Ron Howard are all circling to direct *Blown to Bits,* the story of a Navy SEAL paralyzed in war whose scientist father builds him a state-of-the-art cyborg body to assist the FBI in taking down a new domestic terrorist cell.

Front page *Variety.*

"You see this?" I ask Shane, holding up the paper.

"All I see are seventy-eight e-mails you haven't handled yet."

"Seventy-eight e-mails? That's all? We must be slipping," David jokes as he strides into the offices, holding out a fist in my direction to pound. Our hands connect and grins mirror each other's. "What, no chai latte for me?" he asks.

Joyce and Shane look up, expressionless, then over to me.

"Got it—" I announce.

"No," David interrupts. "Stay here. . . . Sugar, would you mind?"

She sweats anger, staring me down while exiting past my grinning face.

At 12:45 Kevin suggests, "A quick Blvd run?" I usually don't enjoy spending fifty dollars on lunch, but I'm in a celebratory mood and agree to join him. It's about as nice out as L.A.

gets—seventy-three degrees with a slight breeze pushing any cloud in the light blue sky out of existence—so we decide to sit outside. We each order the Blvd burger with sautéed wild mushrooms and foie gras mousse, a shrimp and artichoke pizza for the table, and Arnold Palmers. Kevin puffs a Marlboro Medium to life and mentions Derek. "He's doing well with Larry. People are talking."

"People are always talking," I tell him.

"I popped my head into Larry's office to see if he wanted to join us, but the intern told me they were gone . . . already at lunch . . . together," he says, stubbing out the cigarette, lifting his eyebrows.

"I should have gotten the halibut and chips, you think it's too late?"

"Probably," Kev tells me as the waiter throws the pizza on the table, sending a garnish of wild arugula everywhere.

A rapid set of flashes across the street catch our attention—the assumption being paparazzi are chasing down a celebrity—but it's only European and Japanese tourists, shopping and taking pictures on the Rodeo steps and in front of the fountain.

"This isn't fucking Rome," I blurt out, feta-infused shrimp almost choking me.

"It's weird," Kevin notes, lighting another Marlboro. "Like, don't they know it was built in the nineties?"

"Tourists are idiots."

"Correct."

After the pizza, we both smoke and discuss Ty dropping out of business school and training to surf professionally, and then we argue over the end of *Inception*—Kevin swears it was all a dream. Then we spend a brief amount of time pondering exactly how much Chris Nolan is worth and whether or not we'd represent him for zero commission just to have him on a client roster—I'm in favor of the maneuver. And just as Kevin is calling me a mongoloid, the burgers are placed in front of us and we both dip fries into the foie gras mousse and have our Arnold Palmers refilled.

Then Kev hits me with it. "So, you know Alisa and Greenberg are fucking, right?"

"Perfect." I toss my burger down, licking beef grease off my palm.

"How so?" he asks, humored, chomping on his food.

I pause for a moment, knowing I shouldn't trust Kevin, but quickly decide the truth is the only way.

"How so? Well . . . I've been fucking Laila."

"Who the fuck is Laila?" he asks, inhaling another huge section of the burger.

"Greenberg's wife."

Kevin is finally silent, his chewing slows.

"So, like I said . . . perfect."

A Beverly Hills fire truck screams by us, almost flipping over, making the turn onto South Beverly, which the tourists across the street enthusiastically photograph.

"I guess he found out," he says.

"Is that a question?"

"What do you think?"

"Whatever."

"Perfect," Kevin says while devouring the rest of the burger with a ravenous munch as a smile appears and the check comes and it's back to work.

. . .

I return to find an empty office, soothed by how quiet and calm it all seems with everything halted for the one o'clock hour. The time for chatter over lobster Cobbs at The Grill or McCarthys at the Polo Lounge accompanied by the gossiping, the belittling, the backstabbing, the cheating, the stealing; and it's taking place across the entire city, and it's mean and mostly unnecessary and incredibly toxic, but it's also essential (regardless of what Shane believes), so this is a daily practice and deemed good business.

As the clocks strike two, Shane and Joyce rush into the office and the calls begin, the e-mail notifications sound, and business as usual erupts again. David enters soon after, talking on a Bluetooth headset, unknotting a white Prada tie, which sports a brown stain at the bottom of it, most likely from his lunch with Bernard, his business manager and accountant, at Junior's (the only place in the city Bernard eats), where David usually orders the barley soup, which was obviously the cause for the stain. We're almost certain David is talking into his headset when he walks past Shane, throwing the dirty tie at her, saying, "I'll take care of him for you," then points at me, gesturing into his office. No one made the call for him, so we're unsure if he's actually on a call, and I may have just ruined a new pair of Brooks Brothers boxers. "Follow me," he says, moving quickly into his office. Joyce and Shane stand up, looking at each other, then turn toward me, shrugging their shoulders.

"Was he talking to me?" I whisper.

"Get in here and shut the door," David commands from inside his connecting office. The girls shake their head in confusion as I slowly enter his office, closing the door behind me. David has his back to me, facing the glass wall. I close in on him, passing the round Cattelan Italia coffee table, the matching leather Moroso couch and chairs, the awards from countless charities, all the black-and-white framed photos of David with a who's who of the cast of every issue of *Us Weekly, The Hollywood Reporter,* and *Entertainment Weekly,* and a couple of one-sheets for films David packaged with billion-dollar box office grosses featured on them. And my life flashes before my eyes: playing Marco Polo with my sisters in our old pool on South Whittier; a July Fourth night in Malibu sitting in cold sand, watching fireworks explode over the ocean; the first time I fucked on ecstasy, scared I might die; my first day at the agency, meeting Alisa; and the foie gras mousse may spray out of me at any moment as I reach David, who spins around smiling with a check in his hand.

"You did good . . . real good," he tells me, handing me the check.

"Simon's gonna make four to five million on this Will Smith thing when it's all said and done."

He moves away, behind his desk, and takes a seat, sliding the Bluetooth iPhone headset off and a Bluetooth office phone headset on. "I want you to take that check, cash it, and go to Barneys. Roberto is expecting you."

I look down, unfolding the check—$10,000.

"Three or four suits on me . . . you've earned it."

Shane's voice penetrates the room, "Rupert, line two!"

I turn my head, see her sneaking into the room, and watch her eyes tilt down, spotting the check in my hand.

"Got it," David yells back at her.

She exits. David motions for me to sit down.

"You want this life?" He spreads his arms out wide, past all the posters with billion-dollar figures and black-and-white photos of celebrities.

I nod yes.

"Then take it."

"I will."

"Good, now go," he commands before picking up the call, turning the charm on. "Rupert, I miss that accent . . ."

"Murdoch?" I ask Joyce, returning to my desk.

"Everett . . . an old client."

Shane looks up from her computer. "Ethan and Brian Gottlieb here to see you . . . Shall I send them up?"

"No, I'll meet them in the lobby," I nervously tell her.

"Fine, just be back ASAP, David needs a urine sample delivered to Cedars and the mailroom has no one to do it. Toodles." She wiggles her fingers at me, returning to the phones.

I slowly make my way to the railing overlooking the lobby to find the brothers in matching pink short-sleeve Polo shirts, pacing the marble floor below. I watch them fidget, checking their iPhones at least three times each. Brian runs a hand through his hair, looking anxious, then he inspects Ethan's mouth, pulling something from between his brother's teeth. And I step into a closing elevator, heading to the depths for them.

"Gentlemen, how the hell are you?"

"How the fuck do you think we are?" Brian snaps.

"He's going to pretend he doesn't know why we're here." Ethan is boiling.

"Easy, guys, easy," I tell them, trying to contain the volume. I put an arm around each of them. "Let's get some sun," I say, guiding them to the nearest door leading out to the courtyard.

The brothers slap my arms off their shoulders.

"So you're denying it?" Ethan asks me, sliding a pair of green-tinted aviators on.

"He's fucking denying it," Brian says, stepping next to his brother, facing me.

I act dumbfounded.

"His father taught him *all* the tricks," Brian continues.

I'd love to admit to this "trick," and it's killing me that I can't claim ownership, that I can't scream about my father having nothing to do with this move, that this was innate. That I'm sure my father never had the nerve or had to work half as hard to get promoted. But I'm forced to continue the charade with silent confusion instead.

"Our script!" Ethan says.

"What about it?"

Brian can't contain himself. "What a dick!"

Ethan holds up the front page of *Variety,* hurling it at my chest.

"Fucking dick!" Brian is blind at this point.

"I had nothing to do with"—I look down at the front page of *Variety,* pretending to see the article for the first time—"this."

"Bullshit," Ethan says, now pacing around Brian, who's standing in place, hyperventilating.

"Guys, this is Industry 101. Similar projects get developed at the same time all the time. *Armageddon/Deep Impact?* Hello? They didn't teach you this at Stark?"

Ethan takes a step toward me. "Just so we have it on record. Are you claiming you didn't steal our concept and give it to your boss, who then gave it to his biggest writer client? Is that what's going on here? Because I am *out* of my fucking mind with disbelief."

Brian is now foaming at the mouth.

"For the record, I have no idea what you're talking about. Simon Wilcox came up with this idea on his own," I tell them, looking down at the front page of *Variety* again, pretending to read it for the first time. "It says here, *Blown to Bits* . . . an Iraqi vet fighting on American soil . . . that it's *Iron Man* meets *Avatar.* That's totally different."

"It's called *Blown to Bits.* We said 'blown to bits' in our pitch!"

"I'm not seeing it, boys. And this ridiculous Winklevoss routine you're attempting to pull isn't a good look. I wouldn't push this if I were you. I mean, I never even got the script. . . . You didn't e-mail it to me, did you?"

Checkmate.

The brothers are silenced, their chests heaving in and out.

"Now, I have to run some piss to Cedars. Are we done here?"

The Grove

I wake up gasping for air early Saturday morning and can't get back to sleep even though it's still dark outside. My eyes sting when I attempt to keep them open, and exhaustion blankets my body heavier than the Natori duvet cover my parents bought me when I moved into the Versailles. There are no memories of last night and nothing on TV or interesting enough on the DVR, so I decide to see a movie at The Grove—but would have to wait hours for the first showings.

While walking by a fountain shooting water into the sky on my way to the theater, Italian opera music blasting throughout the empty grounds of The Grove at 10:00 a.m., I imagine this is what it would look and feel like as the only survivor of a virus outbreak or zombie invasion. And I continue enjoying this thought while purchasing a ticket and a bottle of water in the vacant lobby of the theater.

Halfway though the new Ryan Reynolds comedy, in which he morphs into Jack Black when his piggish, male ways become unbearable to the opposite sex, I get a text from Laila: *Jason working in office all day . . .* I tell her to come to The Grove for a movie. We pick the new Kate Hudson romantic comedy because the tracking has been weak, which means less chance of us being seen in public (Industry Fact: Tracking is the ability, through polling, to estimate how a film will perform in its opening weekend). The Ryan Reynolds comedy was actually pretty solid—I'd give it a B. I especially enjoyed the scene in which a girl thinks she's on a date with Ryan Reynolds, then magically sees Jack Black sitting across from her instead, and pukes on his face.

In between films, sitting in the lobby, waiting for Laila, checking my BlackBerry—no new e-mails, texts, tweets, or Facebook messages—I have an urge to scream while watching a few kids rush into the arcade across from where I'm sitting. Laila enters the lobby, buys a ticket at one of the self-service machines, and passes me on her way to the concession stand. Walking into the less than half-full theater, I see Laila sitting in the back right corner. We quickly share a glance and a smile as I find a seat in the last row of the left side of the theater. After a trailer for a remake of *Up in Smoke* starring Josh Blum and Seth Rogen, and a *Baby Mama* sequel called *Baby's Mama's Daddy* (which Tina Fey is only producing, not starring in), Laila quietly makes her way over to my empty row, taking the seat to my left.

The movie starts, and it's so predictable and numbing that I don't notice Laila unzipping my jeans. The shock of her cold flesh snaps me out of the dazed, unblinking trance everyone in the theater is experiencing. Looking around, my dick growing in her small, tan hand with French-manicured nails, I feel like I'm seeing a film with the patients in *Awakenings,* or maybe there actually was a zombie invasion and Laila and I are just blending in. I smile and lean over to share the zombie-thought, but she's facing straight ahead with closed eyes, stroking me. Visions of her piercing our skin flash through my mind, but there's no pleasure, there's no pain, there's only silence and frozen faces. I'm not going to finish (good news for the couple sitting in front of us), so I take her hand, remove it from inside my jeans, and zip up. She opens her eyes, turns to face me, blinks, and turns back to the screen without a word.

After the flick, we share a salad and chicken marsala at Maggiano's, where we're certain no one of any significance in either of our lives will be eating. I'm telling her how lucky Kate Hudson is that Zooey Deschanel turned down the role of Penny Lane in *Almost Famous,* and how Kate is almost not famous anymore due to "the kind of shit we just sat through."

"I liked it," she tells me, gently stabbing whole wheat penne with her fork. "I think I'm going to use that third-act roller-coaster monologue in class this week."

"Yeah? Cool," I answer, sipping Diet Coke, which, surprisingly, is one of the best Diet Cokes in the city.

"They're probably together," she says, and then continues, "Jason and her."

"Probably," I admit while tweeting about Maggiano's having the best Diet Coke in Los Angeles, then listing Baby Blues, Toast, and La Scala as runner-ups.

"You know we've known each other for over a year." She tells me, dipping a piece of bread in a puddle of balsamic vinegar sprinkled with Parmesan cheese.

I look up from my phone, smile at her, then say something pleasant and return to checking Twitter, concentrating on a tweet from Derek, who's bragging about enjoying the new Allan Loeb script, which I've heard is excellent but haven't gotten around to yet.

"Maybe I should try to have children again . . . seems like they'd be fun . . . you know, to play with," Laila says, prompting me to drop my BlackBerry on the table.

"Play?" I ask.

"Yeah . . . play," she tells me.

The Michaelses

The Simon Wilcox deal made me. I'm in, officially David Michaels's boy. And with that comes even more responsibility, greater access, better perks, higher stakes, longer days, and, of course, rampant jealousy. It starts with trust. A key to the house in Brentwood with all the pass codes and introductions to all the maids and Carl the butler, who tells me he's really more of a concierge than a butler and "I'm not going to answer the door for you" when he answers the door for me. The introduction to the wife and kids, who at first keep me at a distance—friendly, but cold—and in time come to rely on the skill set I bring to the house. The weekend house visits to inflate a new pool raft; picking up the kids all across the city when Karen the nanny and driver is PMSing so bad she has to call in sick; the time the wife couldn't start her desktop, so I rushed over and noticed it just wasn't plugged in; countless mornings in the kitchen watching the kids eat egg white and spinach omelets waiting for David to finish his early morning exercises so I can drive him to work while he video-conferences with Europe and the East Coast. The specific reasons and actions that were necessary became moot. He needed me, I needed him, and we both understood.

I cut my hair short in the summertime and am never seen

without a tie, because that's what David does. I make sure to remember everyone's name and always send thank-you notes for even the smallest gestures, because that's what David does. I only drink bottled water at company functions and never eat at Ruth's Chris, Il Pastaio, or Sushi Roku, because that's what David does. It's never: "Let me think about it" or "Maybe"; it's always "Here's the answer" or "Absolutely." It's never "Ya know, my family is going on vacation, sorry," it's always "Oh, you need me to come in at 5:00 a.m. on Saturday? I'll be there." It's Stockholm syndrome. It's obsessive-compulsive disorder. It's "all so fucked up," as Kevin puts it when he hears I left work for an afternoon to help David's daughter complete a five-thousand-piece puzzle of the Ponte Vecchio because she freaked out and wanted it finished after a trip to Florence. I go to school plays and ballet performances to videotape the kids in action. I drive to Oxnard to pick up one of the biggest pumpkins in the state and carve Justin Bieber's face into it. I pick up stuffed bags of makeup from Chanel and dresses from Missoni for the wife. I've lost track of my family but feel at home.

For my twenty-fourth birthday David gives me a $500 gift certificate to Cut with a card that reads:

You're getting close.—DM

He hands it to me, places a hand on my shoulder, and is taken with the texture of my suit. I tell him it's Paul Smith. He asks, "Part of the Barneys upgrade?" And when I answer yes, he smiles and says, "Nice" before taking a call he answers in Japanese. And when I do see my family the night of my birthday for the annual celebration at Mastro's, their gifts and their presence don't come close. We're all sitting at the same table downstairs, but when driving to drinks after dinner, I could have sworn I was upstairs in the corner booth under the Rat Pack poster, alone.

I'm a young Henry Hill receiving special treatment from all my peers and even some young agents—"It was out of respect," I keep repeating to myself. I'm the only assistant granted entry into the Motion Picture meetings, surrounded by agents, absorbing everything. I'm in charge of getting David's Titleist golf clubs cleaned and, on a few occasions, assist the valet workers at David's parties, informing them of the guests' names to make everything affiliated with David a personal experience. But I'm also inside the parties, being seen and talking to clients and higher-level colleagues; getting a taste for how industry players behave outside the office. I balance the shit with the shine, the yuck with the "Fuck, I just had dinner with a client who made twenty million on his last picture." And everyone understands that today's shitstain is tomorrow's shit-eating grin, so I'm looked at as a comer, as "Michaels's guy," as a possible candidate for the town's next big thing.

Kevin reminds everyone again how "it's all so fucked up" at Bar Marmont, where a few of us gather for drinks to celebrate "the boy's birthday." People are actually calling me the Boy, and, when I question Kev about it, he claims they've been calling me that for a while and thought I knew.

"I didn't know."

"Don't sweat it, it's better than Bagel Boy," he tells me, raising his voice over the Madonna remixes that are playing at an obnoxious volume. From across the room I spot Alisa stumbling in my direction, a cranberry and vodka spilling in one hand, her iPhone in the other, a Céline bag (her prized possession of the month) falling off a shoulder with newly dyed brown hair that blends into a tight chocolate top. She's coming for me, so I look down at my phone, searching through e-mails I've already read.

"I'm leaving," she tells me.

"Have a good night." I look up from my phone as a Taylor Momsen cover of "Like a Virgin" plays.

"No, I'm leaving . . . the agency. Thought you should know," she says, sipping half the cranberry concoction away through a small red straw.

It makes sense.

"Well, good luck." I'm looking everywhere and at everyone but her for as long as I can but finally relent and watch her finish the drink, place her phone in the black leather bag, and say, "Bye."

A Katy Perry cover of "Celebrate" rushes past us, through the speakers. "Say what's up to Jason for me."

She turns to face me, looking wounded (but she always looks wounded), and then quickly exits.

Acting

David put me in charge of planning his annual Friday Night Before the Oscars Party, which this year is in direct competition with Bryan Lourd's CAA party at his home in Beverly Hills, Ari Emanuel's WME shindig at his Brentwood Park estate, Harvey Weinstein's TWC soiree at Soho House, Brian Grazer's Imagine dinner at Cecconi's, and a reception put on by all the partners at UTA to celebrate an abnormally stellar season of client performance. I've already confirmed David Blaine to perform magic tricks (he also said he could make people disappear, but I told him David has other people for that); Todd English to re-create the stations he runs at the Plaza Food Hall (except for the sushi station because David is friends with Kazynori Nozawa, who won't be preparing food because he's a guest of the party but will assign chefs from Sugarfish and will personally oversee the offerings); and although live music is usually frowned upon at these things because it drowns out the gossiping, Eddie Vedder will play an acoustic set for half an hour, which will be less hectic. David really liked this idea; I won points with it.

While I'm on the phone with a meteorologist seeking a more comprehensive understanding of the weather patterns and, more specifically, chances of precipitation or any other type of moisture or wind the night of the party, which is still two months away, a package is delivered by Dale, the new, fat mailroom trainee, whose mom works for Ralph Lauren, so he's always squeezed into their shirts, ties, and suits. Today it's a checkered brown thing with a purple tie, and I'm checking him out, baffled by his taste, until the meteorologist screams "Hello?" I grab the package from Dale and rip it open to find a few new iPads, ten $100 Best Buy gift certificates, and a black vibrator. Shane quickly throws her headset off, abandoning a call between David and Donna Langley to retrieve the package and its embarrassing contents. She whispers, "Mostly for David . . . and a bachelorette party," holding up the ribbed seven-incher before hiding the package under her desk, jumping back on the call, and playfully rolling her eyes at me and Joyce, who glances at me briefly, sharing a knowing look.

"It's too early, sir," the meteorologist tells me.

"I'm calling from David Michaels's office, did I mention that?"

"You did."

"And you can't do any better?" I ask, checking out a few celebrity bikini malfunctions on Perez Hilton.

"Hold on, sir, let me get God for you, I'm sure he can help."

"Okay, thanks," I answer, slurping drool into my mouth from the nipples of celebrities I never expected to see. Soon, there's a dial tone and I'm about to ask Shane about the package, but her words beat mine. "D.M. wants a chai tea latte with no sugar added and so do we," and I'm off to the Coffee Bean. I stop in the mailroom before exiting the building to see if they really had no one to pick up the drinks for David—they don't, the room is empty—and return to find Shane in David's office taking notes on a legal pad, Joyce on the phone telling someone "Try me, it won't be tasty," and on my keyboard a new to-do list, which includes an envelope pickup at Montage Beverly Hills, hand-delivering a check to Staples Center's business affairs office, and buying "as much lobster and jumbo gulf shrimp at Santa Monica Seafood as you can."

As the door to David's office swings shut, Joyce hurries out (most likely to take a shit, she's good for a few a week around this time) and the phones erupt. Calls from Jim Nelson, Peter Bart, Lawrence Bender, and a woman who claims her name is Stella, but when I ask for a last name, she refuses to give one; and I tell them all that David will have to return their calls with only "Stella" giving me a hard time, questioning when she might hear back, and no one does this, at least not anyone truly in the business, so I attempt to brush her off.

"I'll tell him you called."

Three more lines light up.

"And that I want to hear from him," she tells me.

Another line erupts with a shrill sound and a flashing red light.

"Yes, thank you."

I quickly hit another line, hanging up on Stella.

"David Michaels's office . . ."

"It's Bobby Biz for him."

And I know they're old friends, but I also know that David won't be taking the gossip website owner's call, so I tell him, "We'll have to return."

That's one.

"David Michaels's office . . ."

"Hi, Dan Lin calling . . ."

"Hold please."

I scream out "Dan Lin" and can barely make out Shane's voice on the other side of the door telling me to "Return!"

"I'm sorry, he's unavailable at the moment, we'll return."

Two.

"David Michaels's office . . ."

"Doug Belgrad calling for David."

"I'm sorry I don't have him at the moment."

That's three, but another call blasts out.

I answer, the older of the two calls, "David Michaels's office . . ."

"Amy Pascal for David."

"Hold please."

I place Amy on hold and answer the fifth and final ringing line.

"David Michaels's office . . ."

"It's Greenberg for him."

"Sorry, Jason, he's unavailable."

"Unavailable? You didn't even try him . . . I know he's in there."

The Pascal call is beeping (a function of the phone, reminding the user of calls on hold). "He'll return." I slam the phone down, move to the closed door, and yell out, "Pascal on four!" The door opens, and Shane's flushed face slides through it saying, "Return, damnit," and she almost slams the door closed on her own head, but not before I notice her blouse is unbuttoned at the top, and I let Amy's office know David will return her call shortly and it's finally quiet.

Joyce reappears with a spring in her step (a few pounds lighter, I'm sure), trailed by a frustrated Jason Greenberg, who walks past me, stopping in front of Joyce, and politely asks, "I'd like a moment with him." The phone rings, Joyce throws on her headset, answers the phone, holds a finger up in Jason's face, signaling she needs a minute, and proceeds to get into a lengthy conversation with the car wash guys downstairs in the parking lot regarding instructions on the interior detailing of David's G550.

"He's not available, dude."

Jason leaves Joyce's desk and approaches mine.

"Who's he in with?"

"Does it matter?" I ask, getting up, straightening my tie, and readying myself to tackle the to-do list left on my keyboard earlier.

"Nice tie, what is that, Nordstroms?"

"Alexander McQueen," I tell him, twisting the tie around, showing off the label.

"Nice gift from Mommy and Daddy?" He grins.

"Actually, from David," I tell him as he heads for the door.

"Let him know I stopped by."

"Got it."

"Seriously, last time I left word, I never heard back." He finally turns to leave.

"That's 'cause I'm fucking your wife."

He swings back from the hallway. "The fuck did you just say?"

"On my fucking life . . . I'll let him know you left word for him, what?"

"Right," he says, nodding his head, gritting his teeth. "Thanks."

Joyce was finished with the car washers downstairs halfway through that little dance and offers a strange expression before asking me to pick up David's dry cleaning as well.

As I'm exiting the office, Shane appears, taking a seat at her desk.

"You're leaving?"

"Yeah, the to-do list." I hold up the buck slip, standing in the doorway.

"Will you also get a couple of swordfishes from The Ivy? David is staying in for dinner; he asked me to join him."

I slip out, into the hallway, adding "Dry cleaners" and "The Ivy" to the list as Dale, the new trainee, passes me, angrily mumbling something to himself, pushing a cart of scripts. I slowly follow behind him, lost in his journey—the newborn existence—until I can't take it anymore. Once in the elevator, descending to the garage, I smile, thinking fondly of my time in the depths of the building.

The minute I hit the car the texts start pouring in, and they're all from Laila wondering if we're still on for tonight (I already told her yes twice this morning), reminding me she has something to discuss with me (again, something she already told me about numerous times that I hoped would go away because I can't imagine what she wants), and I write back: *Yeah, Izakaya, 830,* and she sends me three texts in quick succession: *Okie dokie, Can't W8, C u soon love.* It's only after the last text, seeing the word *love,* that I decide I'm going to tell her we're over; that it's her, not me.

I'm fifteen minutes late to Izakaya on Third because the swordfish was overcooked, and, naturally, Shane had to send me back to The Ivy instead of sending an intern or mailroom trainee or god forbid she remembered she was an assistant and returned it herself, but that's not reality and I don't mind David knowing I put in some extra work, but it backfires when I return with the new entrées and he reminds me that next time I'm picking up food for anyone and they ordered it at a specific temperature, to check the food before leaving the establishment. Excellent.

I find Laila at Izakaya, already seated, biting into a baked crab hand roll, then slurping a remaining dose of red wine. She stands up, wearing a black miniskirt, kissing me on the cheek, which I pull away from her to take a seat. She apologizes, offering me a roll, saying something about starving herself for the past week and how she had to start eating.

"You sure this is cool? Being here?" I quietly ask her.

"It's fine," she tells me. Then she leans in and whispers, "The secret's out."

I grab a passing waitress by the hip, tell her I want two spicy tuna cut rolls with soy paper, an order of rock shrimp, and a beer, any beer she wants to bring me.

Then Laila begins. "So, you know I've been doing that acting workshop?"

Fortunately, the waitress brings my beer while Laila blabs on about her love of the arts and how she finally feels at peace with life because of acting, and I'm downing the bottle in one tilt back, gulping it as she's pouring her heart out in sync with the emptying of my beer.

"So, can you?"

"Can I what?" I'm confused while finishing the foam at the bottom of the bottle, motioning to the waitress on the other side of the room for another.

"Hip-pocket me?"

"Lai— It's a ridiculous request. Assistants don't hip-pocket, we can't."

The sushi and shrimp are served, as well as some toro she

ordered (the most expensive item on the menu). "Christ, this is good," I moan, delight overcoming my senses while I'm chewing a fried shrimp. "Not as good as Koi or Nobu, but still."

"Ridiculous? Can't?" She raises her voice. "My career is going nowhere. What actor makes it after thirty?"

"Hackman," I tell her, moving on to the spicy tuna pieces. "But I think that's it."

A tear forms, rolling down the left side of her face.

"Look, I thought you said things were looking up."

"I need this," she tells me.

"Absolutely not."

"Michaels loves you, you can get away with anything."

"I just fucked up swordfish, there's no way."

"Why?"

"Because."

"Because I'm a shit actress."

"Because you're Greenberg's wife!"

"It's over. The secret's out!"

"So?"

"You don't think I'm talented, you don't think I have a shot."

I say nothing.

"I'll meet with anyone. Tell me who." She's pleading with both hands buried beneath the table, leaning toward me. "You're just like Jason."

I throw a piece of sushi in my mouth, chewing slowly, deliberately.

"We'll see . . ." I tell her.

She's pounding the table, the tips of a few fingers slightly coated in blood from the scabs on her legs she must have just been picking, and a drop of blood is launched in the air, falling on the tempura-battered shrimp in front of me. She's not crying anymore; there's anger, no sadness. I dig into the shrimp with a pair of chopsticks, locate the blood-soiled seafood, lift it, holding the piece close to my face, then eat it.

"You're not going to use me," I tell her, hoping to sound genuine. "I won't let you."

She leans back in her chair, silent as I take a long pull off the second beer and continue, "I think I'm done."

Then she gets up and leaves.

Give Thanks

By the time the second week in November rolls around, business slows, and anyone with any kind of money will vacation at least once during this time period. They won't just rush back January 2 either, they roll in midweek or the second week back, relaxed (this is usually fleeting), tan (this usually sustains), and ready to jump back in; but alas, then it's time for Sundance. And although only a smaller assortment of agents, executives, and clients attend, their absence, and the simple knowledge that something moderately important is happening east of the 10 freeway extinguishes the collective energy of the town.

It begins with Thanksgiving. I'm not in charge of handling anything for David or the household—Joyce is the chosen "lucky" one this year—so I actually get a four-day break. Mom didn't feel like cooking (not the first time). She told us, "When I cook, I nibble, and I can't nibble." She's on a strict diet, preparing for another possible recasting situation on the new season of *The Real Housewives of Beverly Hills* (my sisters pleaded with her to resubmit applications and learn every maître d's and head valet's name in town, desperately wanting to sniff fame, and whatever my sisters have ever wanted, they've received). She asks me to go pick up dinner from Joan's on Third because

"Everyone loves Joan's on Third . . . everyone!" And, according to Jill, the wife of a gay entertainment attorney who gets her nails done with my mom, "they do a fab Thanksgiving."

"But you don't like Joan's," I remind her.

"Exactly, I won't nibble. I can't."

Joan's is packed. There's a very skinny girl wearing denim shorts in front of me, leaning over the counter, lifting a cowboy-boot-covered foot into the air, searching for something behind the counter. One of the cashiers leans over, whispering. "Ma'am, I assure you, that wasn't a rat."

"Then it was a huge fucking cockroach."

"Ma'am, that's just not true."

She drops the cowboy boot back to the ground, pulling a pair of brown Dita sunglasses down to the tip of her pierced nose.

"Well, it was something."

He looks exhausted. "Ma'am . . . this is Joan's . . . I assure you, it was nothing."

I'm contemplating biting her butt cheek, which has slightly made its way out of her shorts, and as I'm moving in, my mouth slowly opening, she spins around with two huge bags of food, saying, "Rats!" to no one in particular as she vanishes onto Third Street.

"Women . . ." I say to the cashier, smiling.

"That's why I fuck men," he tells me.

I blurt out, "gross."

He looks offended.

While waiting for the order, I try six types of cheese, including four different kinds of Parmesan, and a slice of duck sausage, using an Orangina as a palate cleanser; and when my name is called, I get help carrying five boxes of food to my car. About to leave, I hear the cheese guy who was helping me say, "Really?" after I didn't buy anything or tip him. I keep hearing the word *really* on the ride home even though I have a Lil Wayne album playing at maximum volume—I can't shake it. It makes me sick, and my stomach rumbles horrifically while I'm racing the sun west to my parents.

"Food is in the car, I have to shit" is all I have time to say, running into the house, past Emily and Keith playing Scrabble, Cate texting, and my father watching football. While slamming the door shut, coming a little too close to shitting in my pants, I hear Cate yell, "Really?" accompanied by my father and Keith giggling, and the word continues to bother me.

We're all feasting on molasses-glazed turkey, rosemary ciabatta stuffing, chilled cranberry soup with a sweet potato crème fraîche, and everyone is ignoring the brussels sprout casserole Cate made because it's not nearly as good as everything from Joan's. Mom is sipping a kale banana smoothie (the only thing she's allowed to digest), leaning back, watching us.

"Hungry?" I ask.

"This kale is fantastic," she tells us, forcing another straw-full of the green pudding down.

"You have any idea how many calories that thing has?" Emily announces, dabbing the sides of her mouth with a napkin.

"I'm not concerned."

"Well, you should be . . . you might as well blend up some stuffing and eggnog."

"Em, please . . . I'm not nibbling."

Keith and I share a look, shoveling more into our mouths.

Dad is on his BlackBerry. "Hun, not tonight," Mom pleads, sucking in another helping of the smoothie. Dad grunts, slicing an entire piece of turkey into a few portions before placing one in his mouth.

"No business happening anyway, right?" I add.

"Exactly, thank you, honey," Mom tells me, slurping another shot, gagging a bit when swallowing.

Dad stares me down.

I shrug at him, driven by visions of an army of women with bangs, wearing thick doses of onyx mascara, laughing at my mother as she retches from another sip of her diet shake. Anger builds as we lock eyes, but he almost immediately looks away, continuing his meal; and if it were me, I would have continued staring down *my* son.

Cate says something about the brussels sprouts, then adds a spoonful to her plate, but doesn't eat them.

"I heard that guy killed more dogs in Runyon Canyon," Keith says.

"So did I," Cate excitedly announces while texting.

"No texting," Mom pleads again.

"It's not business," Cate whines.

"Exactly." Mom places the shamrock-colored shake down.

"I'm confused, can I text then?" Dad asks.

"What? Absolutely not." Mom is fed up, crossing her arms.

Dad turns around to catch a replay of a touchdown in the football game.

"Really?" Mom looks at all of us, annoyed.

My stomach rumbles.

"Let's all give thanks to Mom for keeping this family so

together." Emily raises a wineglass and continues, "I only hope I can be half as good a mommy as you, Mommy."

Cate's smiling wide, unable to contain herself, and everyone loses their shit that Emily and Keith are finally pregnant. Tears and hugs are followed by Mom raising her green drink and finishing it with a happy gulp as I continue to check Twitter and Facebook under the table, which has somehow gone unnoticed. Minutes later, Keith mentions the game going to overtime, and that's the signal for the end of dinner and I tweet something about being an uncle soon, Joan's ciabatta stuffing, and already shitting twice today, which loses me six followers.

Larry's Office

Derek invited a few of us to hang out in Larry's office after work to watch the Lakers game on Lazar's new fifty-five-inch Viera Panasonic 3D TV, and fortunately David is in a screening downstairs in the theater for one of our biggest actor clients' directorial debut. I lie to Joyce and Shane about my "lunch not sitting right," which is code for having to take a shit. I'm not embarrassed in the slightest, but they are, which works perfectly because they don't want to hear any more from me or about it and I'm out, skipping down the hall toward Lazar's office. The doorway is blocked by an orange gift basket from Bristol Farms featuring lots of fresh whole California oranges, a bag of dried mandarin slices, milk-chocolate-covered sour Seville oranges, and four bottles of freshly squeezed Murcia orange juice sitting in a small half cooler of melting, crushed ice.

Derek jumps out of the seat behind Larry's desk, noticing the gift basket, and drags it into the office. The pregame is on, and the announcers look like they're in the room, and I walk toward them and the TV hanging on the wall behind the image, slowly moving my hand through the hovering glow of light.

"Or-ange ya glad I invited you?" he asks, positioning the gift basket out of the way.

"Funny."

"What the fuck is so funny?" A voice that sounds like Larry's booms from the doorway, causing both of us to quickly turn around, but it's only Kevin fucking with us. "Pussies," he says while taking a seat on the couch lining the wall across from the TV.

Gay Andrew shows up next. "Are you guys only going to talk pussy, because you know I just can't keep up."

"Man-ass is your pussy, you can talk about man-ass if that makes you more comfortable."

"Thank you, Kevin."

"You got it, bud."

The game is under way, and Derek ordered Vito's, which was nice of him, and he's sitting behind Larry's desk with his feet up and a folded slice of white pie in his hand, telling us about a client, Chelsea Silver, who is very close to getting the female lead in James Cameron's *True Lies* sequel; how he's pretty sure Larry doesn't know his name, because he only calls him Pal; and they've been receiving strange phone calls and packages, "like this orange thing," he says, and Larry doesn't seem to care, "but he probably should," Derek says, stuffing himself with a mouthful of pizza, then coughing it up on the floor after choking while celebrating a fast break dunk at the end of the first quarter. "My bad." Derek laughs with all of us while he bends down, cleaning the pizza off the rug.

"What the fuck is so funny?" booms from the doorway.

Derek is still laughing. "Fuck you, Kev . . ."

"What the fuck is this?" Larry asks. Derek was not expecting him back tonight, but it's him, and Derek is not laughing anymore.

"Larry?" he says.

"Larry?" Lazar mimics in a childish voice. "What. The. Fuck?"
Derek is speechless.

"Get the fuck out of my office. Get your fucking Lakers game off my brand-new three-fucking-D television. Get your fucking ass in your shit cubicle and get me my fucking phone sheet. Don't you ever again in your fucking life let me fucking see you behind my fucking desk, with your fucking shoes up on my fucking shit, thinking you are the fucking shit, or I will fucking fuck you into the fucking ether." Larry's tirade has us all in shock; we're statues watching him throw his bag down, rip open the gift basket, pull out a few of the fresh oranges, and hurl them at Derek. "You want to be the man with some feet up on a desk, watching a three-D TV, don'tcha? Don'tcha?" Derek's dodging the fruit, and Larry screams, "Get the fuck out of my face," and we all scatter back to our offices as Larry reaches inside the gift basket for more ammo, and the next day Derek claims it was "standard."

A Very Michaels Christmas

D avid Michaels is Jewish, but the tree he assigns me to pick out, oversee the chopping down of, and drive back to Los Angeles from an organic tree farm in Northern California so that it can be decorated by a crew of professionals with hundreds of handcrafted ornaments and twinkling lights is incredibly gentile. The first two weeks of December bring a simple assignment: handle everything holiday-related for David; and the most important thing holiday-related is client gifts. Each of David's fifty-something clients receives a personalized gift, ranging from Ducati motorcycles to a two-week stay at a home in Belize to cases of Fat Tire beer (for a lesser writer client) to a weekend at LeBron James's fantasy basketball camp to a lifetime supply of See's Candies to season tickets at the Ahmanson Theatre to African safaris and Italian cruises. With the gift comes a personalized note written by David and an invitation to a client-only holiday dinner at David's home, where guests will be entertained by an at-home version of *Iron Chef* between Masaharu Morimoto and Mario Batali, whose competition courses will be served for dinner (you wouldn't believe how much this costs, so I won't bother revealing it). Every single contact in the Rolodex receives an e-mail notifying them David has planted a tree in either Montana, Israel, or India (depending on the person's religion), and the e-mail signifies a conscientious effort to keep things "green" for the holidays, so it looks responsible, but my god if they only knew how much paper and unrecycled cardboard is being used at places like Barneys and Chanel and Neimans for the people who deserve more than just a tree. For the studio heads and presidents of production with green-light power, for the clients at other agencies David wants to represent or used to and still cares for, the top attorneys and managers we share clients with, for the big-dick producers with first-dollar-gross points; for these people it's fuck the environment, fuck the kindness, it's Jerry Ma-fucking-guire time, it's show me the money. And I see the money, too. A thousand in cash from the Michaelses and the following from assorted clients: gift cards to The Shave, Trader Joe's, AMC, Best Buy, and Bloomingdale's; three bottles of Hanzell Pinot Noir 2001; a 1.5-liter bottle of Dom Pérignon (the 2000 vintage, so not the best, but certainly not a cheap bottle); a gift basket of dark, milk, and white chocolate dreidels from Madame Chocolat; a $200 gift certificate for the 76 station in Beverly Hills (that should be good for two fill-ups and some gum); and, of course, credits at spas around town—The Peninsula, Burke Williams, and Four Seasons Thousand Oaks (which I'll be trading to another assistant or selling online, because, honestly, who wants to drive to Thousand Oaks?).

Other things I "handle" for David during the month of December: hand-deliver a script to a client in county jail; arrange over seventy-five Edible Arrangements deliveries for lesser nonindustry recipients; help the kids build a gingerbread replica of the Capitol Records Building and the Walt Disney Concert Hall (easily the most challenging day of the month); and, finally, assist the party coordinator leading up to and during the company holiday party, making sure the guest list is strictly enforced, the kitchen is serving a balanced quantity of regular and truffle-seasoned French fries, and, most difficult for me, staying sober the entire night, not only because that's what David would do but also in case anything needs attention, like when I remove the new receptionist from the hotel after she attempts to give a client in the new Wes Anderson flick a lap dance. Finally, all momentum surges toward getting the Michaelses on a plane to Maui for their annual Christmas to New Year's trip with the kids to the Four Seasons. Most important, making sure the reserved cabanas at the kids' and adult pools every day are truly reserved, and not only are there ludicrous fees involved in these reservations but they also necessitate daily cash tips to the pool staff. With that in mind, an envelope with two thousand in cash in twenty- and fifty-dollar bills is delivered to Carl, the house concierge, who is packing for the family. Other deliveries to Carl for the Michaelses' trip: five bottles of Clarins sunblock spray in different SPFs, new Ralph Lauren bathing suits for David and the children (the wife handled her own), a new Platinum American Express card attached to a recently opened account to be kept separately from other cards and money (just in case), Havaiana sandals for the entire family, and a new iPad and iPhone (again, just in case). Last, I'm on the phone with David while he's boarding the flight, discussing *Blown to Bits* details and how I need to be available for Simon over the next week if he should want to talk anything out, to which I answer, "Of course," and I hear the flight taking off and a flight attendant yelling, "Sir!" as the call cuts out.

• • •

I wake up a few days later and it's warm out so I go to my parents' house and drift in the pool for hours without any interruption—they're in Cabo with the girls; I decided to stay home this year in case I was needed. And I get my hair cut and my eyebrows thinned out; work out with Reggie a few times and start talking to Stacey the trainer again (maybe she forgot she thought I took a "shit" on our "date"); go shopping for new button-downs at Steve Alan; have a meal at Red O and then Red Medicine (I can't decide which one I prefer); have lunch in Westwood with Cohen, who was in from New York and almost cried rehashing a few high school "incidents." I spend New Year's Eve with Kevin and Derek, roaming a house party in Hancock Park that's lit by candles burning on multiple low-hanging chandeliers, where my only goal is to black out. Laila does not call or text. I do not get laid the entire break. On the Sunday after New Year's I finally get a work e-mail, the first one from the office in two weeks, and I'm excited for the action: a tree has been planted in my name in Israel.

Combat

A wards season blows by, scoring the agency lots of Independent Spirit Awards (meaningless), a few Golden Globes (yawn), a handful of guild awards (but not enough PGA victories for anyone to get excited), and Oscars for Best Adapted Screenplay (we would have preferred an Original Screenplay win), Best Actress (the most meaningless of the major prizes—so when Lisa Howard's name was called and the memories of her blowing smoke in my car returned, it didn't sting as much), Best Director (incredible), and a few technical awards for our below-the-line department, but I'm not even sure if those nominees were invited to any after-parties, so excitement is muted. Sundance produces two huge deals for our Independent Film & Financing Department, with lots of positive hype and deals with Fox Searchlight and Sony Pictures Classics (the only companies you want handling an independent film), who will be releasing both pictures. Things are good. Business is solid. Perception remains immaculate. But things can always be better. And since appetites never diminish and teeth are always razor sharp, David implements a bimonthly, all-agent meeting to strategize "combat."

Combat refers to the poaching (stealing) of other agencies' clients. It's the word most often used in the room, and no other assistant has ever been inside the meeting. David asks that I attend to take notes, and, when the invitation is extended, I think back to the text of the birthday card he gave me—"You're getting close"—so I smile and nod, yes.

The first order of business is the location of Larry Lazar, who's been missing since the holiday break, and no one, including his wife, knows where he is. "Nothing new there," someone jokes.

"Fuck." David sighs. "Run down his list, please?"

Not "Geez, where could he be?" Not "My god, I hope he's okay." And never "We need to find him" (especially in Larry's case, he's not that good of an agent). It's just "What's his list?" "Who's making the most money and needs to be saved first?" and "Who do we not give a fuck about?" (other than Larry).

"Maybe that serial killer started targeting assholes," someone in the huge, sun-filled conference room jokes.

"I'd watch your back then," David says.

Chuckles echo off the walls.

David asks, "Where's he going? CAA? WME? UTA? ICM? Maybe Gersh? No way anywhere else, right?" David continues, "Seriously, who does he have that we need to secure, other than Bronx, which I'll obviously handle."

Greenberg speaks. "Honestly, Dave, nothing to worry about. He has no one with a quote over a million in film, and the few winners he does work with in TV will be saved by myself, Drew, and/or Bernstein. We're cool."

"We cool, Ben?"

"We're cool," Bernstein tells him.

"That right?" David asks the room.

The sea of groomed, smooth faces nod slowly.

"All right, le—"

"Sir," I interrupt. "There is one name that should be discussed."

"Who?" David sits up in his seat.

Jason and Drew also move forward as silence grasps the room. The only movement: shards of sunlight slowly crisscross the stained, marble table.

"Chelsea Silver."

"Look"—Jason speaks up—"you're an assistan—"

"Cut the shit, Greenberg." David commands, then insists, "Go on."

"I hear she's close to landing the role of Arnold's daughter in the *True Lies* sequel."

"Bullshit!" Jason huffs.

"This is bullshit, Eliza played her in the original, it's all but done for her," Drew says.

"It's what I hear." I stand by the information, and then continue, "This is James Cameron's next project we're talking about. Why take a chance?"

Silence.

Jason and Drew stare me down. Bernstein is busy typing on an iPad.

"Cameron," David repeats and then continues. "Save her, fuck everyone else he wasn't sharing. Let the kiddies at other agencies eat some scraps."

Jason continues to glare.

"What else, people? This is combat! What do we have?" David stands up, slapping his hands together, looking dapper in a navy Prada suit and Gucci dotted tie. "What do you have for Papa?"

Sharon Margolis, a homely blonde with an above-average motion picture talent list and a face full of freckles, speaks. "I have something."

David swings around, smacking his palms together again, startling a few of us.

"Hit me, Sharon."

"This is big."

"I'm already wet, babe, enough of the fingering."

"Luke."

"Luke," he repeats.

"Luke," she confirms.

"How many times have we heard he's *finally* decided to sign with an agency?" Jason asks as a few colleagues call bullshit on the information, singing "Whatever."

"Luke," David says, quieting everyone, "the fucking *prince* of Hollywood has never had an agent, and never will according to his manager, Ron Best . . . my good friend and occasional golf partner."

Sharon remains strong. "This is good, David. . . . He's finally looking."

David listens, processing it, then slowly begins nodding his head. "Luke."

"Luke, sir." Sharon smiles.

SHARON MARGOLIS

36 years old

Motion Picture Talent Agent

- Just signed a new 4-year deal paying her $450,000 annually, but if this Luke information is good, she'll be seeing a hike

- Drives a tan Camry hybrid with a SiriusXM subscription but only listens to the eighties channel

- Single and is rumored to have never been in a relationship

- Other rumors about Sharon: hasn't had sex in over a decade; blew Nick Rizzo when she was in the mailroom; once barfed in the Dodgers' Dugout Club with clients after eating too many free Cracker Jacks; converted to Judaism and changed her last name before starting in Hollywood

- Formerly represented TV talent, but recently moved into the Motion Picture Department when her clients started successfully crossing over

- Only eats sushi for lunch and only at Sugarfish, Sushi Roku, Hamasaku, and Katsuya

- Never eats dinner, claiming it's the only weight loss remedy

Tana's

On the way to Dan Tana's, I'm barely listening to Palisades excitedly telling me about staying at Two Bunch Palms over the weekend to get through "an epic pile of scripts" for his boss and the hooker he ordered. "She had a scar running from the middle of her back, down her right thigh."

"Sounds hot," I tell him, speeding north on La Cienega, the lights from the hills towering over us like a colony of UFOs; and while making a left on Santa Monica, I almost run over a guy dressed like Jesus, holding a cross.

"Uh, no, it was not hot," he says while lighting a cigarette. "She cost a hundred dollars." He takes a drag, flicks the cigarette at a group of guys in front of a frozen yogurt shop, and rolls up the window, allowing the air-conditioning to devour the hot summer air trapped inside the car.

"I asked her if she was attacked by a shark."

"Was she?"

"No, said she was hit by a truck."

"Cool."

"Yeah, pretty fly . . . pretty disgusting, too."

"You get what you pay for."

"I guess."

Paparazzi are devouring a group exiting the yellow and green exterior of the restaurant as we pull up and valet. Perry is hanging back, trying to get a view inside the storm of cameras, annoying me. "Come on, dude," I tell him, "anyone leaving this early probably isn't that interesting." He surrenders, following me inside, past an eighty-year-old man smoking on one of the green benches next to a small Hispanic dude holding a few dozen roses for sale.

Kev and Derek are waiting at the small, red leather seat for two behind the check-in area sipping martinis.

"Martinis, huh?" Perry questions with a puzzled, almost disgusted look on his face.

"Very weird." I feel the same.

"Fuck you," Kevin says with a smile.

"Nice little love seat you guys have here," Perry says, looking even more disgusted.

"Bar is packed," Kev mentions.

"Speaking of which, scotch?" Perry asks, scoping out the scene.

"Danka," I tell him.

"So," Kev says, picking an olive out of his glass. "What's up?"

"Nothing. Oh, Perry fucked Bethany Hamilton, you should ask him about it."

Palisades returns, pushing a Black Label on the rocks into my hands.

"Anyone here tonight?" Derek asks, as Magic Johnson gets up from the corner booth to the left of us.

"Just a legend," I announce, gripping everyone's attention. "Magic," I alert the group as he starts to leave. We all shut up as he lumbers past us to say good-bye to Christian, the maître d', with a hug and a discreet passing of money through a weak handshake.

"So, he never had full-blown AIDS, right?" Perry asks a little too loudly.

"No, just HIV . . . but who cares?" I snap back. "The guy is a legend. You wouldn't take a little HIV for his life?"

Perry watches him leave, sipping scotch. "Let me get back to you on that."

"Gentlemen!" Christian rests his hands on Perry's shoulders. "You're all looking beautiful tonight. . . . The Wasserman booth awaits," he tells us, swinging both arms gracefully to the left.

Kev and Derek excitedly jump up and follow Chris to the booth Magic just vacated, the southwest corner table in the front room. I place my scotch down and playfully straighten Christian's bow tie, telling him how sexy he looks tonight, and immediately order a round of chilled Don Julio shots for all of us.

"How's your father?" he asks, surveying the room.

"He's good."

The shots come fast, and we all down them.

"Tell him I say hello," he says, his eyeballs darting across the red interior space.

"I will," I tell him, recovering from the cooled tequila.

"And tell your mom I miss her, too."

We both laugh. I tell him he's beautiful, menus are offered and refused (except by Derek, who doesn't yet have the menu memorized like us), and an order of garlic bread, a couple of Nicky Hiltons (chopped salads), and fried calamari are ordered, as well as another round of drinks, including another shot for Christian, who screams "Thank you" over the chaos of a Monday night crowd when our waiter delivers it to him at his station near the entrance.

Tonight it's Larry King wearing suspenders with Rock &

Republic jeans at a booth with his children and a nanny; a group of Persian girls dressed in pastels only eating Nicky Hiltons; a couple of UTA agents with a writer client who, according to Perry, is "pretty talented" but he forgot his name; Todd Phillips sniffing some girl's neck; and Ryan Phillippe and a crew of lesser actors on the other side of the room across from a table of older, gross blondes who can't even eat the Dabney Colemans (New York strips) they ordered because they're embarrassed in front of Ryan.

The food comes, and we attack it, sprinkling Parmesan on everything, and in between bites, while sneaking in breaths, I listen to Kev and Perry argue over certain agents' salaries (Derek chokes when Kevin mentions the top partners at most agencies making our yearly salary every day); what sequel will open biggest this weekend; whether or not genital warts are curable (Perry seems most interested); and once again, the end of *Inception*: was it a dream or not?

Returning from the bathroom, Perry tells us he overheard some "old fart" tell a teenage girl at the bar that it's times like these he's most happy about the money he's made in life. This launches a quick conversation about how old of a woman we would fuck, and when Kev says seventy-two, Derek laughs, I gag, and Perry offers a cigarette, so we go outside to smoke.

While we're devouring nicotine, watching Asian girls in skintight dresses wait in line at the venue next door (it's always changing, I have no clue what it's called these days), Drew Diller's maroon Cayenne Turbo pulls in front of us and Greenberg pops out of the passenger side.

"Look who's here . . . the mailroom," he drunkenly announces.

I flick my cigarette close to him, into the zooming traffic.

Perry gets involved. "You are aware we're not in the mailroom anymore, or are you so old Alzheimer's is starting to kick in?"

"What are you, out here parking cars?" he says, stepping toward us.

"Easy, easy," Drew says, steering Jason away from us and inside the restaurant.

Making our way back to our table, pushing through the lively nest of waiting bodies in the front room, we pass Drew and Jason at the bar, and he screams out "Mailroom" again, prompting me to turn around and extend two fingers under Perry's nose while staring at Jason with a smirk. Perry takes a deep sniff in and laughs hard as we turn around, heading back to the Wasserman booth. Upon approach, passing a couple on my right feeding each other fried raviolis, I'm pushed from behind into our table, my hands planting sloppily into whatever's left of the food, and as I turn around to identify my attacker, Jason swings a fist, which Perry catches with both arms, pulling Jason backward, and he's screaming about Laila divorcing him and her leaving town, about killing me, and about fucking Alisa as Drew holds him back while he continues to scream about the *True Lies* sequel and how I just ended my career, and there's more pushing and disruption as Christian gets in the middle of it all, giving me a *really?* look. The silence is terrible as all the action and chaos and buzz of the night is stabbed in the belly by the incident. Drew and Jason leave, we resume our fight-splattered meal, and later, over scoops of cappuccino ice cream, I imagine Laila on a plane, over Los Angeles, traveling east, refusing to lift the shade on her window, her hands buried between her legs, and we all toss credit cards on top of the pencil-marked bill as Derek asks, "So, is it a dream or not?"

Combat Continues

I get in early the next morning, canceling my session with Reggie, who texted me back: *Why do you hate me so much?* There is no blowback yet: nothing from HR or David, and certainly nothing from Jason. But soon the e-mails from Kev, Perry, and Derek come in all at once while I'm in the parking garage loading David's Mercedes with fifty copies of the *Beverly Hills Courier*—which ran a piece today on a lawsuit being filed against one of the heads of our biggest competitor by ex-employees and clients who were "sexually tortured"—and they all read the same. One word: *Deadline.*

I don't recognize my reflection in the metal doors of the elevator traveling back upstairs, and a heavy layer of cold sweat has formed, encasing the entire body. My heart is thumping but slowed by the pills I ate for breakfast, and my mouth has lost any moisture it ever had as I sit down to read Deadline. The article, entitled "Tana's Tussle," written by Nikki Finke, describes the scene almost entirely, with touches of amazingly accurate detail, such as the sauce on the side dish of pasta that was thrown across the room (garlic and olive oil), the suits we were wearing (me: black Calvin Klein Collection, him: gray Hugo Boss), and the style of fighting (mostly two-handed pushing). Our names, the company we work for, and the nature of the brawl were not reported. Even within the comments section, which grows to over three hundred entries by day's end, no mention of Jason or me by name is written, and though other websites mention our names, they mention other industry suspects as well. The fight was between two studio execs dueling over a project going into turnaround; the mozzarella went flying due to a gay couple breaking up (I took offense at this); two regulars and Christian got into it over wanting the Wasserman booth—it quickly morphed into lore, into a phantom incident.

David pokes his head into the assistants' quarters.

"Can I see you please?" he asks, leaving the door open.

I almost spray puke on my keyboard, Joyce, and especially Shane's face.

David is standing with his arms crossed and his back to the glass wall as I enter the office, closing the door behind me. He's not wearing a jacket or tie, his white button-down shirt is unbuttoned at the top, both sleeves are rolled up, and the sun is glowing behind him through the slightly tinted wall of windows, darkening his face.

"Sharon was right," he tells me, his face almost completely obscured by shadows. He then slowly walks in my direction, stepping out of the black fog, revealing wide eyes and a jumping pulse in his forehead.

"Sharon was right," he tells me again. "Luke . . . He's finally looking."

"What's the move?" I ask after a speechless beat.

"The move . . ." David repeats, walking past me, returning to the spot in front of the glass. "Combat," he says, "that's the move."

"So, we're getting a meeting with him?" I ask.

"Ron Best . . . Luke's manager . . . my *fucking golf buddy* . . . isn't returning my calls. I'm not sure what the *fuck* is going on."

David's body is bouncing up and down, his face still hidden. He regains control, crossing his arms in front of his chest. "Here's what we know," he announces, walking closer to me with a degree of caution and wired eyes. "Ron and Luke have set up meetings all day tomorrow, they're booked solid. I offered Best's assistant a goddamn Porsche to give me fifteen minutes for coffee with them. They had nothing. Our spies around town have all confirmed the intelligence. It's real."

I say nothing. To my left, a phone on the side table next to the couch is exploding with red blinking lights, and outside a prolonged car horn sounds and repeats at least half a dozen times. David steps closer, taking a seat on the matching Italian couch across from me, crosses his legs, drops both hands on the knee in front of him, and speaks.

"You ever see *Wall Street*?"

"Course."

"And?"

"Great film."

"No, an excellent film. Next time someone asks you about *Wall Street,* you tell them it's an excellent film."

I nod. He continues, "You know what makes that film excellent? You know what it is?"

I don't consider answering.

"It's all heart," he tells me, smacking his chest. "That fucking flick and those goddamn characters are *all* heart. It's about wanting something and achieving it. The whole movie, every fucking frame is a lesson in triumph. A lesson in balls!" He jumps out of his seat with excitement and walks up to the glass, gazing out at the city. "So . . . do you know why you're here?" he asks, his back to me.

"To assist," I answer from the couch.

"Do you know who I need you to be?"

I stand up, facing him, staring into the back of his shirt. "Bud Fox," I tell him, confident.

There's a brief pause before he turns his head back at me, and it all seems like it's happening in slow motion when he says, "Then, go."

The Mission

consider renting a motorcycle, but I have no idea how to operate one, and, honestly, the concept frightens me; plus my X5 has tinted windows, which, for this exercise, seems essential. I beg a friend of a friend who plays tennis at Luke's house a few days a month for the address, but he refuses. I offer him a couple hundred bucks and promise seats to any regular-season Lakers home game of his choosing, but he balks.

"The Heat, bro? You're turning down Lakers versus Heat and a few bills for information that will never, not in a million years, get back to you?"

All he says is "Correct."

Then I remember he's a struggling actor and stand-up comedian.

"I'll guarantee you a one-on-one with our head of comedy bookings."

He's not saying no. This is good.

"Fine, the Lakers seats, money, and the meeting."

I've got him. But this presents a good opportunity to practice cutthroat negotiation.

"The meeting, that's all," I tell him, keeping composure.

"The meeting and the tickets," he counters.

"No."

Pause.

A showdown.

"The meeting and the money."

It could all blow up here. I tell him "No."

"Bro, you need this address."

"I could go down Sunset right now, buy a star map from some Mexican with a beach chair for seven bucks, and be at the house in minutes."

I'm lying; I already looked into it and found nothing.

He's considering.

I flinch as if I'm moving to walk away.

"The meeting!"

"A meeting," I confirm.

I'm wide awake at 4:30 a.m. the next day, shower, dress casually—RRL black jeans, a white American Apparel crew neck, gray cardigan my sister and Keith bought me in Japan (whose designer's name is unpronounceable, but they assured me it wasn't cheap), brown leather Frye boots, and a blue Dodgers hat to pull low over my face if and when I get too close throughout the day. Hit the Coffee Bean for a large cappuccino and I'm parked a few houses down from Luke's gated compound, North of Sunset in the West Hollywood Hills, waiting for any movement at 5:05 a.m.

Four hours later, there's zero movement except from me, taking a long piss on someone's front lawn. Howard Stern is on vacation this week, so instead of live shows, they're playing a greatest hits collection called "Mammory Lane." I've already listened to the world's smallest penis contest (a real pleasure at 6:00 a.m.), a queefing contest (ditto at 7:00 a.m.), and an interview with Julia Roberts that made me yearn to hear more women farting out of their vaginas.

9:34 a.m.—We have movement. The security gate rattles open, exposing Luke's circular driveway (with a black-bottom fountain in the middle), a parked black Tesla Roadster (his, which I confirmed studying as much paparazzi media I could last night when I wasn't googling "Tana's Tussle"), and the front door shuts before I have a chance to confirm anyone's location. A white Range Rover rolls out from a corner of the driveway, and I'm pretty sure I recognize the brunette actress with her hair pulled back in a ponytail who's driving—she's incredibly hot and I'm incredibly jealous. There's no one in the passenger seat as the Rover flies by me.

10:51 a.m.—The security gate rattles open again, and Luke's electric sports car explodes out of the compound. He's definitely driving, a hat pulled low over his eyes. I roll out slowly, then rush to keep up, but at a distance. David sends me an e-mail as I'm stopped behind the Tesla at a red light on Sunset. It reads: *Lose him and I'll have someone eat your dick.* I don't imagine this is a good thing. When I look up from the e-mail the light has turned green and the car is gone. I grab my dick, scared, make a quick decision, turn left, and floor it, thankful to find him stopped at another red light. I roll to a stop two cars behind Luke and release my dick. It will not be eaten today.

11:06 a.m.—I'm parked at a gas station across the street from Hugo's in West Hollywood watching Luke pace outside the restaurant on a phone call, fidgeting with the brim of his hat.

11:14 a.m.—The gas station attendant reminds me this isn't a parking lot. I tell him my car broke down and then buy some gum, cigarettes, and a 5-Hour Energy. Walking back to my car, gulping down the caffeine shot, I witness an actor friend of Luke's, Roy, who occasionally works but not nearly enough to make a decent living, approach, and they walk inside Hugo's together.

11:34 a.m.—Standing outside my car at the gas station, I have a perfect view of Luke and Roy eating, signing a few autographs, and taking pictures with young girls. I wish it was colder out so I could stomp my feet on the concrete and rub my hands together like Popeye Doyle in *The French Connection*. I'm enjoying this.

11:52 a.m.—Roy leaves, sliding on shades and lighting a cigarette. These guys have nice lives.

11:58 a.m.—Luke has been on a call since Roy left, the gas station attendant is breathing fire, I'm back in my car listening to Howard interview two sisters who enjoy making out with one another. A second e-mail comes in from David: *Keep. Me. Posted.* I grab my dick again.

12:03 p.m.—Just as the attendant is banging on my window and I'm losing my mind thinking there may be some sort of jihad in the streets of West Hollywood, the day kicks into high gear. Ron Best shows up, enters Hugo's, and within seconds they're walking out together. The Tesla Roadster pulls out of the parking lot behind the restaurant, makes a right, west on Santa Monica Boulevard. I make at least three serious moving violations and settle in behind him.

12:19 p.m.—Back at Luke's. The Tesla is parked, Ron's 600SL pulls in, and the gate closes.

12:35 p.m.—I've heard every second of today's Stern episode and now enjoy silence. No movement.

12:56 p.m.—A Honda Civic pulls in, driven by a Hispanic

woman. It must be the maid or Luke is into some weird shit. Kev e-mails me: *Where you at, playa?* I e-mail him back: *Sick, puking blood.* I think he believes me.

1:07 p.m.—Luke drives Ron in the Tesla. They're off. I follow.

1:19 p.m.—The sports car pulls into the valet lane on Canon in front of E. Baldi. Luke and Best exit the vehicle dressed strikingly nicer than before. I stop behind them, pulling my Dodgers hat down, looking to the left, toward X'ian, as they pass in front of my bumper, heading into the restaurant. I valet and rush inside. E. Baldi is packed. Luke and Best head toward the last open table of the buzzing space. They stop at a table to say hello to Ari Emanuel, who's eating with Kobe Bryant. Everyone is thrilled to see each other, and it's just a little too perfect that they're seated so close. Waiters carrying glass bottles of water and plates of pasta perform figure eights around them, forcing me to push up on the tips of my boots to get a better view.

"Sir." Someone is tugging my arm, pulling me back to the ground. "Sir, do you have a reservation?"

"No, table for one," I tell him, lifting myself up again to witness the two tables, now facing each other, laughing, and Luke shows Kobe and Ari what his basketball shot looks like by holding his right hand up, flicking his wrist, and Kobe nods his head in approval, and now I'm staring directly at the maître d', who's in front of my face. "Sir, we've been totally booked for weeks, you'll have to call next time." He's urging me, placing a hand on my back.

"Don't touch, don't touch," I tell him, raising both arms in the air as I exit the room.

1:28 p.m.—I call David to tell him I think Luke and Best are meeting with WME, that Ari has Lakers ties and probably set up a Kobe lunch knowing Luke is a huge fan. "Ari has the best seats at Staples Center; if that hasn't drawn Luke in yet, nothing along those lines will. It's strictly coincidence," David tells me and then continues, "He's probably trying to sign Kobe, which is smart . . . wish I had thought of that."

David screams to Shane, "Put Kobe Bryant on the phone sheet, please."

Shane clicks on the call, letting David know she doesn't have his number.

"Find it!" He raises his voice, causing her to quickly click off.

David takes a breath and then proceeds with the questioning. "Okay, then what?"

"That's it, I was thrown out without a reservation."

"You should have called, I would have gotten you seated."

"Should I go back in?"

Long pause.

"No," he tells me, "the lunch isn't it. . . . Stay on them."

2:14 p.m.—I'm sitting in a loading zone half a block north of E. Baldi watching a growing pack of paparazzi outside the restaurant readying their cameras when I get another e-mail from Kevin: *Fucking Derek.*

Me: *What?*

Kevin: *Nothing, but since Lazar peaced out, he's kinda taking over the desk, talking to clients.*

I write: *Don't hate the playa, playa.*

But I hate him. I can't believe he's getting this opportunity.

Kevin: *Are you really puking blood?*

Me: *Yes.*

Kev: *Fuck! Where'd you eat?*

I know Kevin is going to Mélisse tonight, so I tell him . . .

Me: *Mélisse . . . brutal!*
Kev: *Fuck, I'm going there tonight!*
Me: *I wouldn't if I were you.*

I begin laughing, thinking how he may now skip the highest Michelin-rated meal in Los Angeles, just as the subjects exit E. Baldi. They quickly jump into the Tesla Roadster while being mobbed by flashing cameras and take off down Canon, toward Wilshire, where they make a left.

2:37 p.m.—They park on Robertson north of Wilshire across the street from Flash headquarters. Luke and Best jay-walk across the street and head inside the Hollywood gossip rag offices. I'm parked a few spaces south of the Tesla, smoking a cigarette.

3:03 p.m.—Luke and Best emerge from the offices. Luke looks incredibly angry. Best calms him down by placing a hand on Luke's shoulder, then says something they both laugh at while crossing the street. Luke has a long history of hating paparazzi. Who knows what that was?

3:11 p.m.—After driving west on Burton, then Wilshire, Luke pulls into the Beverly Hilton; they valet and head inside. I follow a minute later, leaving my ride in front, screaming back at the valet attendant that I'm picking up a guest. He nods at me and jumps out of the way of a limo with flags flying on the windows. I race inside, searching, and see Luke and Best walking toward the back of the lobby. To my right, at the bank of elevators, I see my father and the woman with red bangs and mascara-lined, charcoal eyes standing next to each other. I slow, feeling sick, blink multiple times to confirm the sight, and it's real, but I'm unable to decipher if they just came down from a room upstairs or are about to go up. They don't see me. I can't lose Luke and Best, so I hustle farther back into the lobby, occasionally looking back. I find the subjects talking to massive men in suits with pins on their chests and corkscrew wires falling from their ears; then it hits me—the president is staying here tonight. Luke and Best are escorted to a freight elevator and disappear into the interior of the hotel with a few of the guards. Floating back to my car, past the bank of elevators, my father and the woman nowhere in sight, I hold a few bills out in a catatonic state for the valet attendant. He claws the paper from my loose grip and shuts the door, tucking me into the tinted cabin of my ride. I quickly roll the window down, unable to breathe, and ask the attendant, "The president . . . he's here?" The Hispanic in a red vest smiles, nods, and then dodges another limo, this one bulkier but, again, with flags whipping in the air. The president.

3:38 p.m.—I park a few blocks north of the hotel on a quiet, residential street, sitting in the neighborhood's silence, fighting the urge to curl up in the backseat and cry. But I need to call David and continue the day.

I tell him, "I think I got it."

"Tell me," he begs.

"I just left the Beverly Hilton."

"So?"

"Do you know who's staying at the Beverly Hilton tonight?"

"How the fuck would I know? You want me to send someone to find you and literally eat your dick with a knife and fork?"

"No."

"Then continue," he tells me.

"The president."

"The president," he repeats. "So . . ."

"So, Luke and Best talked to a few Secret Service agents in the lobby, then disappeared into a freight elevator."

"The president," David says.

"Lunch at a table next to Ari, then a meeting with the president."

"WME."

"Luke's an activist, an environmentalist, he's got political issues he wants to see handled. What do you get a guy like Luke? Models? A role in the best script in town? Bullshit. He's got it all. But a sit-down with the president? A dialogue with the president of the United States? What agency can deliver that?"

"Only one run by a man with a brother who's politically connected."

"That's right."

"Shit. I can't top that," David admits.

"No one can."

"And nothing else of interest today?"

"No."

"All right, get back here."

"Actually . . ."

"What?"

"I may have something."

4:16 p.m.—Parked outside of the Flash offices, unsure of my next move.

4:19 p.m.—David e-mails me: *WTFFF?*

4:31 p.m.—I'm on the verge of walking into Flash headquarters and asking to speak with Bobby Biz, Flash's CEO and host of its daily gossip TV show, but, luckily, that's not necessary. He appears in front of the building with a French bulldog on a leash. I exit the car, jogging into his path.

"Cute dog," I tell him.

He sticks an unlit cigarette in his mouth and says, "She's ugly, but I'm fine with it."

I laugh, looking down at the dog, and admit, "She's not pretty."

Bobby lights the cigarette. "It's fine, I'm into ugly."

The dog takes a shit on the sidewalk. I'm lingering, scared.

"What can I do for you?" he asks.

Then it comes to me.

"Ron . . . he said you have something for me."

Bobby throws the cigarette away, looking around. "Ron?"

"Ron Best, my boss. *Luke's* manager . . . I think you know what I'm talking about."

Bobby is silent, stone-faced. But then he steps closer to me; the bulldog, done shitting, is now barking at passing cars on Robertson. "Tell him, there's no . . . deal . . . to . . . be . . . had."

I try to speak, but he cuts me off. "The tape is *not* for sale. Get it?"

I nod my head, yes. He moves even closer, lowering his voice, and continues, "It's bad, sure, but a career ender . . . Who knows in this town? So, you know, I don't know what to say other than bye." And he walks off.

4:47 p.m.—I e-mail David: *I got something.* He doesn't respond.

5:06 p.m.—I dash by Joyce, who's lighting a few of the new D.L. & Co candles, when David sticks his head into the assistants' quarters, waving me inside his office.

"Tell me."

"Before the Hilton, they had a quick meeting at Flash."

He motions with bulging eyes to continue.

"Luke exited the meeting angry. Distraught. I didn't think anything of it at the time. But . . . I went back."

"And?"

"And there's a tape."

"A tape?"

"That's what Best and Luke were doing there. Bobby Biz has a tape . . . of Luke."

"Bobby's an old friend of mine."

I nod.

"Is that all?"

I hesitate, and then tell him. "No . . . He said it could be a career ender."

David smiles, and then asks again, "Is that all?"

I want to tell him my dad is cheating on my mom. That I saw him today at the Hilton with another woman, a woman I've seen him with before, and that, when I close my eyes, I don't see signing Luke or being fitted for suits at Barneys or the endless line of digits on future commissions; that all I see is red bangs and mascara-lined, charcoal eyes. Instead, I answer, "Yes."

Oh, Brother

The next day David is at an early lunch with an "old friend" (that's what's written in his Outlook Calendar from noon to 3:00 p.m.) when Kev and Derek step into the office with a bounce.

"Nate's. You down?" Kev asks.

A swell of anxiety pushes the word from within. "Can't."

"Come on, Gloria's holding a table in her section," Derek tells me while typing on his iPhone.

"Come on, bro, there are things to discuss," Kevin says.

"Such as?"

"Come and find out," Kevin tells me.

Derek's grin exposes teeth while he continues typing with eyes locked on his phone. Then he looks up and says, "You must."

The phones light up, I can't imagine what they're talking about, and I don't care. I didn't sleep last night, and I can't function now, because all I see is red bangs and mascara-lined, charcoal eyes, and all I have are questions.

"Whatever, don't come to Nate's. But tonight it's on; premiere of *The Depths* at the Dome with passes to the after-party at the Roosevelt and a couple of actresses who want to sign with the agency." Kev and Derek both snicker when exiting the office, and as Kev passes through the doorway, he yells back at me, "You're coming whether you like it or not . . . there are things to discuss," without looking back.

Joyce is lost in composing an e-mail while Shane opens a new box from Amazon, pulling out DVD box sets for the full series of *The Sopranos, Seinfeld,* and *Sex and the City,* as I drift, powered by grim curiosity, out of the office. My parents left for New York this morning for a few days—my father working out of his East Coast office while my mother shops at Bergdorfs, and they'll meet at Fred's or Eataly for lunch, then Babbo or the Waverly Inn for dinner—enjoying the city. Parked in the garage, I'm watching kids eagerly hop to their fifty-five-minute lunchtime escape. Then I'm stopped at the red light on Sunset and North Rodeo, ignoring the flashing indicator on my Black-Berry. Soon I'm passing through the security gates of Beverly Park and entering my parents' house. I yearn for nostalgia but find none within a recently purchased home decorated with mostly current photos (my mom and sisters are mortified by their pre-rhinoplasty faces). Passing by a maid, who's busy heating corn tortillas on a stove burner, I begin to search through my father's life for answers.

I attack his dresser in the master bedroom, but it offers nothing: the yellow gold Patek Philippe Star Caliber, keys to the 500 AMG, a BlackBerry with a severely cracked screen, unused Lakers-Raptors tickets from a few months ago, and a stack of head shots wrapped tightly in a rubber band, which I flip through, finding one with a red *X* over the face of a girl who looks a lot like Laila. The name on the top of the photograph reads, "Claire Boise," but the resemblance—a curling, sad smile, dark blond hair, and perfectly waxed, mirrored eyebrows—frightens me, stunting my journey and violently dropping me into my father's office downstairs. More photographs: all of us in Mexico that someone must have taken under duress because it looks slightly blurred; a giant black-and-white shot of my parents hugging on a beach in Big Sur; my sisters and I sitting on a couch together, watching television, unaware of the moment being captured; and a collection of portraits of my father in the Lakers floor seats with his many guests: Jeremy Piven, Michael Bay, Ryan Seacrest, Drew Brees, José Andrés, Joe Torre, Sumner Redstone, and Aaron Sorkin.

His desk is immaculate; only an Apple LED thirty-inch Thunderbolt display and a VTech cordless phone, standing in a charging dock, litter the space. After finding nothing of interest in the drawers (with the exception of an expired Viagra prescription), I'm spinning in his chair, stopping in front of the wall behind the desk where the black-and-white of my parents hugging in Big Sur hangs. I'm standing up now, lightly running my palm against the glass, over their sandy legs, feeling them; the frame gives a bit, pushing in, then swings open, revealing a hidden shelf. On it sits one thing—a brick-thick, worn legal folder with the name "William" scrawled across it. I find a batch of paid bills going back at least a decade for something called The Cabin in North Hollywood for tens of thousands of dollars, memos (most of which, profiling behavioral studies), a few childish paintings, and, finally, a birth certificate dated five years and a few months before I was born, in the same hospital I was born (Cedars-Sinai), and every document has the same name splattered across it, claiming ownership: my last name. I sit there, weakened, while the maid powers a vacuum down the hallway as every document confirms what I never knew—I have an older brother.

Shane and Joyce both ignore my e-mail informing them of a late return to the office, but I'm not even sure what lie jumped out of my thumbs and into the message. I keep straining to conjure any memory, any glimpse back into the past. There was nothing as I rolled through the Cahuenga and Burbank intersection, seconds before killing the SUV's engine in the parking lot of The Cabin. An hour passes. The grounds of the home aren't as institutional as I dreaded they would be on the drive over the hill, fighting the urge to turn around and simply forget.

I finally exit the car.

A black girl at the front desk smiles brightly as I push the front door open, peeking my head inside. "Come on, sugar, I won't bite," she tells me, smiling with a blast of clean, white teeth.

I blink, frozen in the doorway.

"Come on, sugar."

I move toward the voice, nearly blinded by reality.

"That's it, love," she says, welcoming me.

My driver's license is on the counter. "I'd like to see . . . William." I tell her.

She inspects.

Her face morphs colder as she walks away, instructing me to have a seat.

"So, you're the son." The redhead with bangs and mascara-lined, charcoal eyes tells me, intrigued by my presence.

Looking up at her, I jump up, wanting to leave, but extend my hand instead, needing to feel her. Our palms are touching and she tells me her name is Cara, that she can't believe they told me.

"They didn't," I admit.

"You can't tell them I'm here."

She nods, softening to my plea. "They never visit," she says.

"I've seen you. I saw you," I tell her, now hunched over in pain.

She continues to nod, explaining her meetings with my father. "He won't come, but we meet for updates." Then she takes my hand, leading me down a dimly lit hall.

I'm sitting alone in William's room while Cara is finding him. There's a photo of my grandmother holding a newborn—I've never seen this picture before, nor have I ever seen her looking so young. A Lakers Back to Back Championship banner from the eighties hangs above the queen mattress with paintings similar to the ones on my father's hidden shelf filling the rest of the wall. The only item of personal effect: a Grateful Dead *In the Dark* poster. My father's favorite band.

Cara enters quietly. A man with thinning brown, curly hair, wearing a plaid flannel shirt buttoned to the top and tucked into Gap jeans trails her into the room. "William, this is your brother . . . he's here to visit with you."

Rocking back and forth, he stares aimlessly into the ground. *This is your brother.*

"He doesn't really talk, but . . . he'll warm up to you," Cara explains in a hushed tone. She then suggests that William paint me a picture, which he does. I believe it's a lone cactus in a desert.

I accompany him to dinner, watching as he playfully dines on meat loaf and glazed carrots. It's around this time when he comfortably lifts his head to make eye contact. I gently nod my head as the word *hello* somehow releases from my lips. A moan abruptly exits his mouth, followed by chewed chunks of carrot and a crippled grin. I back away from the table, breaking eye contact, racing for an open window, my car now in sight, but I'm miles away.

I write David, Shane, and Joyce: *Sick. Taking rest of the day off, available if you need me.*

Shane responds immediately: *We ALL need you SO much.*

I remain standing by the window, my back to the dining room, ignoring reality, staring at my car.

We return to William's room with Cara as the sun begins its descent in the San Fernando sky. He looks younger now, no longer a grown man. He's painting again—this time the brown recycled paper canvas is filled with two yellow beings and an orange setting sun in the upper-right corner of the frame. He hands it to me. My throat closes in on itself.

"Will you be back?" Cara asks. "He'd love to have you," she says, dropping her head, exiting the room as William climbs onto his bed, sitting Indian style, looking up at the wall of his creations, rocking again—back and forth, back and forth—as the sun disappears and the room darkens and Derek e-mails me: *The Depths?* And I don't respond.

I return to the Versailles hours later—sometime near morning—after being pulled over for driving too slow and given a sobriety test. I don't know exactly when my eyes welled or when an e-mail came in from HR alerting me I've made it to the two-year mark of working at the agency and am eligible for a 5 percent raise or when a neighbor was desperately punching my door because of the continuous weeping from inside my unit or even venture to approximate when I finally faded into a prolonged, puffy-eyed wink, but it happened.

Parents' Thirtieth

I call in sick Friday and spend two days alone, ignoring everyone, ordering in food from Ago and Chaya and BLD, but eating nothing, and I can't sleep. Early Sunday morning I leave the Versailles for the first time in what feels like weeks, and drive east on vacant streets, guided by an overcast sky. I'm pulling over and parking on Franklin, then I climb a steep concrete hill, lined by meager apartments and rundown cars, and enter the base of Runyon Canyon joined only by dogs and a few bums wrapped in bulky, dark blankets. I ascend the paved path, winding higher into a mist hanging low over the scene. When I reach the bench at the summit of the mountain, hikers scatter the dirt trails at the base below—pulling on stubborn dogs, anxious for their climb—and all I see is gray. I sit here for a while, blindly staring ahead at a blanketed cityscape, until the sun suddenly breaks through and the clouds vanish, revealing an incandescent panorama. The dogs below finally relent, joining their owners, and in time, a stranger sits beside me, shielding the light from his eyes, something metal glistening in his grip, and he turns to face me, and begins to speak, so I return home.

I find myself reading a few scripts that piled up for David over the last few weeks, which demand attention and offer an escape. It comes in waves, the panic, eroding my psyche, so I nosh on more pills. Then something happens. Something no drink or food or medicine could achieve—I read an excellent screenplay. It's *Die Hard,* but more entertaining. It's *Terms of Endearment,* but more heartbreaking. It's *Psycho,* but more thrilling. It's get-your-fucking-tuxedos-out-'cause-we're-walk-ing-the-red-carpet excellent. It's called *Heavens,* and all the hor-ror fades. I read the script again (something I've never done) to validate my opinion. And it's confirmed; I'm Daniel Plainview, I'm Monty Brewster, I'm Billy Ray Valentine—I just lucked out. (Industry Fact: 99 percent of screenplays are absolute gar-bage.) I celebrate with beer and cigarettes on the rooftop of the Versailles, in a lounge chair with my shirt off, thinking about presenting the script to David, what clients would be perfect for it, and how this assists in the end goal.

The family usually does Madeo on Sunday nights, but we're switching it up for my parents' anniversary and taking it to Giorgio Baldi, which is arguably the best Italian food in the city; and I'm on autopilot. Sunday nights are usually a who's who of the L.A. beach scene, just east of the Pacific Coast Highway; and tonight is no different. Sean Penn is wearing shorts and flip-flops on the patio, smoking at a corner table with his kids. Inside, Tom Hanks, Rita Wilson, Kate Capshaw, and Steven Spielberg have the table closest to the kitchen, all looking impossibly happy, having wine poured for them (Dad and Mom rush over to say hello). Ovitz is eating with his son, daughter, and some woman, and they're all typing away on phones until Mom and Dad leave the first table of hellos and move toward them. Dad shakes Michael's hand, points to me, eliciting a nod of recognition from the ex-most powerful man in town, then the parents return as we're shown our usual table in the front east corner. I point out an agent across the room, telling everyone how he's known for pissing out of his office window when he's too busy to get up and go to the bathroom, and I'm pretty sure he's sitting with Rupert Murdoch. I ask if that is in fact Murdoch and am told, "No, it's just some other rich white guy with a hot Asian wife." We share a laugh as champagne is being poured. "I thought we'd celebrate," Mom tells us.

Dad places his hand over hers, and I watch them kiss.

"You guys are so fab." Cate squeals in delight. Mom says something about wishing Emily and Keith could be here (they're in Positano on a "babymoon"—one final vacation of peace before children ruin any fun you're capable of for decades to come), and then she flinches and drops her head, whispering to my father, "The Normans." Ken and Kay Norman were part of my parents' scene before a Ponzi scheme took it all—$16.6 million to be exact. They're older than my parents; Ken was a top entertainment lawyer in town before retiring, and now he's back to work, teaching at Loyola Law. My parents are hiding their faces, somehow hoping they won't make contact in one of the smallest restaurants in the city, praying the Normans will be seated on the patio to avoid them, but alas, no such luck. On the way to their table, they stop and say hi. The parents begrudgingly speak to them and force smiles. Kay says they haven't been here since "It happened," and, though it's probably not a wise decision, they had to, "we just miss it so much . . . maybe we'll just split the veal," she says, trying to make light of the disaster. Mom holds a champagne glass out. "Well, cheers," she says and downs it.

Kay looks at her husband, then back at us.

"We must make plans," Kay says to Mom as Ken stands to the side, looking weak and uncomfortable.

"We must," Mom says. They walk away to their table, stuffed in a corner by the bathroom, and Mom dramatically exhales. "She can't be serious. Plans? What would we do, go to a park?" Cate giggles, and a glass breaks near the kitchen as two Hispanic busboys rush past us to clean the spill.

"Something's wrong," I announce, cutting into the Milanese, the words falling out of me.

"Not good tonight, hon?" Mom asks with mouth full of sweet corn ravioli.

"Did you finally realize you need to upgrade to an iPhone?" Cate asks, displaying her Apple device, smirking.

"Hon, you okay?" Mom questions.

I regain control of my voice, dropping my fork and knife on the breaded meat. "No."

"Yeah, but the scene is excellent," Cate says, her hand gliding out and to the side like a game show model.

Later, we're all eating our own servings of citrus sorbet served in hollowed-out, frozen lemons. Then Derek appears in the doorway, looking beach casual—khaki shorts, white short-sleeve Polo, and brown Sperry Top-Siders with no socks—so I wave him over. He smiles, appearing in front of me in seconds. Introductions are made, but the family couldn't be less interested in him and more interested in their dessert; I'm not sure anyone even looked at him. We chat about work (the Larry Lazar disappearance is "weird but kinda cool" because it's generating helpful exposure with the clients, and he even made sure a few didn't sign with the competitors); the weekend box office (it baffles both of us that Nic Cage is still starring in blockbusters); Derek's new Beverly Hills—adjacent apartment ("moving up in the world," he tells me with a wink); and Kev (whether or not he's "got what it takes"). A few men who love Brioni suits and Cut enter the space, causing me to burp up a mouthful of frozen veal. They see Derek and wave him over to the table Tom Hanks and Steven Spielberg just got up from.

"Who are those guys?" I ask, needing to know.

"You're kidding, right?" He laughs, blissfully patting my shoulder.

I look to my father, but he's staring out of a window behind him at the valet scene in the parking lot, which is now swarming with photographers, flashing away.

Derek continues to laugh.

"Gotcha!" I tell him, winking, and joining in on the laughter.

Derek's laugh kicks up a notch, and it's darker now, the candles at each table illuminating the room. "Well, it was nice meeting you." Derek addresses the table while slinking away.

Dad is struggling to sign his name on the bill as Cate and Mom are applying makeup. I lean over and ask if he recognizes the guys at the corner table, pointing at them. He strains for vision in Derek's direction. "Helen fucking Keller in here," he says, unable to see, returning to the credit card receipt, searching for the line to sign.

Cate smiles at me with a freshly painted face and I thought she knew, but she doesn't. My sisters can't know; they've never spoken of him, and they couldn't contain this information if they tried.

Mom kisses Cate on the cheek, moves a few strands of hair out of her daughter's face, and tells us how upset she is that

Emily and Keith aren't here tonight. "I can't bear being without you guys."

I smile across the table as Mom smiles back and Cate moves away from more incoming kisses while Dad is still straining to read the bill and Mom can't bear being without us, except for William.

Back to Work

David is working through the one o'clock hour and treating all of us to a sushi lunch, which I have to pick up because apparently, since I left the mailroom, its inhabitants have been rendered completely useless. As I return to the office, three bags of Sugarfish Brentwood dangling from my arms, Jason exits David's office silently and flashes by me without any contact. On his approach, I drop the bags, readying myself for a Hebrew school shoving match, but it never comes. Joyce and Shane stare at me curiously, saying nothing, amused by my behavior.

"What?" I ask.

"The food, what's wrong with you?"

I'm about to answer as honestly as possible when David's voice booms out of his office. "You back? In here now, please."

I look to the girls, who break apart chopsticks and begin devouring raw salmon and blue crab as I slowly enter David's office, closing the door behind me. The room appears empty; then two hands grab my shoulders from behind, startling me, and I grab my dick, protecting it, as a voice whispers "Luke" in my right ear.

I relax, swinging around to see a smiling David.

"We got him?" I ask.

"Meeting—is—set," he tells me, thrilled with the information. "He's ours."

Relief coats my innards as he tells me to put together a plate of sushi for him. Then he steps closer. "You made this meeting possible, so you're in it."

Nobu with Eisenberg

L arry Lazar is back at work with our biggest competitor. It's all over Deadline. He wasn't murdered in an abandoned studio, tied to a chair, his eyes scooped out of his head, a heavy coating of weeks-old, dried blood cementing him to the cold, concrete floor from countless stab wounds—the victim of the serial killer—like so many people thought . . . and hoped. No, he's just chained to a new desk in Beverly Hills, bleeding internally from ulcers brought on by failing to bring most of his clients with him. Eisenberg, who's working on Kevin Huvane's desk and loving life at CAA, guzzles a vodka soda, telling us everything he knows about Larry's move; but more specifically, he tells us about Larry's disappearance and how Larry has no memory of his recent whereabouts. He claims he woke up in an empty Montage suite days ago, without any knowledge of how he got there or how long he was gone. Perry from the Palisades and I stare back at him, laughing, sipping full glasses of Black Label on the rocks at Nobu on La Cienega, bragging about the Lazar clients we were able to save. Eisenberg says he heard Derek was instrumental in the agency keeping Chelsea Silver, who was just cast in the *True Lies* sequel.

"Who said that?" I ask.

They both stare at me, looking amused.

Eisenberg asks, "Could you imagine if he *was* murdered?"

"Who, Derek?"

They both laugh at me. "Take it easy," one of them says.

"I'm cool," I tell them, turning away, forcing a long, controlled breath out of my system.

"He did land Bernstein's desk," Perry says.

"Derek?" I ask.

"No, the serial killer."

They laugh, which I soon mimic with some forced noise.

"Did you hear the new theory?" Eisenberg asks.

Perry and I slowly shake our heads no.

"They think he's targeting people in the business. The last few victims, all in entertainment."

I want to ask if they're talking about Derek but don't. Paranoid, Palisades looks around the room before speaking. "Fucking serial killers."

"Relax," Eisenberg tells him. "I don't think he's here ordering the creamy snow crab."

Palisadess keeps eyeing the room as Eisenberg continues, "Who knows, they're still investigating . . ." He trails off, checking a message on his iPhone.

"Fuck" is all I can muster.

Another round of drinks is served as well as sushi and some girls are dancing in the distance to the new Justin Timberlake single, but it's too dark to make out their faces. Eisenberg answers a call and says, "I'm making cunt pâté tomorrow, so bring your fucking crackers!" This impresses me.

Then he tells us over a few ounces of Australian Wagyu beef that CAA is close to landing a Luke signing meeting (I nod at this but say nothing) and how he recently spoke to Ty, who gave up surfing professionally and has been in Mexico filming an *Endless Summer* remake and that he may have lost his mind.

"Can you remake a documentary?" Palisades asks, sucking on an empty edamame pod.

"I'm not sure, but he's bad, dude. He told me he's ready for the end."

"Of the documentary shoot?" Palisades asks.

"No."

"Fuck" is all I can muster.

Luke

Nick Rizzo successfully orchestrated Jason Greenberg's signing with his new agency, and he's taking more clients with him than we thought possible. David is pacing behind his desk in a Dior suit with a chili pepper red tie, strategizing with Drew Diller at a low volume for the Luke signing meeting that's about to commence, and every once in a while I hear, "Fucking Rizzo." Drew's older brother, Dean, is a club promoter and friendly with Luke, so Drew is in on the meeting, as well as Sharon Margolis, who first brought the Luke information to David's attention. I'm helping Shane with last-minute touches: a platter of various sandwiches from Bay Cities deli and crunchy chocolate chip cookies from Tavern are displayed on the black marble table under David's plasma, which is firing out muted images of a U.S. embassy bombing somewhere in the Middle East. A box of Padron Anniversario cigars are opened and placed in a brand-new humidor (Luke loves cigars, David hates them). Finally, black-and-white photos of David with Al Gore, Ric O'Barry, Nelson Mandela, and Marlon Brando are displayed more prominently right behind family photos. When returning to the outer office, David reminds me to stay, triggering poorly masked hurt faces from Shane and Drew.

Luke and Ron Best enter six minutes later.

• • •

David is taking a different approach; he's calmer, dropping the agent hyperbole for something else, something almost serene. He's telling them a story about being a young agent and meeting Jimmy Stewart, Frank Sinatra, and Marlon Brando (his hand motioning to the nearby black-and-white photos of them); how working for them as he was just starting out raised the bar for everything he would do in the future, for everything he's doing now.

"That work . . . those relationships planted a seed that has blossomed into an unrelenting desire to work with the chosen ones, to do something special in life. I hope you can give us that opportunity."

Clean and simple. No fluff or fangs. He's not saying: we'll put you in this movie, with that director, for more money than you've ever made, and deliver Oscar gold and Tinseltown glory; because Luke already has it. But even more important, because those are the exact words every other agent would be reciting.

"That's beautiful, man, thank you for sharing that," Luke tells David.

"Of course," David says, moving closer to the center of the room.

"But, do I really *need* an agent? I'm not so sure," Luke says, wanting more out of David's presentation.

"I see." David holds it together as Luke chomps down on a Genoa salami sandwich while Best sits back into a bed of pillows, nervously twirling a phone in his hand. David moves to his desk, away from all of us, searching for something. Drew has an odd look on his face, which I assume is because Sharon just broke a cookie in half, leaving a piece she touched on the serving plate.

David continues, "Hold on, I want to show you something. I want to show you how, even before you make a decision, we will be working for you." He pulls a VHS out of the old safe in the corner of the room behind his desk that was once robbed by John Dillinger.

Luke's about to get more out of the presentation.

"Anyone know what this is?" David asks, holding the VHS up in the air, walking back toward the party in the center of the room.

"No, what is it?" Luke asks, enjoying himself.

David jokes, "It's a VHS, silly." Drew forces a laugh.

"Thank you, Drew."

David hands me the VHS, motioning to the plasma, which now has a VCR connected to it. "It's a little something I got from an old friend," he says, moving back to the couches.

Bobby Biz.

David hits a button on a universal remote, dimming the lights, lowering the shades over the glass wall, and switches the TV off CNN and on to a video input. I could destroy the tape right now, before this goes too far, before everything veers quickly off the rails. I'd be fired at best, blackballed into real estate or finance and possibly out of Los Angeles. Luke and Best appreciating my effort and offering to hire me wouldn't matter. The worst-case scenarios are unthinkable. My father wouldn't even be able to save me; I'd be finished.

I shove the tape into the archaic machine and press Play.

All color has been neutralized. Luke is much younger, with longer hair, and his face is fuller, but it's him, and he looks lost, wearing jeans and no shirt. Others in the "cast" enter the small bedroom setting, and at one point, after they're all making out and spitting on each other, someone unseen by the camera says,

"Do it. Fucking do it." And the younger Luke drops out of the frame, down another boy's bare stomach, and I look away.

Luke's eyes widen to an indescribable shape as the scene plays out. Best launches into the air, demanding to know, "How the *fuck* did you get this?" and "Is it out there? Did Bobby put it out there?" Drew maintains a straight face while Sharon sits frozen, one of her eyes lightly watering.

"Shut it off," David commands. I eject the tape and walk it back to my boss.

"We want to give this to you, it's our gift to you. I know for a fact it's the only one in existence, and other than Bobby, who understands I'll cut his tongue out of his head if he talks, the only people who know about it are in this room. It will never get out. As of this very second, it ceases to exist. You have our word on that." David extends the tape, and Best grabs it, holding it close. Drew nods sincerely as Sharon remains speechless. Luke and Best exchange glances. I slowly step backward, out of the epicenter, as David reminds them, "You have our word."

From the look on Luke's face, he gets it. It's: we know what you did and have the proof and it disappears in an instant if you do the right thing and sign with the agency. But if you should decide to pass on signing with the agency, if you ever decide to leave the agency, we may remember another copy exists out there in this big, bad world that can be uploaded in the stroke of a button to every household, office, and coffee shop in existence.

They're both stunned as they exit the office in silence, tape in hand, and a single tear slides down the left side of Sharon's face as David tells them to "take your time, we know you're busy men." He nods at Drew, then walks to me, places both hands on my shoulders, and says, "You made this happen, you're with me on this." And I'm not sure if it's a question or something else. His eyes are piercing, waiting for any sign of communication, and it's all intersecting here—my future at the agency.

"I'm with you," I tell him; the words trickle from my cold lips as he smiles and continues to nod at Drew and I float away—the rapid beat in my chest gaining speed, dominating any sound in the room—until my back rests firmly against the glass wall of the office.

Another Sunday Night at Madeo

I stop returning e-mails, texts, and phone calls after the Luke meeting, and, in time, my phone dies. Friday night I do coke in the Versailles with my air-conditioning set as low as possible, playing the oldest video game I can find (Madden '01) until sunrise. Unable to sleep, I drive into Beverly Hills and drink eight cups of coffee at Nate 'n Al, trying to read the *Times,* but unable to comprehend the Calendar section. A surge of loud, old Jews infiltrate the vacant deli, so I leave. Not wanting to go home, I find myself driving in circles around the Beverly Center as a scorching late summer sun rises. Then I'm on a freeway, dipping into the valley and coming to a stop across the street from The Cabin in North Hollywood. But I'm paralyzed, unable to exit the car, so I drive away, eyes glued to my rearview and the shrinking image of William's home.

Universal Studios is nearby, and I accelerate up a giant hill toward the theme park. I ride the Studio Tour tram three times and begin mumbling along with the conductor, having memorized certain narration of the attraction, and I'm almost thrown out of the park for jumping off the tram during the *Psycho* section of the tour to hug Norman Bates. I'm removed from the *WaterWorld* show for multiple shirtless standing ovations. I stumble around, waving fried chicken drumsticks behind a green-haired Beetlejuice, shadowing his prancing routine. I hand a tourist my phone, ask him to take a picture of me shaking Shrek's hand, and then tweet the picture out with no words. People stare and whisper. Children appear as leashed guide dogs. I smell every old person hovering in my vicinity, examining maps of the park while pointing to their next destination as a symphony of different tourist dialects surge into my eardrums and the park soon cools with a set of clouds blanketing the valley sun. A few key bumps in the Frankenstein parking lot to keep me from drifting off road get me home as night falls. I sleep past 6:00 p.m. the next day; and I'm starving, so I meet my family at Madeo.

Everyone gives me shit for being late. "No Parm and olives for you, young man," Emily says, feigning disappointment with my tardy arrival. Keith points out the entire Hilton family sitting a few tables away, which leads to a serious discussion between my mom, Cate, and Emily about the number of nose jobs Paris has had and how Emily and Keith's baby daughter is probably going to need one.

"Obvs," Cate says.

I want more coke and consider texting the Hasidic drug dealer who Lance put me in touch with but decide to get drunk instead, ordering a Peroni and scotch, instantly downing both.

"Guess what?" Cate asks the table. Mom instantly slaps away her excitement and reluctantly tells us they made the final cut for a new Housewives series—*The Real Housewives of Malibu*—and they just purchased a house on Malibu Road and "It's so happening," Cate howls, jumping up and down in her seat.

"To fame." She holds a glass of wine in the air.

Dad and I don't join in on the celebration and each order another round of drinks.

I'm having the Bolognese as a starter, and it's easily the highlight of the weekend. Check my phone, and, finally, activity begins. Tons of everything: work e-mails, curious texts, messages from an assortment of acquaintances, including, most recently, an e-mail from Derek: *We should talk*. My father abruptly gets up from the table, answering a call on his way to the bar, and, like phantoms gliding in slow motion, the entire Gottlieb family pass me with Brian muttering something I can't hear, sporting a mean mug, still foaming at the mouth, while Ethan whispers into his dad's slicked-back, sunburnt head, pointing at me, and the senior Gottlieb nods, staring at me, his snake eyes snapping shut and peeling open again; then they're gone.

The girls are discussing an interview they had with Andy Cohen, who "couldn't be nicer or gayer," and I look to Keith for comfort, but he's trying to discreetly frame a picture of the Hiltons with his phone, and I down a glass of wine and the rest of the scotch in front of me to relieve the creeping anxiety that only subsides in the bathroom hallway, outside the dining room, where my legs give out and I'm forced to lie down.

Six wood-fire-baked lobsters decorate the table as I return to the family ripping pieces off the platters, devouring the dripping meat, and texting and mindlessly talking. It's while observing my family—now busy examining every new face that enters the room and arguing over what high school Emily and Keith's baby will go to: Brentwood or Harvard-Westlake—that I start thinking about the painting in William's room of a cactus in a desert. The truth that claws at me, the truth we'll never speak of, one that my parents will never hint at, one that my grandmother, who I loved, hid from me. And as Cate and Emily decide on Brentwood, I run back to the bathroom hallway, hand over my mouth, cheeks stuffed with vomit.

Your New Star

My family is throwing a party at the beach—which is to be filmed by Bravo, so I invited a few friends (around seventy) to celebrate my twenty-fifth birthday at the Beverly Park house for a pool party; and Emily is friends with a girl in PR who represents The Counter, so it was free burgers for everyone. More young agents show up than I expected, bringing clients with them, including Ashley, this perfect brunette from Florida (not a Jew) who just got booked on two network pilots. We connect immediately and start dating and we'll probably break up if one of her pilots gets picked up (at which point she'll dump me) or both get dropped (at which point I'll dump her), but we'll enjoy each other's company for now, and she looks the part as my date at the premier of *Blown to Bits* at Grauman's Chinese Theatre, dazzling everyone, including my father, who takes me aside and says, "Remember what I told you about actresses? It should probably be disregarded."

The Real Housewives of Malibu airs to record numbers for a Bravo premiere (most likely because this is the best-looking cast, which obviously it pains me to admit), beating Bethenny Frankel's first spinoff from *The Real Housewives of New York City* by half a million viewers. The episode is highlighted by two scenes. The first features a producer's ex-wife at Capo, choking on BBQ calamari, knocking over an entire table of food in the process of her phony death throes, and being rushed to a hospital, where she later accuses an internist of fondling her. The second highlight of the series premiere stars my family but, more specifically and unfortunately (for him), my father, who for some reason agreed to be on the show and was portrayed throughout (but especially in a scene at Neimans while being fitted for a suit, fighting with my mother over single- and double-breasted styles) as a "vain industry douche bag" according to Nikki Finke and a "castrated donkey" in "Page Six." Dad claims, "They fucked me with editing," and for the first time, I think about him outside the business, contemplating his post-pulse, "retired" life.

My mom and sisters join Twitter, each generating a few hundred thousand followers in twenty-four hours, and all Ashley wants to know is why I'm not on the show, and when I forward her all the commentary on my father, she writes back: *but you're so much cooler than him.* I get so many e-mails, calls, texts, instant messages, Facebook messages, Twitter mentions, office memos, face-to-face compliments, and pats on the back, all saying how great my mom looks, how well Cate came off, what great parents Emily and Keith are, how hilarious my parents' relationship is, and everyone, including Kev, is curious why I'm not on the show or if I'll be featured later in the season.

"You just fucked up in a big, big way," he tells me at Wolfgang's as Derek, who's dressed in a Brioni suit and tie, annihilates a shrimp cocktail to my left, with Palisades on my right, sipping from a small glass bottle of Diet Coke.

"First thing someone says about you, do you want it to be 'reality star' or 'agent'?" I ask, playing with my new iPhone, which Ashley demanded I purchase or, as she joked (I think), "we're through."

"'Tis true, 'tis true." Palisades agrees with me, finishing his drink, turning in his seat to find our waiter.

Kev is just shaking his head. "You know how much pussy you're losing over this?"

"I'm with Ashley now." I remind him, flipping the phone in the air, then pocketing it.

"Oh, isn't that cute?"

"That is nice," Perry adds, cracking the cap off Diet Coke number two with a twist.

Derek chuckles, licking cocktail sauce off his thumb.

"It is nice, thank you," I tell them, annoyed, waiting on my cheeseburger and giant French fries, dreading going back to the office to deal with all the fallout the afternoon promises to bring from last night's broadcast.

"Anyone down for Cut tonight?" Derek asks.

"Steak houses for lunch and dinner? Fine," Kevin says.

"I'm down," Perry tells us as the burgers are served, and the new iPhone rings: an e-mail comes in from Joyce, alerting me to get back quick, "per David."

I'm back with half the burger in a bag, and Joyce looks up from her computer having nothing to say, just pointing into David's open office; so I drop the leftovers at my desk and enter, closing the door behind me.

Luke and Ron Best are nearly sitting on top of each other, whispering on the couch as David stands over them, motioning for me to join them.

Luke looks up at me. "Heard you put in work to get me here," he says. I look to David, who nods slowly back, so I answer, "I did."

"And not only did this kid find the magnificent *Heavens,* he assisted in bringing *Blown to Bits* to the world," David tells them, placing a firm hand on my shoulder.

"That's headed for some serious business," Ron mentions, impressed.

"I got lucky."

"And *Heavens,* that's a hell of a read."

"The read? You should see the talent we're putting on it," David tells them.

Ron and Luke carefully inspect my face, then settle back into the couch. "The kid behind *Blown to Bits* and *Heavens . . .*" Ron says.

I nod my head as David smiles.

"I wonder what else you're behind . . ." he says before pausing, then continuing, "Okay, he's in."

David walks excitedly around the couch to his desk, quickly types something on his computer, and returns to the center of the room.

"In?" I ask.

"Luke has decided to sign with me, with the agency. . . . Sharon and Drew will also be on the team . . . and . . . so will you." David crouches down in front of me and says, "It starts now."

Ron joins Luke off to the side, against the glass wall, as David jumps on a phone call, leaving me suspended, gasping, desperately trying to remember if my dad was promoted when he was twenty-six or twenty-seven; I need to know how much I beat him by.

"Let's go introduce you," David says, slamming the phone down, throwing on his jacket. Ron and Luke follow us out of the office into the assistants' quarters, where Joyce's and Shane's desks have been left unattended, into the hallway, to the railing, where every single employee of the agency, over three hundred people on four floors, from the lobby up to where we're standing, can be seen.

"Ladies and gentlemen," David announces to the hushed crowd, "your new star!" Everyone looks to Luke, David, Ron, and me, applauding, and I step forward to get a better view of all the faces; looking down over the railing to the lobby, where Stan is surrounded by all the new trainees, looking up, smiling. It continues, morphing into wild animation, and I see Kev and Palisades standing by their bosses hollering like maniacs next to Bernstein, who's grinning wide, and Drew and Sharon walk toward us clapping, joining Joyce and Shane, who look thrilled, and Derek is across the railing, his enthusiasm muted, saying something to a younger assistant wearing a blinking Bluetooth headset, who begins nodding as the clapping builds, reaching its peak decibel, and they're all looking at me, beating their hands together like wound-up, cymbal-banging toy monkeys, cheering.

Acknowledgments

To my agent, Alex Glass, for the tireless hours and undying positivity: without you, there is simply no book. Lauren Spiegel, my tenaciously determined, gifted editor, and everyone at Touchstone/S&S, I'm unbelievably grateful for your belief in the material and focused diligence. And to my friends (you know who you are), thank you for being you.